To Jen A —
Hope you enjoy this!

BRITTLE BONES

Paula Hunter

BRITTLE BONES

PAULLA HUNTER

CAMEL PRESS
Kenmore, WA

CAMEL PRESS

A Camel Press book published by Epicenter Press

Epicenter Press
6524 NE 181st St.
Suite 2
Kenmore, WA 98028

For more information go to:
www.Camelpress.com
www.Coffeetownpress.com
www.Epicenterpress.com
www.paullahunternovels.com

Cover design by Scott Book
Design by Melissa Vail Coffman

Library of Congress Control Number: 2022936118

ISBN: 978-1-68492-061-7 (Trade Paper)
ISBN: 978-1-68492-062-4 (eBook)

Printed in the United States of America

I dedicate all my works to God, St. Philomena, my husband, Roger, my daughter Stacie, my son of my heart Zach, and my three beautiful granddaughters, who have always encouraged me and loved me through this journey of mine. I could not have done this without you.

ACKNOWLEDGMENTS

I WANT TO THANK MY CHEYENNE Critique group: Elizabeth Roadifer, Jeana Byrne, Michael Shay, Dean Petersen, Tina Olson, and David Hopkinson. They were kind but thorough in their critiques of this book. If there are any mistakes in this book it is solely my fault.

I also must thank D.P. Lyle, MD who is the author of Forensic For Dummies and who was incredibly kind about answering some of my fairly bizarre questions.

CHAPTER 1

DARCY MORELAND GLIMPSED THE YELLOW police tape flapping in the cool autumn wind and slid her baby blue Audi into a parking spot behind Detective Hank Nelson's black Ford 150 pickup. She grabbed her notepad and clipped her press badge to the collar of her denim shirt as she ran up to the house and ducked under the crime scene tape.

"Hi. Darcy Moreland, KCWY News." She flashed her brightest smile at the officer standing on the small, covered porch and gestured to her laminated ID. "What's up?"

The uniformed woman by the door looked stoic. She was about the same age as Darcy, mid-twenties, and wore her glossy black hair cropped short.

"Can't comment, ma'am."

"Is it a death? As I was driving by, I recognized Detective Nelson's pickup out front. He works homicide, doesn't he?"

"Can't comment, ma'am. Please step behind the yellow tape."

"Aw, come on. Throw me a bone here. I need enough information to call it into the station. A camera crew will be here eventually, and this way I can impress my boss. It'll make me look enterprising."

The young officer opened her mouth to reply, but Detective Hank Nelson interrupted, slamming through the wooden screen door.

"Don't let her con you, Clark," he said on his way past. "Her boss is one of her old college friends. Trust me. Enterprising wouldn't even hit the top ten adjectives he'd use to describe Ms. Moreland."

Hank took Darcy's elbow and steered her off the three small steps of the porch.

Hank Nelson, infuriating as he was, was still disconcertingly handsome with his dark brown hair and icy blue eyes. They had started dating last summer during Cheyenne Days while they were both investigating the murder of a young girl. Just the look of him could make her heart beat faster and heat rise up her back. She could feel her cheeks flush.

"Who do you think you're pawing?" Using feigned anger as a defense from her traitorous hormones, Darcy pulled her elbow from his grip and narrowed her eyes.

"I know exactly who you are." Hank stared down from his six foot something height, stuffed his hands into his back pockets, and smiled. The lines around his eyes crinkled in his tanned face.

Darcy squirmed. This man had seen her almost naked last summer. It was distressing and distracting. She closed her eyes and forced herself to focus.

"Right now, I'm a reporter," Darcy blustered, "and I would like to know what is going on at this crime scene."

"I'll just bet you would." Hank bowed to the inevitable. "For the record, we know nothing yet except that there is a body we are extracting from the basement."

"Body? As in dead body?"

Hank laughed. "If it were alive, we'd walk it out."

"Feeling sassy this morning, Nelson?"

"That would be Detective Nelson to you, Ms. Moreland. Right now, I'm a detective and I would like you to move your cute little butt away from my crime scene." He smiled at her when she winced. "We have no more information to add." He lifted the tape and nudged her through to the other side, turned, and walked back up toward the house.

"What do you mean, extracting? Was it buried?" Darcy raised her voice but didn't dare follow him beyond the yellow tape.

Hank turned and walked back. "Yes, it was buried. A contractor found it when he was checking the foundation. We are done now."

"Don't you wish." Darcy tapped the station's speed dial number.

"Wendy, Darcy Moreland. Can you have Zach send a crew to 515 East 18th? We have a body buried in a basement. Thanks." Darcy turned her phone off and grinned into Hank Nelson's adorably frustrated face.

"I'll just wait out of the way till my crew gets here." She propped herself against the front fender of her car.

"Do that." Hank said and disappeared into the house.

She might as well get a feel for the neighborhood and the house, she thought. Glancing down the street in both directions, she admired the golden yellow of the leaves broken by an occasional splash of red on the trees lining both sides of the street. Old-growth trees matched the old houses on both sides of the street Her eye followed the path down to Celebration Park where the street dead-ended for about three blocks.

The park, originally called City Park, because it was the only park in Cheyenne at the time, had the obligatory swings and things for the kids, but it also boasted a small lake that was inhabited by a large community of ducks and geese. Darcy remembered reading that when it was first allocated as a park, it had a series of canals that young courting couples could float away a lazy summer day. Hampered with floods later, the boats disappeared, and the canals were joined into one lake.

The houses fronting this old neighborhood street were a hodge-podge of Victorian gingerbread and red-bricked-bungalows. 515 was of the latter variety. Although two story spacious, it squatted on the corner plot like a roosting hen.

The eaves, painted a dark green to match the wood trim on the door and window frames, hung low over the small front porch. On either side, the newel posts and short banisters looked like guards rising out of red-bricked bases rather than welcoming arms.

No peeling paint or broken gutters, Darcy thought. Whoever owned it maintained it well. The yard was a little scruffy, but that could just be the result of the warm fall weather and the continuing drought that was always plaguing the Plains states.

Darcy breathed in the air, savoring the soft, musty, dried-leaf smell of the season. Closing her eyes, she turned her face to the welcome glow of the sun. She leaned back across the hood of her car and let the warmth soak through her. The crash of a door slamming wrenched her from her autumnal daze.

Shading her eyes from the glare, she saw a white van emblazoned with the KCWY News logo splashed along the sides. Darcy took two steps toward it before she froze, her welcoming smile slipping from her face.

"So, sweet-cheeks, where's the action?" Bryce Adkins, Darcy's least favorite person at the station, sidled over from behind the van and propped his butt against the front fender of her car.

Darcy shot Adkins an I-want-to-barbeque-your-balls-for-breakfast look. "Off the paint job," she said, waving her hand as if batting away an annoying bug.

Adkins stood, but watched the front of the house like a cat at a mouse hole. "Seriously, what's going on?"

"Seriously," Darcy planted herself, blocking his line of vision. "This is my story. I called it in, and I requested a crew, so back off Adkins."

Adkins aimed his perfect Chiclets smile at her. Darcy wondered for a moment if all that smarmy charm actually ever worked on anyone, anytime.

"Technically Darcy, you haven't checked in at the station yet, so I convinced Zach to give this to me. I think he has you slated to do a feature on the quilting club or something like that."

Darcy clamped her jaw shut, and by sheer force of will swallowed the inappropriate phrase that wanted to fly from her mouth. Adkins looked so smug; she knew what he was telling her was essentially true.

"Dead body found in the basement. Knock yourself out." Darcy turned away and pulled out her phone. Hitting Zach Horton's number on speed-dial, she listened to it ring as she stomped through the rustling leaves in the gutter.

Pickup was swift. Darcy smiled.

"Yeah, Darcy. I figured it was you. I had to give it to Adkins. His uncle said he wanted to see him get more important face time. Since Uncle Arnold pays both our salaries . . ." Zach dribbled off, surprised Darcy hadn't interrupted him yet. "Darcy? You still there?"

"Yeah. Yeah. I figured it was something like that. Call you back in a minute. Okay?" Darcy stuffed her phone in the back pocket of her black dress pants. She moved toward where Adkins stood by the side of the house and listened to his ramblings for a moment.

"It is our guess that this house has been the scene of a murder, but the police are, at present, unavailable for comment and we don't have confirmation of whether the body is that of a male or female. We will continue to follow this story for you. This is Bryce Adkins reporting for KCWY News."

Nice non-story story, she thought as she passed. Darcy's focus was on the coroner she recognized from last summer. He had just finished a phone conversation, then walked over to talk to an investigator on the scene. Darcy edged closer, keeping her back to them.

"Close down the scene as soon as they've finished taking photos and got whatever samples they need, Detective Connors," the coroner said. "I've called Dr. Dan Moss at the Community College to do a consult, but I doubt he'll be able to tell us too much since he's only a regular anthropologist. We'll probably have to send the remains to Laramie. I think Professor Villars at the university is the closest forensic anthropologist we have, but I like to use the local boys first."

"Okay, Chuck. And thanks." Detective Connors disappeared back into the shadowed dimness of the house without ever noticing Darcy.

Walking up to the coroner, Darcy stuck her hand out. "Darcy Moreland, KCWY News. I was wondering if you would mind answering a couple of background questions for me?"

Charles W. Thompson peered closely at Darcy's laminated ID clipped to her shirt. He was a tall man in his late forties, Darcy guessed. Prone to premature balding but what little fringe left was pale blond and went well with washed out blue eyes. He looked like he'd been left out in the sun too long. Mr. Thompson looked behind her for a camera crew and relaxed when he didn't see one.

"It depends, Ms. Moreland. What would you like to know?"

"I overheard you talking to Detective Connors about having the remains examined by an anthropologist and then shipped to the university. What does an anthropologist have to do with an investigation like this?"

Thompson looked a little surprised by the question, Darcy thought, probably expecting her to ask him to speculate about the cause of death or other issues about the investigation.

"Anthropologists are a handy resource when you find bones rather than a full body. In this case, Dr. Dan Moss will help determine the genders of the bones and to make sure we've sorted them correctly before we send them to Laramie for forensic evaluation."

"Did you say genders? Bones? As in more than one set of bones?"

Thompson's eyes shifted from hers briefly searching for help, then gave it up.

"I suppose it will be common knowledge soon enough. Yes, there are two sets of bones. Now if you'll excuse me, Ms. Moreland." Thompson left her standing on the front sidewalk.

Darcy glanced behind her and saw Adkins hand the mic to the crew, then strut off to get into his chili-red Mini Cooper convertible parked behind the station's van. As he slid into the black and red leather seats, he looked at Darcy and sent her a mock salute and a grin.

Tempted to return a salute of her own, she resisted, barely. Comforted by the knowledge she knew more about this story than Adkins did, Darcy was sure she could convince Zach to let her cover the anthropologists at least as a sidebar.

Darcy returned to her baby blue Audi and slipped behind the wheel. She punched Zach's number.

"Nice of you to remember me, Darcy."

Zach sounded irritated, but not full-blown-pissed.

"Sorry about that. I was listening in on a conversation between the coroner and a detective, and before you ask, not *my detective,* and guess what I found out."

"Working here, Darcy." Zach was edging toward aggravated.

"Working here too, boss. They found two bodies. Actually, two sets of bones. Thompson, the coroner, is waiting for a consult with Dr. Dan Moss from the community college here before he sends the bones over the hill to Laramie. The university has a forensic anthropologist who will look over the remains and try to determine cause of death."

"Damn! Did you tell Adkins?"

Darcy smiled. "Nope. He zoomed out of here after doing an underwhelming report about all the stuff we don't know yet. I will hang around and see if I can talk to Dr.Moss if that's okay."

"Okay Darcy. Nice hustle. I gave Adkins a chance. Uncle Arnold will have to live with the fact that his sister's kid is at best unprepossessing, and at worst, incompetent. Come back to the station as soon as you can, and we'll do a report with you from the newsroom."

"You got it, boss." Darcy grinned as she snapped her phone off and stuffed it into her pocket.

Punching up the stereo, Darcy reclined her seat and basked in the warm glow of success.

Dr.Moss appeared less than twenty minutes later, unfolding his lanky frame from the cab of a dusty gray Chevy pickup, and striding over to talk to Coroner Thompson. His brown suit hung on his frame and made him look like a scarecrow, and his unkempt, wispy white hair added to the affect.

Darcy scrambled after him.

"Dr. Dan Moss?" she asked, extending her hand to him. "I'm Darcy Moreland KCWY News. I understand you're an anthropologist from the community college here. Is that true?"

Dr. Moss blinked his watery, pale green eyes at her behind some seriously correctional lenses in wire frames. It made him look like an owl, Darcy thought.

"I understand," Darcy rushed on before Thompson could stop her, "that you're being asked to consult on this case. Is that true?"

Dr. Moss's head swiveled from Darcy to Thompson.

Thompson smiled at the trapped look on Moss'face. "You might as well confirm it, Doctor. It's no great secret."

"Yes, though I don't know as I can be much help." Moss smiled with unspoken apology at Thompson who smiled back.

"Would it be all right if I wait and get a statement from you after you've concluded your preliminary examination of the remains?" Darcy sent him her most winning smile.

"I . . . I don't . . ."

"It's okay, Doctor. It can't hurt to give the media a little of the preliminary information."

Charles W. Thompson was well aware of the bad press law enforcement were receiving recently, so he was anxious to accommodate the press if it didn't impede the investigation.

"Well, if you think it's appropriate." Dr. Moss looked doubtfully at Thompson, then back at Darcy. "I don't know how long I'll be." He pulled a handkerchief from his back pocket and dabbed at a little dribble hanging from his long pointy nose.

"No problem." Darcy smiled. "Take your time."

Dr. Moss nodded dismissively and paced up the walkway in a long-legged, shambling-stride.

Half an hour later, Darcy slid from the hood of her car and dashed to cut off Dr. Moss's retreat to his pickup.

"Doctor Moss, can you tell me what you think of the bones?"

"Huh? Oh, Ms. Moreland. Can't tell you much. Both skeletons are male. One much larger than the other. If you want exact measurements, I gave them to Mr. Thompson . . ."

"No. I'm just asking for your general impressions now. Did it look like a murder/suicide?"

Moss blinked his watery eyes as if trying to process a question for which he had insufficient information.

"No. The men died at vastly different times. The smaller of the men has been dead for decades if the discoloration and deterioration is considered. I don't have the laboratory capabilities to pinpoint the more recent man's death, but I presume Dr. Villars can help you there." He shot his cuff and glanced nervously at his watch. "You must excuse me. I have a class in a half an hour."

"Oh of course, doctor. Thanks very much for your help." Darcy watched as his gray pickup belch smoke, jerk once, then rattle down the street.

"Two bodies. Both male. Died at different times?" Darcy muttered to herself as she got into her car. "Dang!" she shouted and slammed on the accelerator. "Zach is sooo not going to believe this."

By the time she entered the newsroom, she was grinning so hard her cheeks hurt. She loved scoops—and more—she loved scooping Adkins.

Ensconced in the tiny closet she called her office, she punched Zach's extension.

"Horton," Zach's voice blared over the speakerphone.

Darcy propped her feet on the desk in front of her. "I'm back, boss. I talked to the anthropologist from the Junior college, and he said both bodies were male."

"Murder/suicide?"

"My question exactly, but nope. Different times of death, one decades older than the other. How much time can you give me?"

"Why?" Zach sounded wary.

"I will try to get get some background on the house."

"See what you can do. Twenty minutes max and then we go with what you have. Kim will segue to you in studio after Adkins's tape." Zach clicked off.

"And a pleasant goodbye to you too," Darcy dialed her cousin Cathie's number.

"Cheyenne Title and Abstract. How may I direct your call?" Darcy grimaced at the perky receptionist's voice. "Cathie Garner's extension, please. Darcy Moreland calling."

By the time Cathie answered, Darcy had sketched out a few questions.

"Darcy. Nice to hear from you, but it's too early to plan Thanksgiving."

"Nice one. I need a favor."

"No preliminaries? Jeremy's fine. I'm fine. I'm dating a new guy in case you're interested."

"Cath, I really am, but I'm under the gun here. I need a title search on a house at 515 East 18th. ASAP."

"For a story?"

"No. I'm stalking a guy! Of course, for a story."

"Okay. Okay. It'll take a while."

"Define a while."

"At least a day. I have to dig through the records at county."

"Call me back as soon as you find something."

"Yeah. I've got to go up there today anyway, but I expect payback."

"Like?"

"Like you watch Jeremy for me on Saturday while I get my hair and nails done."

"You got it, but hurry. This will all make more sense to you if you watch the news at noon. Thanks."

Darcy hung up, propped her elbows on the desk, and glared at the yellow legal pad in front of her.

She put a check next to: Who owns the house?

She looked at what was left. Murder? Both? Any DNA? Cause of death? Extent of wounds? Any identifying marks or clothing? How long buried?

Darcy let out an explosive sigh. Not much chance of finding any of this out until the ME did the preliminaries. She'd check with Hank about what the ME learned about the bones before they sent them to Dr. Villars. She took her computer off sleep mode and typed a few notes.

It took a grand total of forty seconds to type what she knew, but even at that, it was more than Adkins managed to find out.

She leaned back in her chair, gulped down the now-cold dregs of her morning coffee, and chuckled. She was delighted, but her friend Abby, her former English teacher who lived in the same apartment building as Darcy, was going to be orgasmic or the post-menopausal equivalent.

CHAPTER 2

WITH AN AUDIBLE GROAN, ABBY MCNEILL dropped her slight frame into her favorite Chesterfield chair. "Damned arthritis," she muttered and rubbed her right knee, knowing full well the twinge would come back as soon as she stood again.

"Let this be a lesson to you," she aimed her teacher voice at a ball of brown and blonde fur, Guinness Murphy McCann, a cairn terrier, who lolled on his back in a patch of sun. "Old age ain't for sissies, as Bette Davis used to say."

At the sound of Abby's voice, Mac, who loved visiting Abby, rolled from his back to his side, obviously deciding her tone didn't indicate danger or a forthcoming treat, and therefore not worth getting up all the way.

"Let's see what our Darcy girl is up to today." Abby punched the TV on, balanced her lunch plate in her lap, and tried not to dump her chicken sandwich on the floor as she snuggled into the depths of the chair.

The noon news report, already in progress, filled the screen with a medium shot of Bryce Adkins standing in front of a red-bricked house draped with yellow crime scene tape.

"Little snot," Abby bit viciously into her sandwich, then squinted to look past Adkins and pointed her sandwich at the screen. "I know that house. I know who used to live there."

Responding to the excitement in Abby's voice, Mac scampered

to her and rising up on his hind legs, placed his front paws in her lap. Abby scratched his ears then pushed him down.

"Sorry boy. Darcy' d skin me alive if I let you sit in my lap while I was eating. She already thinks I've spoiled you beyond repair." Mac curled at her feet, unconcerned, and Abby turned up the volume

. . . we don't have confirmation of whether the body is that of a male or female. We will continue to follow this story for you. This is Bryce Adkins reporting for KCWY News.

Abby snorted her disgust. The scene shifted to Kim Davis, the Noon News anchor.

That was Bryce Adkins with an earlier KCWY breaking news report. Some further developments have occurred in the case and for that we go now to our studio and Darcy Moreland.

Darcy tucked her blonde hair and the earpiece wire behind her ear, looked earnestly into the camera and waited for the silent countdown to cue her.

"Darcy, what have you been able to find out?" Kim spoke to the monitor on her left.

"Kim, this story has been unfolding in some dramatic ways. After the police responded to an unpretentious brick bungalow home on 18th Street. earlier this morning they began their investigation of some unidentified bones discovered in the basement crawlspace."

Abby scooted to the end of her chair.

"Do they have any information about the identity of the remains?" Kim asked.

"No, Kim. The Investigation became complicated because as the exploratory team gathered evidence, another set of bones was discovered during the initial extraction. I spoke to the county coroner Charles Thompson . . ."

Darcy glanced down at her notes, then back up to the camera.

". . . and he confirmed there is little evidence that can be ascertained without an extensive examination on both sets of remains. Dr. Dan Moss, an anthropology professor from Cheyenne Community College, was brought in to do a consult. His determination was that the bodies were probably both males but had been buried decades apart and that their deaths were unlikely to be connected."

"Could he give any indication about the cause of death of these two men?"

"Not at this time. The bones have been collected and are on their way to the University Forensic Anthropology Laboratory in Laramie. Dr. Aaron Villars(thank God for Google) is going to attempt to study the remains and determine more information. We will, of course, be following the details of this intriguing and sad story."

"Thank you for that information, Darcy. We look forward to learning more about this bizarre investigation."

Abby snapped the TV off. "Oh boy, oh boy! I can't wait, Mac. Maybe our girl would enjoy a little spaghetti tonight . . . with a lot of Chianti on the side." Abby practically skipped to her dollhouse-sized kitchen and began rattling pans.

An hour later, when Darcy got the call from Abby with the dinner invitation, she had no illusions that Abby just wanted her company. Abby was dying of curiosity. That was okay with Darcy, first because she was a non-recovering pasta addict and second, because talking things through with Abby always helped clarify her thoughts.

Darcy spent the rest of the afternoon setting up an appointment with Dr. Villars at the University and leaving a callback message for Charles Thompson, the coroner. She figured she'd have to go to or through Hank to get anything off the Me's report.

She also drafted some notes about skeletal identification from information she had accessed from the internet. She listed the specific points she wanted answers for: race, age, and something called endocranial suture closure, which delineated age.

Damage to both skeletons might determine cause of death and clues to when they died . . . according to the website.

She was saving all her notes in a file marked BONES when the door to her tiny office burst open. Darcy's breath whooshed out in a gasp then morphed into an infuriated growl when she saw

Adkins standing in her doorway. She shut her laptop with more force than necessary.

"Who the hell do you think you are, using my story to escalate the details like that?" Adkins snapped.

"Listen, charm-school dropout, I did what you should have. I stuck around and I asked questions. Zach says I can investigate the forensic angle since I found it. So back off. And don't you ever barge in here without knocking again. You got it?"

Adkins looked surprised that she hadn't just withered. For a moment, his mouth opened and closed like a goldfish dumped on the carpet.

"You don't want me for an enemy, Moreland."

"Well, I most certainly don't want you for a friend, Adkins." Darcy leaned across the desk and glared at him. "Now get out."

"Don't think letting that police detective jump your bones is gonna help you around here. Uncle Arnie knows all about your sneaky tricks."

Adkins stormed out and Darcy sighed and sat again. She really did want to get along with the people she worked with, but Adkins' ego and arrogance had been swelling to hot air balloon proportions since they'd had a couple of run-ins last summer.

He resented that she'd broken a huge story about a murder during Cheyenne Days, and she resented that he had no training or experience. Because of his relationship to the station's owner, he wasn't likely to get either.

Darcy admitted to herself she wasn't all that experienced, but she did have a degree in journalism, a year and a half at a Kansas City station, and not to mention, common sense.

Adkins had nothing. Darcy smiled, remembering a saying her dad used to use: "He's all hat and no herd." That was Adkins to a T.

Darcy pulled the scrunchie from her long blond hair and shook it loose, then stuffed her laptop and a collection of bits of paper and sticky notes she'd assembled into the new briefcase her folks had given her for her birthday. She still got a thrill when she looked at the red leather perfection of it. It even smelled new.

The ride home was uneventful, and she even found a parking place right in front of the Algonquin, a delicately decaying apartment building she called home.

The wide stone steps and the four stately white pillars which flanked the front porch, always made Darcy feel a little like she was entering an antebellum mansion. She liked that it had a historical, bedrock quality about it.

The heavy oak doors were decorated with matching beveled and etched ovals of glass and led to the mosaic tiled foyer and the dimly lit staircase.

Darcy sprinted up the stairs, impatient to change into jeans and sweatshirt and drop the cares of her day in her apartment before she went down to join Abby and Mac.

As she toed off her black flats and wiggled out of her black dress pants, she wondered in passing when she had begun to think of Abby and Mac as an indissoluble duo like PB&J or salt and pepper.

Mac was her dog, but Abby's sidekick, she decided as she pulled a fleecy light green sweatshirt on and zipped her jeans, which was simply fine with her. They kept each other company, and they both loved her. What else could she want?

The greeting awaiting her was all she could hope for. Abby handed her an oversized round glass half full of dark red Chianti and Mac leaped into her lap as soon as she'd nestled into the overstuffed comfort of Abby's small settee.

Abby plopped into the chair across from her and leaned forward.

"Okay. Give." Abby's soft blue eyes brightened with unadulterated interest.

Darcy took a deep sip of the surprisingly mellow wine and smiled. She wondered if she could draw this out a little, but then took pity on her friend. After all, the air was redolent with the comforting smell of marinara sauce bubbling in the kitchen. Darcy's stomach growled in anticipation.

"I suppose you saw the news this afternoon?"

"I grow old, I grow old."

Darcy laughed and took another fortifying sip of wine. "I don't know what I can tell you other than what I said in the report, except that Bryce Adkins would like to feast on my liver for that little coup."

"A happy little by-product," Abby chuckled and sipped her wine. "Who lived there last? Do you know?"

"No. I have my cousin Cathie working on it, though. She agreed to do a search if I watch Jeremy for her on Saturday."

"Wonderful! I haven't seen that little rascal for weeks." Abby sank back into her chair, relished another taste of her wine. "I used to know the old lady who owned that house. Recognized it as soon as I saw it."

Now it was Darcy's turn to lean forward. "Who? Who?"

Abby rose. "In a minute. Let's get dinner on the table and I'll tell you everything I know."

Darcy could barely contain her curiosity, as she helped set the salad bowls and plates on the table. Slightly mollified by the wonderful smells of yeasty, tangy garlic bread and the enticing pasta topped with meatballs the size of small fists, Darcy pulled out her chair and sat at the solid round oak table.

Waiting until their plates were heaped, Abby smiled.

"Okay. Back in the mists of time when I was small, we lived in a house on Seventeenth Street. Every morning and afternoon my friend Doedy . . ."

"Wait. You had a friend named Doedy?"

"Technically, her name was Annie, but her Grandpa had a fondness for the infamous Leadville, Colorado beauty, Baby Doe Tabor whom he'd met once, and nicknamed Annie, Doedy. Why do you care?"

"It just sounded like an odd name for a girl is all. Go on." Darcy carved into one of the over-sized meatballs.

"As I was saying, every day Doedy and I would walk by the witches' house on the way to school and back . . ."

"Whoa! Wait!" Darcy choked on a morsel of meatball. "Witches' house? A witch used to live there?"

Abby smiled. It wasn't often you could capture someone's

undivided attention. She savored the sensation as she sipped some more wine.

"Abby!"

"Oh alright. Just stop interrupting. I doubt if she was a real witch, but she was a recluse. Almost no one saw her except when she'd carry an old basket to the market on 20th Street once a week.

"She dressed all in black . . . like she was in mourning, and she wore those chunky black shoes my grandma used to wear. You know—sturdy two-inched heels that laced across the vamp on top. Must've been made in the thirties."

"Never mind the fashion report. Get on with the story." Darcy twirled her spaghetti on her fork.

"The fashion report is important. It's why we thought she was a witch. Remember the old witch in *Sleeping Beauty*?" Abby waited for Darcy's distracted nod. "Well, this lady looked just like her. She wore a shawl over her head and what we could see of her hair was white, though looking back now, I don't think she was really all that old back then. Her face didn't have any moles or chin hairs, or even wrinkles, which sparked a lot of playground debates about whether you could be a legitimate witch without them."

Darcy chuckled. "I'll just bet it did. Did you ever talk to her?"

"Not really. There was something about her manner that made it clear, even to insensitive brats like us, that she didn't want to be disturbed. Once though, I remember we made May baskets at school to take around and leave on porches in our neighborhoods, and I made a special one for the witch."

Abby grinned at the memory. "It was a confection of pink construction paper, globs of brown glue we used to call 'mucilage', and a dainty lace doily. I'd filled it with sticky jellybeans, blue Easter grass and wrote her a card wishing her a Happy May Day, as I recall, and signed it 'Your Friend, Abigail.'"

"I'm surprised you had the guts to go to her door."

"Me too. I had to talk myself into it, I tell you true. Doedy was sick that day, and I was alone, you see. But eventually I screwed up my courage and knocked on the door.

"I waited for the longest time on her little porch. I could see her shadow behind the lace curtains covering the window of the door. She twitched the corner of the curtain and I saw one jade green eye peer out. I stood there and waved at her inanely, and the curtain dropped.

"I remember I waited a little longer and then bent down to place the basket by her door. I was halfway back down the sidewalk in front of her house when I heard her door creak open, and I turned back to look.

"She was standing there, dressed all in black. Her white hair was uncovered and rolled in a horizontal sausage at the nape of her neck, sort of like Barbara Stanwick. I remember wondering how she did it that way. Anyway, she stooped and picked up the basket, plucked the card from the fake grass, and read it. I watched her face closely, afraid if she hated the card, she'd turn me into a lawn statue or something."

Abby paused, and Darcy had the odd feeling Abby was back there all those years ago. Darcy didn't dare breathe.

"She smiled at me. I remember thinking she couldn't be a witch and have such a beautiful smile. It lifted her whole face, and she looked young again. I just stood there and smiled back like the village idiot. Finally, I waved goodbye and took a couple of steps down the walk.

"I heard her clear her throat, as if it were raspy from disuse. 'Thank you for your thoughtfulness, Abigail,' she said, and went in and closed the door. That was the last time I ever saw her. We moved up to the Avenues soon after and I never went back. I felt kind of bad about it, because she seemed so nice, but then as is the way with children I forgot her until I saw her house on the news today."

"Do you remember her name?" Darcy prodded.

"No." Abby rose and began to clear away the dishes. "I do remember hearing, though, that she belonged to an old ranching family, but I don't remember which one. Sorry."

"Probably no connection to my bones, anyway." Darcy followed Abby to the kitchen with more dishes.

Abby handed her the half-finished wine. "Go sit down. I can do these up later."

"Okay, but I can't stay long. I have an appointment with Dr. Villars in Laramie tomorrow, and I want to be really fresh."

Abby held out her glass for a refill, then sank back into her chair. "Still, it is intriguing to think of two bodies being buried under that same old house."

CHAPTER 3

THE DRIVE GOING NORTHWEST West from Cheyenne to Laramie was one of Darcy's favorites especially in early autumn. The Vedauwoo rock formations on the right side of the highway were breathtaking.

Darcy knew that the word Vedauwoo was an Arapaho word meaning earthborn spirits and the description fit the enormous rocks looking like solidified globules of mud huddled amid patches of vibrantly gold Aspen trees.

The summer and autumn had been unusually moist so the prairie grasses, which were often brown by now, retained their deep green hue and splotches of purple, blue, and yellow wildflowers were still flourishing. Her dad always told her that if you can get water to the prairie it is astounding what would grow.

Framed by the bright blue, cloudless sky, Darcy thought few places in her world were so beautifully primal. Any minute, she imagined a dinosaur lumbering around the rocks to graze on the tops of the trees.

Laughing at her whimsy, Darcy slid open her sunroof to enjoy the cool thin air as it whooshed over her. She waved jauntily at the bronze bust of Abraham Lincoln perched at the highest point of the Lincoln Highway, over 8,000 feet above sea level.

Once past the summit, she swooped downward through red-rocked bluffs and aimed for the Laramie exit. She knew the

Anthropology College was tucked in a building North of Prexie's Pasture, a large grassy commons area in the center of campus. Quickly finding a visitor's parking space nearby, she gathered her notes, and stashed them into her tote.

Striding purposefully toward the front door, she thought how young the students looked now as they meandered toward the Student Union or across Prexie's Pasture to class. Maybe it's not that they're so young. Maybe it's just that I feel so old, she thought.

"Twenty-five is not old," she muttered to herself, attempting to bolster her flagging spirit." I won't even be twenty six for another two weeks."

Once inside the doors, she checked her appearance in the reflection of the glass-fronted office guide. She smoothed down her hair that had been ruffled by the wind and made sure her white shirt was tucked snugly into her navy pencil skirt. Darcy found the office listing for Prof. Villars, Ph.D. and climbed to the third floor, glad she had opted to wear her low heeled boots. His secretary, a cheerful blonde in her late thirties Darcy guessed, said she was expected and showed her through to the inner office.

The office was crammed with shelves of books and stacks of papers, while boxes of files took all available floor space except for a small pathway to behind the desk. A dust-covered computer nestled on a cluttered, scratch-scarred credenza behind the main desk and a laptop perched on the only other chair.

Professor Villars, who was almost as thin as the skeletons he studied, smiled in greeting, then followed Darcy's glance at the chair.

"Sorry about that," he said as he snatched the laptop up and motioned for her to sit.

Managing to find a small square of floor to rest her tote between her feet, Darcy extracted a pen and her notebook in one fluid motion.

"I really appreciate your taking the time to see me, Dr. Villars. I know how busy fall is on a university campus."

"Not at all, Ms. Moreland. Beginning a semester is easier than it used to be. That's why God made grad students." Villars tilted his cadaverous head back and laughed heartily, then wheezed and coughed.

On the corner of the overflowing desk, an enormous ashtray saturated the air with the reek of stale tobacco.

Noticing her fleeting look, he shrugged philosophically. "A nasty habit that. I picked it up when I was interning at Broward County residency program in forensic pathology. I had a weak stomach back then and the smell of the smoke helped. Now it's just an addiction." He lifted the short sleeve on his shirt to show a nicotine patch.

"I keep that there as a reminder of how disgusting smoking is, but I fear it has become a friend in the manner of the Stockholm syndrome—" He smiled at Darcy's puzzled face. "You know—where you start defending and befriending your captors."

Darcy laughed. "A lot of people are battling with it, Dr. Villars. Hope you win." Darcy smiled at him to defuse any implied criticism. "The reason I'm here is to get some background on the bones sent to you yesterday from Cheyenne."

"Of course." He picked up his phone and said, "Joan, could you call down to the lab please? Ask Dr. Larson if I can bring him a reporter from Cheyenne. Thanks."

Darcy raised her eyebrow.

"Don't fret. Dr. David Larson is not only a medical doctor but an expert in Forensic Anthropology. If anyone can determine who the bodies are, it is Dr. Larson." Villars stood. In an old-world gesture, Dr. Villars grasped her elbow and steered her to the door.

"Joan, I presume David was okay about bringing Ms. Moreland down?" His voice rose slightly at the end, but it was not really a question.

"Yes, sir." Joan of the ash-blonde hair and blindingly perfect teeth held the outer office door.

"Have you ever visited a forensic lab before, Ms. Moreland?" Dr. Villars asked as they waited for the antediluvian elevator to rattle up from the basement.

"No. I never have. I took Chemistry and Biology in college though."

"You'll find this a little different." He smiled and remained silent for the short ride down three flights, then gestured to the large set of frosted, swinging doors just steps away marked as LAB in black block lettering.

Darcy's first impression of the lab was size or lack thereof. Two stainless steel examination tables took up most of the floor space. Glass fronted cupboards filled with sterile supplies hovered over the ruthlessly soap stoned counters which ran around the circumference of the room crowded with gadgety-looking machines.

"Dr. David Larson, this is Ms. Darcy Moreland from a television station in Cheyenne. Would you give her what, if any, background information you can?"

Darcy was amused at the friendly smile on Dr. Larson's face. He shook her hand with unbridled enthusiasm.

"So glad to meet you, Ms. Moreland." He unconsciously pulled her into the lab while he shook her hand.

"Please call me Darcy, Dr. Larson." She forced herself to look into his soft grey eyes because the alternative was to look at the piles of bones on the two tables.

"I am always so pleased to talk about our work here." His hand still held hers and Darcy gave a little reminder tug.

"Oh!" he let go and folded his hands behind his back like a child in Grandma's parlour.

Darcy thought there was a lot about him that was childlike. His voice vibrated with anticipation and excitement which seemed at odds with Darcy's preconceived notions of a scientist.

His round face looked boyishly open, and if he hadn't had thinning red gold hair that barely covered the top of his head, Darcy would have guessed his age at about 17.

"Let me show you what we have so far." He waved her between the two tables until she stopped at the head while he took the space in the middle.

"Mr. Smith here—"

"You know his name?"

Dr Larson barked a short laugh. "Heavens, no. Not yet. I just assign names to them, so I don't forget that they were once human beings."

Darcy smiled at him, oddly touched by his compassion.

"This is Mr. Smith, and this is Mr. Jones." Dr. Larson smiled at her half ruefully, but Darcy reassured him with a nod and jotted down the names in her notes.

"Mr. Smith is the older and younger of the two."

"Pardon me?" Darcy glanced back at Dr. Villars and wondered for a fleeting moment if Dr. Larson was mentally stable.

Dr. Larson laughed and picked up Mr. Smith's skull. "By looking at the endocranial suture closure we can determine Mr. Smith was likely around his early twenties. If we check the teeth and look at the wrist development, we can approximate an age."

"So, if Mr. Smith is in his early 20s, Mr. Jones is younger?" Darcy scribbled in her notes.

"I'm sorry, I was just having some fun with you. Mr. Smith died long before Mr. Jones . . . which makes his bones older."

"I see," Darcy ran a line through the notes she'd written and made some corrective additions.

"About how long ago was Mr. Smith killed?" Darcy asked.

"Did Dr. Larson say he was killed?" Dr. Villars raised a brow as he snapped on some surgical gloves, then relented with a sigh. "We estimate that 'Mr. Smith,'" he sent a weak smile in Dr. Larson's direction, "died from a blunt force trauma to the head. That doesn't in and of itself imply that he was killed, though.

"See, this side of the skull is cracked, likely from a rough fall against a hard surface. It is deeper on one end than the other. If someone is hit with say a poker, the wound would be more uniform."

"It could have been an accidental fall." Dr. Larson explained. "The brain bounces in the skull when that occurs. If it bounces a little, we call it a concussion. If it bounces a lot, we call it fatal."

"How long ago?"

"About sixty years. That's an educated guess based on the protein matrix of the bones." Dr. Villars picked up an ankle bone.

"Is there an easy way to say that?" Darcy asked.

"It just means that as the bones become more brittle once the flesh decomposes and leaves them unprotected, the protein begins to break down. See, Mr. Smith's bone is so soft you can leave a mark with just your fingernail." Dr. Larson pressed his nail slightly and left a small indentation. Darcy winced.

"Now Mr. Jones over here is much less degraded." Dr Larson swiveled to pick up the other skull. He pressed his fingernail into the bone and left no mark.

"So, when do you figure he died?" Darcy felt her eyes drawn to the bones laid out on the table like a giant jigsaw puzzle.

"About five to six years ago. A male will lose about 3 pounds a day of soft tissue due to decomposition, so it loosely fits the math. He was wrapped tightly in a sheet, like swaddling a baby, and the sheet was still mostly intact."

Darcy glanced around looking for the sheet.

Dr. Larson smiled indulgently. "All artifacts found with or on the body are examined by the Criminal Investigation Lab. We just do bones here."

"Oh, sorry. This is all fairly new to me. What was Mr. Jones' cause of death, do you think?"

"Ah, now in his case, we're pretty sure this poor fellow was murdered." Dr. Villars moved to face Mr. Jones table, gently replacing the skull, and picking up a thighbone. "See these marks on this femur?"

Darcy peered at the bone. "What are those dents from?"

"Those are evidence of multiple blunt force traumas. We don't yet know the weapon, but I think we can rule out a hammer or tool of some kind, because the indentations seem to have irregular patterns that can't be accounted for with varying levels of force."

Darcy was so fascinated, she forgot for a moment she was looking at the remains of a human being. She leaned into the table and ran her finger along an irregularly dented arm bone.

"Ms. Moreland. We'd prefer you not touch the bones with an ungloved hand."

Darcy jumped back, embarrassed. "Oh, I am so sorry, Dr. Villars. Did I compromise anything?"

"Not likely. We've done most of the tests already."

"Tests?"

"In Mr. Smith's case, we wanted to find out if he had died before 1950, so we tested for radioactive isotopes. Because of the use of nuclear weapons and further testing in the 50s and 60s the global environment had an increase of C14, strontium 90, cesium 137, and tritium, so these markers are found in people's bones who died after 1950. Mr. Smith died before 1950."

"And Mr. Jones' chemistry?"

"Mr. Jones died considerably later. He had a higher preponderance of amino acids than did Mr. Smith. We also tested for nitrogen levels."

"Wow. You sure have been busy." Darcy was sincerely impressed.

Dr. Larson's face blossomed into another boyish grin. "So pleased to have made that point. We are justifiably proud of our work here."

"Is there any way to positively identify Mr. Smith or Mr. Jones? DNA or something?"

"Ah, the ubiquitous DNA." Dr. Villars laughed then wheezed and coughed.

"Everybody has heard of it, but most don't understand the limitations. In Mr. Smith's case, we are unlikely to be able to compare any sample we might find, and that is assuming we could extract a viable sample.

"In Mr. Jones' case," Dr. Larson picked up the narration seamlessly, "because he died more recently, we might be able to track down a sample we could use as a comparison. Seriously though, where would we begin to look?

"It becomes the proverbial search for the tick in the tester."

"What? I thought you were going to say needle in a haystack. What's a tester?"

Dr. Villars peeled his gloves off with a snap. "It's an old saying my grandmother used and, in this case, is more apt than a needle. A tester is a bed canopy with multiple layers of cloth, in which a moving tick would be almost impossible to find—like DNA to identify our gentlemen here."

"So, we may never know who they are or why they were buried in the basement? Isn't there something else we can do?"

"Take heart, Ms. Moreland." Dr. Larson smiled with that open optimism that Darcy still found charming. "Forensic science has made amazing strides in the last few years. There are many options to investigate."

"Like?"

"For instance, if the investigators request it, the skulls can be sent for facial reconstruction. Doctor Larson fairly beamed.

"What is that? More testing?" Darcy asked.

Dr. Villars wheezed and coughed. His rendition of a laugh, Darcy now knew.

"No. It is more an art than a science. When we finish extracting as much information as we can, if directed to do so we send it to a forensic artist who makes some educated guesses based on skull structure. and any other information we can provide like race or approximate age.

At that point, they try to reconstruct with clay how the person most likely appeared when they were alive. It has proven useful for identifying remains in the past."

"That sounds promising. Even with Mr. Smith, there still might be someone left to recognize him. By the way, do you know the race of the men?"

"Both men have triangular nose holes, so they were undoubtedly Caucasian."

"And Mr. Jones' approximate age?"

Dr. Larson pointed to Mr. Jones' elbow.

"Based on bone, joint, and teeth wear, we're approximating his age at mid to late forties. Mr. Smith, we judge to be much younger mid-twenties or early thirties."

Darcy made note of the last details, then snapped her notebook shut. "Thank you so much, Dr. Larson. Dr. Villars. You've been a big help and amazingly informative."

Dr. Larson shook her hand. "Come back anytime, Ms. Moreland. It was a pleasure to talk to you."

Darcy was still smiling when she started her car. According to the clock in her dashboard, she had been in the lab about an hour, yet it seemed like mere minutes. The doctors were certainly fonts of information.

"Now those are men who love what they do," she said aloud and steered down 15th Street in search of the Interstate on-ramp.

To pass time on the short forty-five-minute drive back to Cheyenne, Darcy snapped her Bluetooth into her ear and punched Zach Horton's number."

"Darcy. Where the hell are you?"

"Hello, Zach. Even with caller ID it's okay to begin with hello. I am on the road back to Cheyenne after talking to Dr. David Larson and Dr. Aaron Villars at the university. Remember I told you I was going to follow up on those bones they found."

"Yeah. So?"

"So the good doctors gave me a lot of information about the bodies so save me about a minute for the noon broadcast. I'll come in and tape a report. Okay?"

"What's your ETA?"

"I don't know. If traffic stays this light, about thirty-five minutes. Why?"

"I want you to do a live feed in front of the cop shop. See if you can corral one of the investigators on the case to comment on camera about the case."

"Do you want me to check into the station first?"

"Yes. I'll set up Netters for you and have him prep for a remote. Oh and Darcy—"

"Yeah?"

"When you get here, keep a low profile. Adkins still wants your hide nailed to the wall."

"Gotcha, boss. Everything on the QT. See you soon."

Darcy tossed her Bluetooth into her tote and turned up her stereo. She didn't want to think of Adkins. She didn't want to think about the challenge of getting one of the investigators to go on camera.

She had an uncluttered highway, a sunny autumn day, and a great CD in the stereo. Life was good.

CHAPTER 4

DARCY BREEZED INTO THE STATION and slipped quietly over to the front desk.

"Hi Wendy. Is Netters waiting for me?" she asked the red-headed office manager/receptionist.

"Oh Darcy. Yeah. I'll just buzz him. Adkins is looking for you too. I think he wants to take body parts. He's really steamed."

Darcy smiled. "Yeah, I know. Zach told me. I can't help it if he didn't follow through on the bones story. It was my catch in the first place, but now it turns out that my little sidebar may turn into a really interesting story."

"Really?" Wendy tucked the ends of her chin-length hair behind her ears. "Tell me." She leaned toward Darcy across the counter.

"Watch your local news," Darcy said.

"Ah come on. Have a heart. I'd tell you if I knew something juicy." Wendy almost whined.

"Ready?" Bill Netters seized Darcy's arm and steered her toward the front door. Netters stood over six foot with a wiry, but well-muscled build. Considering Darcy stood about five foot three, it wasn't easy to keep up as he strode out of the building and into the parking lot.

"Netters. Let go. I'm moving. I'm moving."

"Calamity," he said, using the nickname he'd burdened her with when they first started working together last summer, "I just saved your life." He slid open the side of station's remote van and tossed a duffle bag into the back. He slammed the side door closed, then opened the passenger door for her.

"I drive." His look dared her to disagree. When she didn't, he dipped his head in an almost nod and rounded the van to slip into the driver's seat.

"Buckle up."

"Dang, Netters," Darcy struggled with the buckle then finally heard it click home. "Who peed in your breakfast cereal?"

"Guilt by association." Netters merged on to Lincolnway and maneuvered into the right-hand lane. "Adkins can't seem to separate his hate and loathing for you, from his distrust and dislike for me. In his gnarled little brain, we are joined at the hip, so if you piss him off—"

"Okay. I've got it. Just one point though. It's not my fault Zach keeps assigning you to me." Darcy could feel her good mood evaporate in the late afternoon sun.

"True. And I must admit you're never dull, Calamity." He aimed his big-toothed smile in her direction.

"And stop calling me Calamity."

"It fits, babe. Who stumbled onto the bones story in the first place?"

"A contractor."

"I mean from the station."

"Okay. Yes, I called the story in—then Adkins stole it—then I stole it back. Nothing calamitous in that chain of events."

"Unless like me, you get caught in the crossfire."

"I don't see you ducking."

"If you and Adkins go picnicking on each other, everybody leaves me alone. That suits me fine." Netters parked the van in front of the police station. "Show time!"

Darcy snatched up her tote, slid to the ground, then leaned her head back in to talk to Netters. "Set up by the building logo. I'll go in and search for a spokesperson."

"You got it," Netters was already halfway out, but he ducked his head in and smiled at Darcy. “Try not to get into trouble in the next ten minutes. Okay?”

“Cute, Netters. Real cute.” Darcy slung her tote onto her shoulder, squared her shoulders, and marched through the double glass doors.

The lobby was coldly professional, uncluttered by any non-public warmth. It was all chrome and glass with chairs scattered around. The chairs were basically faux leather slings. Not uncomfortable but not comfortable as it should be in a waiting area, she remembered last summer sitting in those chairs, waiting for Hank to come get her to take her statement.

“It’s all beige,” she thought not for the first time. “They can’t even commit to a color.”

Her boot heels hitting the hard tile on the floor echoed cavernously as Darcy crossed to the receptionist.

“Hello. I’m Darcy Moreland from KCWY News. I was wondering if I could speak to the person heading the investigation on the bones that were found yesterday.”

Darcy flashed her station ID at the 20-something mousy blonde behind the desk. She smiled, but Darcy knew it was meaningless. The woman was the vigilant guard at the gate, and she took her job seriously.

“I’m sorry, Ms. Moreland, is it?”

Darcy nodded, already trying to summon a game plan.

“Well, Ms. Moreland, Detective Nelson is heading up that investigation, and he left clear orders to—um now let’s check—” She looked down at a steno notebook filled with scribbles.

“Here it is,” she sounded thrilled to have found the right memo. Her voice made Darcy want to gnash her teeth. It reminded her of a congenitally-cheery third grade teacher.

“Detective Nelson said to tell you if you asked, ‘The ongoing investigation is continuing and the CPD has no comment at this time.’”

“Is that a memo for all news personnel, or is it specifically for me?”

The receptionist blinked her baby-blues like a matinee moviegoer coming into the noonday sun. “Um—I mean to say—um.”

"It's okay. Detective Nelson and I have a unique relationship. You can tell me." By now Darcy was leaning forward on her elbows on the high half-moon-shaped reception desk.

The receptionist instinctively leaned back to put more space between them. "Detective Nelson did tell me it was for all news personnel, but to assure you specifically it definitely and especially included you."

Darcy laughed, then took pity on the poor receptionist. She looked like she had her finger ready to press an alarm.

"It's okay. I'm much harder to offend than that. Why don't you call him and tell him I am standing in the lobby, fresh from the anthropology lab in Laramie, and I wanted to share some of the preliminary information about the bones."

"Okay. Um—"

"I'll just take a seat over here and wait." Darcy flashed the anxious receptionist a smile and slid into a simulated-leather and chrome waiting room chair. Reminds me of the swings in the parks now, she thought. The rubberized seat bent in and was pinchy and uncomfortable. She much preferred the swings of her youth, made of either rigid plastic or wood. She loved swings. It was always relaxing and exhilarating to pump your legs to climb even higher.

She had barely turned more than a few mangled pages of a year-old *People* magazine when Hank appeared.

"Been to Laramie and back, I hear."

Darcy took a purely selfish moment to look up the full length of Hank Nelson as he loomed over her. Six foot or more, dark, thick hair that needed a trim as it curled on his collar. He was, as usual, dressed all in black. His soft blue eyes could turn glacially cold if annoyed, but right now they looked soft. Almost like he was happy to see her.

"That's right," she smiled at him once her eyes reached his face, "and I thought you might want to know some of the preliminary findings as of this morning, rather than having to wait until Dr. Villars has finished his full report."

Hank sat in the chair opposite hers. Darcy wondered how he could sprawl in a chair and still look poised for a fight.

"And just what preliminaries on the forensic report do you have?" Hank asked.

"Not so fast, cowboy. I want some *quid pro quo*."

"Don't be absurd. If it weren't for the fact that I like looking at you, and that you came at a good time, I wouldn't even be out here. I can pick up the phone and get prelims from Villars whenever I want."

"Ah yes, but you'd have to interrupt him to get the information I can give you right now," Darcy didn't try to mask her triumphant tone.

"You know when you're on the hunt like this, your eyes sparkle. It's not an unattractive look."

"Cut the corn syrup, Detective. Do you want to know or not?"

Hank sighed as if wounded. "I'm giving you all my best stuff."

Darcy stood and looked at her watch.

"Love to banter with you Hank, but I'm on the clock. Here's the deal; you do a standup with me out front, and I'll tell you everything I know."

"I'd be happy to, Darcy, but we really don't have any information yet." Hank stood as if he was ready to leave.

"Well then, just say that. Please, Hank? Zach really wants a taped remote for the early news."

Darcy felt a whisper of uneasiness slither across the back of her neck. She wasn't sure if what she'd told him was true.

"And that's all you want me to say?"

"Well I do want you to comment on some of the groundwork forensics that Dr. Villars has done."

"If I don't know what they are, I can't comment on them." Hank smiled.

Netters opened one of the outside doors and leaned in. "Come on. I'm waitin' out here."

Darcy's head swung from Netters back to Hank. "Hank, please? It will be a taped report and I promise to edit anything you think might compromise the investigation in any way."

"Okay. Since you're such a *quid pro quo* fan, how about dinner tonight?" Hank cocked his brow at the question and Darcy felt her joints melt into pudding.

"Do you practice that?" She tilted her head to one side as if studying him. "It's not an unattractive look." Darcy grinned up brazenly at him.

"Point taken. How about that dinner?"

"You are a truly obstinate man. Okay. Yes. Dinner, but nothing fancy. Now come on." Darcy took his arm and pulled him toward the door.

Netters looked up from adjusting his camera. "About time. Stand by the logo and make sure you're not in shadow." Darcy took the microphone and stood with the grey stucco walls at her back.

"Levels?" Netters asked.

Holding the microphone down from her mouth, she enunciated carefully, "Brevity is the soul of lingerie—Dorothy Parker."

Netters chuckled. "Okay Detective, can you stand to her right please? Otherwise, she'll have to look into the sun. It gives her a piggy-eyed-squint."

Hank laughed and joined Darcy in front of the wall.

"We'll start with a medium closeup and after your intro, tighten up so I can get a two shot," Netters rattled off.

"Just stand right here and I'll come to you after the intro." Darcy translated for Hank. "Oh and Hank, lose the toothpick." Hank looked surprised but remove the toothpick and tossed it in one of the concrete ash trays by the front steps.

"And three, two" Netters counted, then pointed to her on one.

Darcy squared her shoulders to the camera and began:

"This is Darcy Moreland at the Cheyenne Police Department where I'm talking to Detective Hank Nelson, who is heading up the investigation of the grisly discovery of two sets of bones buried in the basement crawlspace of a local home. Thank you for speaking with us, Detective."

Darcy angled her shoulders three-quarters into the two shot. Without waiting for his response, she began.

"Have there been any new developments in the case so far, detective?"

"We are still conducting a general investigation. We'll have to wait to get the forensic report to help narrow the scope. We expect a full report in a few days."

"I've just returned from speaking to Dr. Villars at the anthropology lab at the University. Were you aware that the cause of death of the most recently buried body is being attributed to multiple blunt force trauma inflicted over most of his body?"

"I have not yet received the report, but yes. At the scene, it was evident that the body had sustained multiple blows."

"Do you have any theories about what caused the injuries or why he was buried wrapped in a sheet?"

"I'm not inclined to be theoretical until the evidence has been collected, Ms. Moreland."

Darcy recognized the icy tone in Hank's voice, but she pushed on.

"The second body is also male. Is that correct, Detective?"

"Yes."

"And he seems to have sustained a single blow to the head. His cause of death is also temporarily listed as blunt force trauma. Is that right, Detective?"

"That's correct."

"Dr. Villers and Dr. Larson at the lab told me that the bodies were buried approximately 60 years apart. Given that information, do you think it likely that these deaths were connected in any way?"

"We won't be able to determine that until we investigate further."

Darcy heard in his voice that he was done. "Just one more question, if I may, Detective. Are you going to authorize the use of a reconstructionist for the skulls?"

"I suspect we will." Hank turned full into the camera. "We are asking if anyone has information about these deaths, to please contact the Cheyenne Police Department."

Hank glared at Netters, gestured for him to cut, and turned to Darcy.

"Was it your intention to make me look incompetent or just uninformed?"

"I just wanted your reaction to the causes of death and the separation of the time of burials."

"For future reference Ms. Moreland in case I didn't make it abundantly clear on our last go around, I do not speculate on camera during an ongoing investigation. Is that clear?"

"Crystal."

Hank headed for the door.

"Does that mean our *quid pro quo* dinner is off?" Darcy called after him.

Hank stopped and turned to her. "No. It just means now *you're* buying." He disappeared into the building.

"That went well," Netters said as he relieved Darcy of the mic.

"I think he's annoyed, but not permanently pissed," Darcy said as she continued to stare at the now empty doorway.

"I'd tread lightly. The man doesn't strike me as someone who likes to repeat himself."

"I know." Darcy opened the van door. "Zach wanted a talking head, and I didn't think Hank would be open with the details unless I blind-sided him."

"Did you learn that technique in Journalism 101?" Netters asked as he slid in behind the wheel.

"No. Contrary to the evidence, I had good instructors. It's no excuse, but sometimes when I'm rummaging for information, I forget to be professional." Darcy clicked her seat belt. "I'm hoping to improve with age and experience."

"Well, it was a performance worthy of Jerk-Adkins in case you need any aversion therapy."

Darcy shuddered dramatically. "That image ought to smother my enthusiasm."

"Calamity, I don't think there's any image that tough. Just try not to antagonize your sources."

"Got it."

Once at the station, Darcy collected the three sticky notes by her name on the check-in white board. One stated her cousin Cathie called from the title company. Darcy stuck that on the front of her notebook as she moved toward her office.

The second note was from Hank saying he'd pick her up around six. Darcy crumbled that and the note from Adkins telling her to find him ASAP and tossed them in the hallway trash.

Closing the door on her mini office, she fished her phone from her purse and hit the number for Cathie's office on speed dial.

"Cheyenne Abstract and Title. How may I direct your call?" said the perky voice.

"Hi. Darcy Moreland for Cathie Garner please."

Darcy flipped open her notebook and put a bullet heading: Title Search: 515 East 18th street house.

"Hi Darcy. That was fast. I just called about fifteen minutes ago."

"Yeah, I just got in. What did you find out?"

"Well the title search was pretty brief. It seems that house has essentially been owned by the same family since it was built. It's an old house so we have a list of details, but I'll e-mail you the salient points. Okay?"

"That would be great. Thanks a lot, Cathie."

"Oh, you'll earn it, cousin. Remember you're watching Jeremy tomorrow. I'll drop him by about 10 o'clock. Try to be awake."

"I'll be there, but awake might be iffy. Call me when you're on your way. I thought we might walk down to the park with Mac. Jeremy likes Mac."

"Okay by me, but it takes about three hours to get highlights, a facial and a pedi. You can try putting him down for a nap after lunch. I'll bring stuff for him. See you tomorrow. Bye."

Darcy didn't need to respond as the line was dead. Clicking to access her e-mail, she saw the normal numbers of forwards and jokes and then Cathie's e-mail scrolled into view. It opened with no preliminaries.

"Paul Starks who was an accountant/bookkeeper for the Swan Cattle Company built the house in 1870."

Wow! Darcy thought, the Swan Cattle Company was way back in the day. She scooted closer to her screen.

"Later Starks' daughter, Cara, married stock foreman, Phillip Romero, of Warren Livestock in 1900."

Warren was a huge name in ranching and power circles. He was mostly known for his years in the United States Senate and being the first Governor of Wyoming. Streets were named for him as well as the local F.E. Warren Air Force Base. Darcy made a note to check on the progression of the associations of Swan, Warren, and Romero men often described as cattle barons, making Cheyenne a city of millionaires.

"When Philip Romero died, the house was eventually willed to their eldest son, Fremont Romero, who also owned a ranch out on Iron Mountain and died in 1936 leaving his ranch to his oldest son, Robert and the house on 18th St. to his two youngest children Marie Wilton Romero and Charles James Romero."

Darcy highlighted the names in the e-mail for future reference.

"Marie Wilton Romero never married and lived off and on in the house until she moved to Sage Hill Assisted Living in 2015."

"C. J. died in a car accident in the early 40s. His share of the house reverted to his older brother Robert and younger sister, Marie."

"Marie Wilton Romero signed over her interest in the house when she moved to Sage Hill. The current owner of record is Gary Romero, Robert's grandson and great-nephew of Marie."

"Well . . . hello again, Mr. Romero!" Darcy said aloud. She cocked her chair back cautiously and put her feet on her desk.

She grinned as she remembered the handsome rancher, she'd met during Cheyenne Days last summer when investigating the death of a young girl. He had been the Rodeo Chairman one of the Committees that ran the celebration Cheyenne was famous for. He was a handsome hunk of man she thought, but she had already been infected by Hank Nelson's charm, or sometimes the lack thereof.

The email went on,

"This is as much as I could get from the fast search. I don't know if Marie Romero is still alive, but I think Gary Romero still runs a ranch on Iron Mountain. Let me know if you need more information."

Darcy leaned back further into her chair and let the implications swirl around her head.

The more she thought about it, the more she was sure that Gary Romero would not be thrilled about her snooping into his family.

A Romero was bound to be involved with at least one of the bodies. How could they not be?

Maybe it would be better to bypass Romero for now, and go right to the older woman, Marie Romero if she were still alive. Often older people had clear memories of things that happened fifty years ago when they couldn't remember what they'd just had for lunch.

Flashing back to Abby's story about the witch, Darcy fervently hoped this story wasn't going to be a scene from *Arsenic and Old Lace* where the old ladies poisoned men and their crazy nephew buried them in the basement.

Darcy shook her head in disgust. Gary Romero was perfectly sane. She was almost sure.

CHAPTER 5

Darcy bypassed Abby's door on the way up to her apartment. She took a quick shower, fluffed her shoulder length blonde hair through her fingers, and let it air dry.

Picking out some black jeans, she paired them with a soft black sweater that had a deep ruffled neckline. She loved the sweater. It was both sexy and demure and she felt special in it.

A quick pass with mascara and pink lip-gloss, and she was out the door jogging down the dark oak stairs to Abby's.

They had long ago passed the knock-on-the-door formality, so Darcy breezed right in.

Mac, her Cairn terrier, cavorted at her feet as soon as Darcy closed the door behind her, and she stooped to pick him up. Calling out, "Abby. It's just me," Darcy plopped with Mac onto the overstuffed sofa in the living room. She scratched behind Mac's ears and nuzzled his rough fur.

Abby bustled in from the tiny kitchen, wiping her hands on the towel that hung from her apron pocket.

"Tell me everything. I want to know what you know and what you suspect." Abby dropped into her favorite Chesterfield chair and drilled Darcy with her soft blue-eyed-stare.

"No hello? How are you? How was your day?"

"Hello. Nice cleavage. I saw the interview you taped with Hank, so I know how your day went. Now I want to know the stuff that didn't make it into the report. Give." Abby wriggled in the chair like a setting hen.

"There's not much to tell." Darcy mentally ran through her day in Laramie. "It's no use. I can't do this dry. I need a glass of wine."

"Oh, for heaven's sake. Help yourself." Abby wafted her hand in the direction of the kitchen. "There's a little Pinot Grigio in there, I think. Bring me a glass too."

Juggling the bottle and two glasses, Darcy almost tripped over Mac who barely scampered away in time to avoid a catastrophe.

"For the love of Saint Rocco! Guinness Murphy McCann, stay out of the way!"

Abby's brow shot up. "Saint Rocco?"

Pouring the golden hued wine into small glasses, Darcy answered, "Patron saint of dogs. I'm trying to break myself of cussing."

"Commendable." Abby took a deep taste of the cold wine. "Okay, enough foreplay."

"Well, I met Dr. Larson and Dr. Villars, both forensic anthropologists, in Laramie," Darcy settled back into the sofa. "They are massively excited about what they do."

"Admirable that they enjoy their job, but what did they tell you?"

"Dr. Larson gave names to the bones. Says it reminds him they were once people who'd had lives. I thought it was sweet."

"What did he name them?"

"The sixty-year-old bones he named Mr. Smith and the six-year-old bones he named Mr. Jones."

"Not very original," Abby muttered.

"No but helpful when you're talking about them. Anyway, Mr. Smith was about in his late twenties and Mr. Jones was about in his late forties."

"How could they tell that?"

"Dr. Larson told me about all these complex tests they can do to determine how old a person is when they're dealing with skeletal remains. Has to do with the skull and the wrist bones.

"He also told me about how he could test to identify when they lived by the amino acids in their bones and the presence or lack of radiation. It really was fascinating."

"I don't get it," Abby said. "What do you mean lack of radiation?" Abby pounced on the one condition she recognized.

"You remember the bombing at Hiroshima and Nagasaki to end the war with Japan? VJ Day if I recall my history correctly."

"I know I don't look like it, but I am not that old," Abby said wiggling slightly in her chair with annoyance.

"Sorry. Didn't mean to imply you were around back then, but you do remember celebrating both VG and VJ anniversaries. Not as predominate today, but those were big days. I always have to remind myself that our winning that war was not a foregone conclusion. People were terrified and for good reason." Darcy sipped her wine.

"But what does all this have to do with Mr. Smith and Mr. Jones?"

"Evidently, if you died before the bombing raids in Japan and the subsequent nuclear testing in the desert outside of Las Vegas, you wouldn't have any radiation in your bones. If you were born after, like most of us were, we all have a little bit of radiation residue. Mr. Smith had none, because he died before the bombs were dropped, and Mr. Jones had trace amounts so the forensic anthropologists can determine that he died after." Darcy twirled her wine and watched Abby think about that for a minute. She was well and truly gob-smacked, Darcy thought.

"Fascinating is right. Who knew? I remember doing bombing drills at school in case a nuclear bomb was dropped. We were in danger because Cheyenne is surrounded with missile sites. Looking back, they were a horrible joke. We were told to duck under our desks if the alarms went off. I even remember a film that told us to hide in a ditch alongside of a road if there weren't any bomb shelters nearby. After the Cuban missile Crisis, we were all afraid of Castro, who was being supplied by the Russians with nuclear weapons. We were terrified that they would bomb us in our sleep. People began building bomb shelters under their homes. My friend Patty's dad had built one under their house." Abby chuckled a little at the absurdity of it. "And just think of it. Here we all are, nuclear storage centers walking around."

"It is pretty funny, not ha ha funny but peculiar funny that the average citizen of the world is sublimely ignorant of the long term effects of nuclear weapons," Darcy said.

"How did Dr. Larson think they died?" Abby scooted forward in her chair cradling her glass in her hands. "I mean I heard all that 'blunt force trauma' stuff on your report, but did they give you anything else?"

"He said Mr. Smith could have died from a simple fall. The crack on his skull was wide at one end and small on the other. Dr. Villars said that's the kind of skull crack you can get from falling against something. It could have just been an accident in his case."

"But if it was an accident, why was his body stashed in the basement?"

"I don't know. Like Hank is fond of saying 'we have to wait to have the evidence before theorizing.'"

"And Mr. Jones—" Abby kibitzed.

"Murdered. Said they were sure. Mr. Smith was crudely wrapped in an old rug which implies his death was an unplanned for event. Mr. Jones however was all wrapped up in a sheet when the police found him, so it not only helped to keep the bones of the bodies separate but pointed to a preplanned event. An execution done with malice and forethought."

"How does that point to murder?" Abby said.

"It doesn't exactly, but it just adds to the mystery. See, Mr. Jones' bones, instead of having just one wound in the head like Mr. Smith, had dents all over all over his body".

"Some of the dents were large enough to cause fractures. One thighbone was broken clean in half. In other places, you could see smaller dents in the bones varying from about baseball sized to golf ball sized—but all irregular impressions. It was weird."

"What do the doctors make of that?"

"They said they didn't know yet. They had never seen a set of dented bones before, but they did say they thought Mr. Jones had definitely been murdered."

"My goodness that is intriguing." Abby poured them both a dollop of more wine. "What's your best guess about how?"

"I think he was literally beaten to death. I also think more than one person participated."

"Why do you think that?"

Darcy sipped some wine while she tried to order her thoughts. Finally, she said, "Because the damage was beyond what would likely be inflicted by one person—even someone deep in the throes of rage."

"I'm not sure I'm following the reasoning here . . ."

Darcy sipped her wine. "Think about it, Abby. If I were beyond angry with you—angry enough to kill you—I might pick up a candle stick or a golf club and swing at you until you went down."

"What a pleasant thought. Purely theoretical, I assume."

"Do you want to interrupt, or do you want to hear my theory?"

"I hang on your every word." Abby's eyes twinkled with mischief.

"Any more sarcasm and I'll take my theories and drop them on Hank over dinner tonight." Darcy flopped back into the settee.

"He's taking you out? He didn't look particularly pleased with you on TV—or was that his serious-on-the-job look?"

"No. That was his, Darcy-has-imposed-on-me-again-look. I kind of manipulated him into doing a taped report. Zach wanted an official statement and I—" Darcy twirled her glass and watched the golden liquid swirl up the sides. "Anyway, I'm buying him dinner."

"Where are you going?"

"Bob's Barbeque for the baby back ribs. Thought it would be thematically apropos with all this talk about bones."

Abby laughed. "Hope he appreciates the *Fried Green Tomatoes* symbolism. Okay, finish your theory before he comes."

"My theory is, if I were in a fit of passion and wanted to kill you, I'd swing and hit several times, until you went down. Once down, I might take some last shots to make sure you weren't moving anymore."

"That all seems reasonable, but . . ."

"But if there were several of us, a frenzied mob, countless blows would be inflicted—way beyond the death blows. There is a quality of a fanatical beating on the remains. Like over-kill. It is disturbing." Darcy finished off her wine in one small gulp.

Abby sat silently, then asked, “Are you really taking Hank for ribs?”

Darcy laughed, and it diffused the melancholy moment. “No. Actually, I think I’ll take him to Café Zen and make him eat salad.”

“That will be much better.” Abby wiped away a non-existent ring on the marble-topped table.

“Oh, I almost forgot to tell you. My cousin Cathie called me back. I asked her to trace the ownership of the house and guess what.” Darcy leaned toward her.

“What?”

“I think the name of your ‘witch’ was Marie Wilton Romero. Ring a bell?”

“Only that Romero is a prominent ranching family like the Warrens and the Careys. Isn’t there a Romero Street up by Bar X development?”

“I don’t know about that, but I do know she’s related to Gary Romero one of the Cheyenne Rodeo Days Committee Chairmen. How’s that for ‘small world’?”

“A little cramped—especially if you’re intending to accuse someone from one of Cheyenne’s oldest families of a double homicide.”

“I’m not going to accuse anyone of anything—yet. First, I want to see if Maria Romero is still alive.”

“How can you track her down? Are you going to call Romero?”

“Not right away. Cathie told me that Marie’s last known address was at Sage Hill.”

“That assisted living community on the east side?”

“The same. I thought I’d try to check on it on Monday.”

“Why not tomorrow?”

“Because in return for all this information, I agreed to watch my cousin’s three-year-old tomorrow while she goes to get fluffed and buffed. Monday will be soon enough.”

“Are you going to be sharing this information with Hank later tonight?” Abby picked up the now-empty bottle and the glasses and headed for the kitchen. Darcy followed her and leaned against the doorjamb.

"Truthfully, I'm not sure. On the one hand, he might appreciate the information and feel like we're sharing sources, but on the other hand he probably has already tracked down the title on the house and I don't want to give him an opening to tell me to stay out of it."

Abby rested her butt against the counter and faced Darcy. "That is a problem."

"What would you do, Abby?"

"Me? I'm not to be trusted. I always blab everything I know. Stems from being a teacher. Sometimes I think teachers are the intestines of the world. Whatever we ingest, we want to compact and push out as soon as possible."

Darcy laughed. "That gives a whole new slant on being full of . . ."

"Saint Rocco!" Abby finished for her. "Don't forget your resolve."

"Seriously though, I can see both sides."

Walking past Darcy, Abby went back to her chair. When Darcy didn't say anything more, Abby pulled Mac onto her lap and ran her hand slowly down his back.

Finally, she said, "Why don't you try to see what he already knows before you give him the whole enchilada? If he knows what you know, no harm no foul. If not, you can decide what you want to tell him."

"What if he tells me to stop interfering in a police investigation?"

Abby chuckled deep in her chest. "Because that's always worked so well before?"

"Abby, this is fundamental. Netters told me today not to abuse my sources, and I think he's right. I just want to find the ethical line here between doing my job and not getting in the way."

"Look, honey. If it bothers you, just tell him what you've got. This is a small city. You're likely to continue to overlap on stories, and this might buy you some good will."

"Okay, I'll try it." Darcy leaned over and kissed Abby's cheek. "I'll let you know how it goes when I get home. I think I'll wait for Hank on the front steps."

"Have fun. Mac and I will just be hanging out watching TV."

Darcy planted herself on the concrete steps of her building and rested her chin in her hands. A cool-but-still-comfortable breeze lifted her slightly damp hair. She could smell wood smoke in the air and smiled. It wasn't cold enough to have a fire in the fireplace, but some folks loved to jump the season. Darcy thought the scent was evocative of dark fall nights and mulled cider.

When she was younger, she remembered the excitement of starting a brand new school year. It was liberating in a way. All the mistakes of last year were gone. You got a do over. You got new notebooks and a new box of crayons. It wasn't until later she found out the teachers talked to each other about some of their memorable students that she lost faith in the theory of rehabilitation.

She hoped Hank would give her a do over. It wasn't just that he was a source, she admitted to herself. She really liked him, and she hated when they got sideways with each other. She wasn't altogether sure that just acknowledging faults was going to be enough.

She hadn't waited long before Hank pulled up in his pickup. He looked surprised to see her waiting for him, but he had the good grace not to comment.

As soon as she was ensconced and seatbelt engaged, Hank looked over at her. His eyes strayed south then snapped back up in supreme restraint.

"You look nice. Where do you want to go?"

"Good question. I toyed with getting ribs—because of the case—"

Hank winced in appreciation of her ghoulish humor.

"Then I thought I'd make you take me to Café Zen just to punish you."

"Salads?"

"My final choice is the Tavern. That way we can drink, and you can get a chicken fried whatever."

Hank slapped his truck in gear before she could change her mind.

The Tavern was a cozy restaurant downtown by the Plaza that traced its roots to Cheyenne's earliest history. Decorated with high-backed wooden booths and vintage pictures depicting various views of the old railroad/ranching community from the mid-1800s, it was a favorite place to get an excellent meal and a strong drink.

Hank ordered a beer and Darcy just ordered water, then waited for the waitress to scurry off before probing the sore topic on both their minds.

Darcy sighed dramatically. "Okay, I'll start. I'm sorry I put you on the spot this afternoon. It was unprofessional and I regret it."

Hank sat across from her and didn't respond.

"Well?" she asked.

"And . . .?" he pushed.

Darcy fought a defensive squirm. "And it wasn't nice. How much groveling do you need here? I'm buying you dinner for hell's sake."

"I like the present level. Are you going to share information, or do I have to pull it out of you?"

"I had every intention of sharing everything I know with you in the spirit of professional cooperation." Darcy smiled up as the waitress put a frosty glass of water in front of her.

Hank's face said clearly, he didn't believe her.

"Wipe that smartass little smirk off your face, Hank. I said I'll share, and I will. Are you going to share with me?"

"Within the confines of an ongoing investigation, yes."

"Uh-uh—not good enough. I want access. I will promise to keep things off the record if you ask me to, but I want to be actively imbedded in this investigation."

"Darcy, you know the difference between me and the Pope?"

Darcy scowled for a second, trying to make sense of this side trip. "You mean besides the obvious ones?"

"Yeah." Hank paused. "The Pope only wants you to kiss his ring."

While Darcy processed this remark, the waitress returned to take their order. Darcy pretended not to see her. "Why, Detective Nelson, did you just imply you want me to

kiss your— "

"Don't finish that if you want our new truce to hold," Hank said. "Order."

Feeling like she'd won that round, she ordered a French Dip sandwich and Hank got the chicken-fried chicken.

Hank sipped his beer and waited for Darcy to begin.

She filled Hank in on her initial contact with Dr. Dan Moss from Cheyenne Community College at the crime scene and her subsequent meeting with the Doctors Larson and Villars at the university earlier that day.

"Did he say anything more about the cause of death—beyond what you bludgeoned me with on camera?"

"Not really. But Hank, I have a theory about the newer bones. I think several people beat him to death. You should've seen the dents all over the remains."

"I did."

"Oh yeah. You would've. Anyway, what do you think of my theory?"

"Plausible. But at this point almost anything is plausible. What else you got?"

Darcy summarized the information that her cousin had dug up for her about the house. Hank's raised eyebrow was the only clue he gave that he was surprised.

"So, I presume you called your old friend Romero?"

"No, I didn't. And I might not in any case. I want to see if I can talk to Marie Romero, if she is still alive, before Romero is alerted and runs interference."

"You're going to browbeat poor old Marie for information? Romero won't like that." Hank smiled as if he enjoyed the idea.

"I'm not going to browbeat anyone. I'm just going to go visit Marie with an old friend."

"An old friend? Who?"

"Abby. She used to know Marie. Abby was really young when they met, but she remembers her clearly." Darcy ended triumphantly. Convincing Abby to accompanying her on Monday should be a cinch. Darcy was pleased with her instant inspiration.

"What do you intend to ask her? I don't want an old lady stirred up needlessly because you want a good story."

"Is this where you tell me to back off because this is your case?"

"Close, but not exact. I'm asking you to be as discreet and gentle in your questioning as you can and share any pertinent information you may get."

Darcy blinked in disbelief. "Is that all? And what do I get?"

"Off the record?"

"If I must."

"You get the information that the bones were buried under a pile of stones which I had collected at the crime scene and had taken to the lab."

"Why? Were they special stones?" Darcy was oblivious to the sandwich placed in front of her.

"I have a hunch they were the weapon used on Mr. Jones."

"You think he was stoned to death? Do they still do that? I thought that was Old Testament."

"I think my hunch and yours about it being more than one person who murdered him go together well. Don't you?" Hank raised his beer, and she answered with a clink of her glass against his.

CHAPTER 6

CATHIE APPEARED BRIGHT AND ANNOYING the next morning with young Jeremy in tow and two cups of double-shot lattes from the coffee shop down the street.

As soon as Darcy opened the door, Jeremy ran past to scramble onto the straight-backed oak chair under the window.

"Cars!" he yelled and pounded on the glass with his open hands.

Windex, Darcy thought as she watched more smudges appear on the window.

Cathie laughed.

"I'd wait until he goes home, and you can survey the total damage. He's just fascinated by all the cars down here. He hardly ever sees this many unless I bring him to town. Thinks they're magic."

"You mean they aren't?" Darcy took the brown paper cup with its cardboard finger protector and smiled gratefully at her cousin.

"Only when they work. Reminds me, I need to get my oil changed." Cathie sipped her latte cautiously, setting it on the side table by Darcy's overlarge brown sofa and dropping a large navy-blue bag on the floor.

Darcy plopped down next to her cousin. "How long are you going to be gone, for heaven's sake?"

"Easy, cupcake. I'll only be gone a couple of hours. Here is the number where you can reach me if my cell goes to voice mail."

Mac squatted beneath Jeremy's chair and barked excitedly, while the boy squealed in delight. Cathie scooped him from the chair and bent to Mac's level. She reintroduced her son to Darcy's dog.

"Remember to let him smell your hand before you touch him. Mac is okay. He's an old friend, but it is important that you remember all dogs are not like Mac.

Mac ran his tiny pink tongue up Jeremy's cheek and Jeremy shrieked with joy.

"See, he likes you," Cathie hugged her son close. "He just kissed you."

Darcy smiled and said softly, "Actually he's just trying him out for his taste bank in his little mind. Let's just hope he doesn't file him under 'food.'"

Cathie stood and faced Darcy, picked up her latte. "Nice try. I'll come get him in under three hours. Try not to lose him."

She kissed and hugged Jeremy, leaving before the child knew she was going. The eruption hit as soon as Cathie closed the door behind her.

Darcy spent the next fifteen minutes trying to calm the distraught child before Mac jumped up to join them on the couch to distract him.

Jeremy blinked his huge light hazel eyes and smiled his baby-toothed smile. Darcy was lost.

She split a strawberry donut with both Jeremy and Mac.

"Don't get used to it, buddy," she said to Mac. "You helped me out, and I owed you."

Mac ran his tongue around the outside of his mouth and practically slurped.

Dressed for the cool autumn weather in a mock Aran sweater and some elasticized jeans, Jeremy, holding Darcy's hand, followed Mac slowly down the oak stairs to Abby's place.

The door was cracked open. Darcy pushed through into the living room.

"Grab a jacket, we're going to the park," Darcy announced.

"Sounds like fun," Abby said.

Moments later, the foursome wandered down the uneven sidewalks; Abby and Darcy shoulder to shoulder, Mac on his leash, and Jeremy toddling along grabbing the taut leash occasionally for balance.

"How did it go last night with Hank?' Abby asked.

"Actually, pretty well. He didn't even tell me to back off about going to see Marie. He just asked that I try not to upset her if I could help it. I don't think he considers her a serious lead, but we agreed to share information."

"Well that's progress, isn't it?"

"I told him you were going with me because you were a friend of Marie's."

"That's stretching the truth a bit, isn't it?"

"Jeremy! Put that rock down. You don't know where it's been." She turned to Abby and lowered her voice, "That was stupid. Just where could a rock have been? God help me, I'm channeling my mother."

"He's barely three. What does he care what we say to him? Hank, however, is considerably older, and I don't appreciate you including me in your little lie fest. I was clear when I told you that story. I only met her once for five minutes. We did not have a relationship and you know it."

"I know but I needed to boost my credibility." Darcy grabbed Jeremy's hand as they crossed the street.

"That was an even more stupid statement than the rock one. Since when does lying improve your credibility?"

"When it forces you into going to see Marie with me and it reassures Hank that I won't do something stupid. Please say you'll go with me. After all. You signed your note Your Friend Abigail."

"Okay, I'll come, but I don't like being manipulated like that. Don't do it again."

"No, ma'am," Darcy replied, and tried to look suitably chastened.

Abby and Darcy found a bench in the shade. Darcy undid Mac's leash, and he took off running, with Jeremy fast on his trail. It was comical to watch Mac run ahead and then wait for Jeremy to catch up before they were off again. Occasionally Darcy would call Mac to come back when boy and dog got too far away. They ran full-out for a half an hour when Darcy called an end.

Back at the apartment, Darcy settled Jeremy on her bed and allowed Mac to join him. Both fell asleep for about an hour. Cathie would be pleased.

Cathie picked Jeremy up a little before noon. Darcy had managed to clean off most of the vestiges of a chocolate pudding after nap treat from his face.

"Just how much chocolate did you feed him?" Cathie asked as she dabbed at some pudding in the cracks of his smile.

"Well, he also got a nap so that's something. I fed him just enough sugar to keep myself in good standing. You never know if you'll want to leave him here again and now, he will want to come back," Darcy said. "It's a win, win, win." Darcy smiled at her cousin.

"Except that he'll probably be high octane for the rest of the day," Cathie muttered as she picked up all of Jeremy's toys.

"That's why you live out in the country. Just let him loose in one of the corrals."

"Not helpful, Cuz."

"Well anyway you look gorgeous. Those highlights really brighten everything."

"Thanks, Darcy. And thanks for watching Jeremy. I really do appreciate it." Cathie hoisted Jeremy on her hip and Jeremy reached for Darcy.

"Dar Dar" he cried.

"You can come back again to visit me Jeremy," Darcy said as she ruffled his soft brown hair.

Darcy heard him screaming as Cathie went down the stairs and out the front. "Maybe that last pudding cup was a mistake," she said to herself.

As soon as she was sure Cathie and Jeremy were well away, Darcy grabbed her keys and ran down to get Abby.

"I don't want to wait. Let's go talk to Marie today," she said as she burst through the apartment door.

Abby put down the book she was reading. "What are you going to ask Ms. Romero, assuming we even get in?"

"Try not to be so overly optimistic, Abby. It just pumps up my confidence." Darcy grabbed a sweater from the front closet and passed it to Abby.

Abby tossed it on the back of her chair and folded her arms in front of her. "I'm serious. You need to have a plan. I will not intrude on that woman's privacy if you don't have a plan."

"My plan is to see how awake and aware she is before I ask any specific questions. Hank asked me to be discreet and sensitive and I can't do that without getting a feel for what we're dealing with."

"Fine."

"Is that 'Fine, I think that's a great approach.' or 'Fine, I think you're wrong but I'm not going to argue anymore.'?"

"Truthfully, a little of both."

Darcy laughed. "Then we're fine, right?"

"I guess so." Abby's lips curled into a reluctant smile as she grabbed her sweater on the way out the door.

After a short drive, they pulled into the curving drive of the Sage Hill Assisted Living Home. Darcy fixed Abby with what she hoped was a stern look.

"Let me do the talking when we get in there. I'm not sure I want the office to know I'm a reporter, okay? At least until I get a read on the receptionist. No point alarming her for no good reason."

"Yeah. I remember. I'm your credibility."

Darcy winced at the deliberate sarcasm, but she held one of the large doors open to let Abby go in.

The lobby was decorated in what Darcy thought of as Santa Fe sand-painting. Splashes of rust and ochre yellow in confident lightning-like slashes on lush pillows. A sand-colored sofa and love seat faced a large fireplace. Side tables topped with lavish bouquets nestled next to the wall so as not to interfere with walkers or wheelchairs. It looked like a setting even Gorgia O'Keeffe would feel comfortable in.

"I could live here," Abby said as she watched a resident shuffle past with her yapping Yorkie tucked under her arm.

"Nonsense." Darcy swerved toward a hallway marked Office.

"You're too young, and as a retired teacher on a pension, too poor. This place is for people with a whole lot of money or a whole lot of guilty relatives."

Gratified by the 'too young' comment, Abby didn't argue.

"Good afternoon," Darcy said to the middle-aged receptionist. "We wanted to visit one of your residents, Marie Romero. Could you please tell us her apartment number?"

The attractive steel-gray-haired lady looked over the top of her red-framed reading glasses and studied the two women in front of her. The look was obviously meant to be intimidating.

"Is there a problem?" Abby arched her white-blond eyebrow as if slightly offended.

"Um . . . no. We do need to be careful of our resident's security and privacy. You understand."

Abby inserted herself in front of Darcy and smiled like an angel incarnate.

"Why, of course we do. Don't we, Darcy?" She half turned as if expecting an answer, then swung back to the receptionist.

"I am an old acquaintance of Ms. Romero's. We used to live in the same neighborhood, and Darcy here is a friend of her great-nephew Gary Romero. Is that satisfactory?"

"I'm sure it is perfectly all right but let me call and make sure it is a convenient time." She lifted the phone to her ear, "Could you please tell me your names?"

"I am Abigail McNeil, and this is Darcy Moreland." Beaming another beatific smile, Abby nodded as if that was all that had to be said.

The woman punched in an extension and turned her back to Abby and Darcy with a mumbled "Excuse me." Following a short, muffled conversation, she hung up and smiled.

"Ms. Romero will be pleased to see you. It is apartment 242 just turn right as you get off the elevator."

"Thank you so very much for your help, Ms. . . ."

"Halpen."

"Ms. Halpen. Thank you." Abby gripped Darcy's arm and steered her quickly out of the office and over to the elevators.

"Abby, you're amazing. I can't believe how smoothly you got Marie's apartment number."

"Darcy, focus. Doesn't it bother you a little that Ms. Romero will allow two perfect strangers up to her apartment?"

"Frankly, no. I thought your explanation was clear, concise and truthful. I don't know what sold her, you as an old acquaintance or me as Romero's friend, but I don't care."

The elevator ride was short and smooth. Darcy utilized the mirrors on the back wall to fluff her hair and try to pull the wrinkles out of her light blue sweater.

The corridor delicately lit by strategically placed lamps, and augmented by small pod lights at floor level, illuminated the muted, textured carpet.

Apartment 242 was as Ms. Halpin had said, just to the right of the elevator and sported an inconspicuous number and doorbell combination.

Darcy depressed the button and heard the soft chime beyond the door. She smiled at Abby, and both waited for the locks to be turned and the chain removed.

The door swept open to reveal an impeccably well-groomed lady with silver hair pulled back in a low bun. Her hair color was echoed by large silver Concho earrings she wore.

Darcy noticed that Ms. Romero was a petite five-foot, slim of build and dressed completely in black. The only touch of color was a squash-blossom necklace, resplendent with turquoise and high gloss silver.

"Won't you please come in?" Marie motioned them into the tastefully appointed room.

Darcy thought of all the ballet classes her folks had paid for. She would never be as naturally poised as this beautiful woman. Darcy smoothed her sweater once again self-consciously before she took a seat in one of the matching white linen wingback chairs flanking the fireplace. The gas fire flickered.

"I know it isn't really cold enough yet to have the fire, but I enjoy the aesthetics of it, and with these new remote controls," she shrugged her cashmere covered shoulders, "why not?"

Abby sat on the facing dark green love seat while Marie perched on the edge of the other chair by the fire.

Darcy watched, fascinated, as Marie crossed her ankles and folded her hands as if she had gone to "Princess Training." Darcy tugged at her sweater once more and vowed to get an iron.

"Ms. Romero," Darcy began, a little appalled at how thin, and reedy her voice sounded, "Thank you for agreeing to see us."

Lifting her chin slightly, Marie graced them both with a practiced smile. "At my age, I find that I am cursed with curiosity, and there seems to be no twelve-step-program to address it."

Silence fell over the room. Darcy and Abby exchanged looks.

"The truth is, Ms. Romero . . ." Abby began.

"Please call me Marie. No need for ceremony with an old acquaintance," she nodded at Abby, "and a friend of my great-nephew." She said with a nod to Darcy.

Darcy fought the urge to squirm. "Marie, my friendship with your great-nephew is not really germane."

"I didn't think it was."

So much for dementia or creeping senility, Darcy thought.

"I am a reporter with KCWY news—" Darcy waited for a reaction. Marie didn't blink. "And I have been investigating a story about your old home—"

"My father's old home," Marie interrupted her. "I saw one of your earlier reports."

"So, you know about the bones they found?"

"Only insofar as you reported on them."

Abby scooted forward on the sofa, capturing Marie's attention. "I'm here because I remembered you from when I was younger and lived in that neighborhood. I told Darcy about trying to deliver a May basket—" Abby dribbled off when faced with Marie's stony silence.

"I'm sorry. I have no memory of that."

"Well, of course you wouldn't. Long time ago—" Abby was now red with embarrassment. She signaled to Darcy that they should leave.

"If you knew we weren't quite what we represented ourselves to be, why did you let us come up?" Darcy felt responsible for Abby's mortification.

"I am always diverted by visitors, whatever their reasons for coming. At least you're not trying to sell me anything."

Darcy bristled in sympathy with Abby's discomfort. "Well I'm glad we could amuse you."

"Please, don't be offended, Miss Moreland. My days are long, and visitors of any kind are few." Marie brushed at non-existent crumbs on her lap. "Now you came here to ask me some questions. It would be a pity for you to leave without accomplishing that."

"All right. How is it that there are two sets of bones buried in the basement of a house owned by your family for decades and you don't know anything about them?"

"Your question is poorly phrased, as I'm sure you'll agree, Abby." She smiled at Abby as if uniting with her against impetuous youth. "I cannot speak to something I know nothing about. I suspect what you want to know, is when and how long I lived in that house. Is that correct?"

Abby snorted softly, trying to suck her laughter back down her throat. "She has you there, Darcy." Abby and Marie shared a conspiratorial smile, and Abby was put at ease. Marie had grace that had nothing to do with money. She was the real thing, a fourteen carat lady.

Darcy was pleased at Abby's laughter even if it was at her expense.

"All right. Marie, when and how long have you lived in the house on 18th Street?"

Marie nodded as if to acknowledge a lesson learned. "My father, Fremont Romero, deeded the house to my brother J.C. and myself on his death in 1940. I would have been—my heavens—barely 17. I had forgotten I was that young when Papa died. J.C. was twenty-one." Marie looked beyond Darcy briefly and then shook her head slightly.

"In any case, my brother J.C. and I lived in the house in town and alternately at the family ranch run by my other brother, Robert.

I didn't like the ranch in the winter. It was too cold and too quiet. I loved going to the theater, the Saturday night dances, and the church socials, and especially to the movies."

"How long did you live there?"

"I lived in the house in town about five years before I left to go live in Jackson Hole for a while."

"May I ask why you left?"

"I had suffered a painful, personal loss. I needed to get away for a while and my family had a summer home on Jackson Lake."

"But you were living on 18th around 1956. I was about nine years old when I brought you that May basket." Abby leaned forward.

"Ironically, I had to return because of another painful, personal loss." Marie sighed as if she had made some crucial decision.

Abby and Darcy waited quietly while Marie smoothed her already smooth skirt once again.

"I left for Jackson Hole after my fiancé was killed in the war. Thomas was with the Army Air Corps. I didn't even get to tell him goodbye." Marie's sherry-colored eyes brimmed with tears she tried to blink back.

"Soon after that, J.C. asked if I'd mind him renting out the house so he could go to California for a while. I wrote him back and said I didn't care what he did with the place. Two years later, J.C. died in a car accident in Los Angeles. Robert, my older brother, asked me to come home. Robert was so upset about J.C.; he said he needed to have me nearby. And so, I stayed at the house in town."

"May I ask why you never married?" Darcy asked softly.

Marie chuckled cheerlessly. "I never could stop comparing other men to Thomas. Looking back, I suppose I would have been diagnosed as clinically depressed, especially after J.C. died. I just wanted to hide from the world—and I did."

"I can certainly understand that" Abby said. "It took me a long time to get over losing my husband."

Marie smiled at Abby acknowledging their sisterhood of loss. Darcy felt a little like an intruder.

"May I ask, Ms. Romero?" Darcy continued. "When did you come to live here?"

"Marie," she corrected automaticly. "About seven years ago, I had a very mild stroke and Gary, my great-nephew, insisted that I either go live with him back at the ranch or come here. I didn't want to clutter up his life, so I moved here. It has actually been a God-sent solution. I have friends and activities. I'm ninety-four years old and I feel like a young girl."

"Thank you for your hospitality and your candor," Darcy said, rising. "We won't take up any more of your time."

"Not at all." Marie rose and walked them to the door. "I enjoy company now. By the way, young lady. How deep is the friendship between you and Gary?"

"Slightly more than acquaintances." Darcy smiled in apology.

Marie nodded as if it confirmed her suspicion. "Good luck on your investigation, Darcy. Let me know what you find out, won't you?"

"Absolutely." Darcy said, as the door closed softly behind them.

CHAPTER 7

THE NEXT MORNING, DARCY BOLTED straight up in bed. Roused from a deep sleep she tried to separate the sounds. Someone was banging violently on her door. Her heart raced, and she reached for the old wooden bat she kept under her bed and slowly lowered her feet to the floor. Mac barked loudly as the doorbell echoed shrilly and insistently through her small apartment.

Padding toward the door, she kept the bat at the ready. Mac scurried around her feet, yapping, aggressive as a Doberman. Darcy appreciated the effort.

She peeked through the spy hole, but before she could focus, the banging began again, replacing the clangorous trill of the bell and she jumped back.

"Stop pounding on my door!" she shouted regretting the late night movie she had watched with her chicken salad sandwich last night. A dull ache radiated from the back of her head and settled in her temples. "Who is it?"

"Gary Romero." The pounding stopped, but Darcy still felt uneasy. He did not sound friendly.

"Uh, okay. Hang on a minute." She propped her bat by the door and wrestled with the bolt lock and then the chain.

She picked up Mac's wriggling body to keep him from zipping out and attacking. She slowly opened the door.

Gary Romero, a big bear of a man, filled the doorway. Darcy

had to gulp to catch her breath. She'd forgotten how massive his shoulders were and how impressive his GQ/Cowboy sense of style.

"Come in." She propped Mac on her hip and stepped to the side.

He removed his 40X gray Stetson from his head in a practiced gesture. Darcy thought it was romantic in an old-fashioned-courtesy-way.

Romero looked at Darcy starting from her pink, pedicured toes, up to her Miss Kitty sleep pants, pausing to read the gold lettered Princess that marched across the front of her tank top, and finally let his gray eyes rest on her face.

Flustered, Darcy stepped back once more.

"Hi, Gary. What time is it?" she ran her hand through her already tousled hair.

Romero lifted his arm, shot the cuff of a well-tailored fawn colored western cut leather suit jacket, and glanced at his understated gold watch.

"It is nine-thirty, Ms. Moreland. Sorry to disturb your morning."

"Nine-thirty? Damn! I have to be at the station in less than an hour." She fought the panic of the unprepared and ran to the kitchen to put her teakettle on.

"You want some coffee? All I have is instant."

"No thank you, Ms. Moreland. I won't keep you long."

Again, with the Ms. Moreland? She drifted to her sofa and dropped into the soft cushions tucking her feet under her.

"Sit." Darcy motioned to the straight-backed chair.

Romero perched on the edge of the worn, green velvet seat and twirled his hat between his widespread legs.

"Well?" Darcy prodded, a little annoyed that he was taking so much time to get to the point.

Romero's head came up, and he glowered at Darcy. "Leave my Great Aunt Marie alone. You have any questions; you bring them to me. Understand? And pass that message on to your trained monkey while you're at it."

"You are *not* referring to my friend Abby as a trained monkey, are you?" Darcy felt a flush of indignation wash over her face, and she balled her fists at her side.

Romero looked confused, then once more resolute. "No. I mean your partner from the station—that Adkins fellow I almost had to throw off the park this summer. He came to talk to my Great Aunt soon after you left."

Darcy jumped up. "Are you fringgin' kidding me? That rat bait, sleazy, son-of-a-bitch is NOT my partner. I never discussed Ms. Romero with him nor told him to talk to her."

"Good to know, but I still don't want you talking to her anymore about the house on 18th. Is that clear?"

"Crystal. But why? Is there a problem? She seemed to be happy with our company." Darcy remained standing.

"You told her you were a friend of mine."

"Did I overstate it?"

"Time will tell," he smiled. He stood and towered over her. "But I meant what I said. Don't bother her about those damn bones." He headed for the door.

"Well, then how about I bother you with some questions, since you're the owner of record?"

"You are a pushy little gal, aren't you?" He folded his arms across his chest.

"Don't confuse determination with size." Darcy echoed his gesture folding her arms.

"Okay. What do you want to know?"

Darcy slouched against the back of the sofa, bracing her hands on either side. "Did you know about the bones before they were discovered?"

"What kind of question is that?"

He took a step toward her, and her chin ratcheted up a notch.

"A fairly pertinent one, I think. Your family built and owned the house after all."

"But rarely has anyone in my family lived there," Romero said. "Get your facts straight, Darcy."

"That's what I'm trying to do—*Gary*." She smiled, barely. "What was the chronology of the time Ms. Romero and her brother J.C. lived there?"

"I couldn't tell you for sure unless I looked at my dad's old records, but it seems to me, she and my Great Uncle lived in the house sometime in the late thirties or early forties. J.C. couldn't join the Army because he was 4F, I think."

"Really? What was wrong with him?"

"They said he had a heart murmur. I can remember my Grandpa saying that it's probably what really killed him, even though the official cause was listed as a single car accident."

"So when did he go to California?"

"I don't know exactly, but it was after Great Aunt Marie left to go live in Jackson." Romero twirled his hat once more, clearly uneasy talking about private family matters. "She was pretty desolate when she got the news that her fiancé was dead, or so my grandpa always said."

"And she never married? Never wanted to? She said no one could compare, but that seems a little out there."

"It was a different time, Darcy. People hadn't yet adopted the Kleenex mentality of use-it-up-and-throw-it-away. They had lived through a massive depression and a world war. They didn't take things or people for granted.

I knew an older lady who saved everything. Her doorknobs were unusable because she saved every rubber band she ever got," Romero continued.

Darcy laughed. "I knew that lady too, only mine saved old clothes and newspapers."

"Yup. Same thing. Anyway, she didn't seem to be able to get over the loss, so Grandpa let her be. It was only after J.C. died that he asked Great Aunt Marie to come back to the ranch. She did for a while, but then told Grandpa she'd rather live in town."

"When was that?" Darcy crawled onto the large, padded arm of the sofa.

"I think in the early fifties. I'd need to check." Romero unconsciously tapped his hat against his thigh.

"Will you?" Darcy cocked her head to the side. She didn't really think he'd help her.

"Police asked the same thing. Why don't you get the dates from your police buddy?"

"You mean Hank? I don't know if he can release that information yet since it's an investigation still—but seeing as how we're old friends . . ." She raised her eyebrows.

Gary laughed. "You told my great aunt that we were little more than acquaintances when she pressed you."

"She seems like a nice lady. I didn't want to lie to her any more than I had to."

"I tell you what. I'll get the records sorted out and make a copy for you if you'll have dinner with me."

Her stomach did a flip. He was a handsome man, and he had intrigued her before—before Hank. Technically, she and Hank weren't exclusive. Not in any committed sense.

"C'mon, Darcy, it isn't a Nuclear Peace Accord. It's dinner." He took the two steps to the door and rested his hand on the knob.

His eyes, a deep mocha brown, sparkled when he was amused, and Darcy's stomach did another half gainer.

"Um, okay. Sure," she finally ended the stutter.

"I'll pick you up at seven o'clock." He closed the door behind him softly.

Feeling vaguely guilty, Darcy threw on some clothes, took Mac, and dropped in on Abby. It took less than a minute to bring her up to speed about her talk with Romero.

"Well," Abby looked thoughtful, "except for the tummy-tumbling thing, this is really just a business dinner."

"You can wipe that smile off your face, Miss Abby. I don't have any control over what my stomach does. Besides, I thought you liked Hank."

"I did and do, but it never hurts to have another bull in the pasture."

"That's a disgusting analogy." Darcy took another sip of deep roast coffee Abby had brewed on her Keurig.

"Isn't it just?" Abby agreed with a chuckle and then sobered. "Will Romero also give you information about the other set of bones, if the police share with him? The more recent ones?"

"I think so. With this Marie business, I haven't had much time to work up any angles on the other bones."

"Whatever you find out, you need to hold your cards close to your vest. That weasel Adkins is just waiting to trump your lead."

"Enough with the mixed analogies, but you point is well taken. I need to talk to Zach about pulling him off my story. Speaking of Zach, do you want to hang out with Mac-mutt for a little while? I have to do a short standup on the new restaurant opening. It shouldn't take more than an hour, but Zach may assign me to something else after."

"Sure thing."

Forty-five minutes later, Darcy was camera ready and zooming east on treacherous Del Range Boulevard, the most perilous street in Wyoming if the studies were to be believed.

Darcy was certain the reason for the large number of wrecks was the cluster of shops and restaurants clamoring for the attention of drivers unused to flashing marquees and turning lanes.

Executing a sharp left into the crammed parking lot by the balloon bedecked Mexican restaurant, Darcy smiled to herself as she remembered getting used to driving in Kansas City. She was lucky to be alive, she thought.

She spotted Bill Netters on the wrought iron bench with his camera in his lap.

"Sorry," she said as she squatted to get the mic from the duffle at his feet. "Been waiting long?"

"Nope. Just got here." Netters unwound his tall, lanky frame and hoisted his new DVC Pro camera to his shoulder.

"Give me a sec to line up the owner." Darcy handed Netters the mic and moved toward the small crowd at the front door.

In moments, she had pried the basic information from a camera-shy franchise owner. The trick was to make your subject look just at you and block out the camera and mic.

A part of her brain marveled at how smoothly she and Netters worked together. He'd handed her the mic as soon as she had nudged the owner into position and framed the shot in seconds. He gave her a slight nod, and they had the video done in one take.

The owner walked off, wiping his sweaty hands down his pants legs and Darcy wrapped up the mic to put it away.

"Thanks, Netters. That was painless."

"Supposed to be." Netters finished packing up his camera and stood. "See you at the station later?"

"Um, yeah. I have a couple of things to check on but tell Zach I'll be there in plenty of time to do the noon broadcast."

Netters turned to leave. "Will do."

"Oh Netters—"

"Yeah?"

"Have you been giving Adkins any info about my bones story?"

"Get serious. I wouldn't share what I had for lunch with that tool!" Netters slung his bag across his broad, but bony back.

Darcy swallowed a rumble of a chuckle. "Well, he's been following me around, talking to my sources. I just wondered if you'd heard anything."

"Nope. You might check with Zach though. See ya."

Darcy watched him get into a Silverado Classic 3LT parked just steps away.

"New truck?"

"Yeah. It was between this and a house. I picked this."

"Sweet."

Netters waved and drove off.

On the drive to the house on 18th, Darcy reviewed her options. She had about an hour before she had to be back to the station, so she decided to try to question some of the neighbors. Sometimes all it took was to find one person in the neighborhood who knew everything from who a wandering dog belonged to, and who was having an affair.

The yellow crime scene tape was still in place, but there was no overt police presence around the bone house.

Darcy played with the idea of trying to sneak in and get some pictures but decided to play it straight and ask Hank for permission.

Parking up the block, she spent the next forty-five minutes canvassing the neighborhood. She felt like she was running for office.

This older area was filled with an interesting combination of yuppie professionals, intrigued with "rehabbing a classic" and old-time residents who were only glad no one was selling crack on their street—yet.

Darcy got a better feel of the surroundings, but no real leads after five houses. She almost skipped the brick bungalow across the street, but since it was on her way to her car, she made a stop.

The door was large Victorian, beveled oval glass, with a turn wheel doorbell. Darcy twirled the brass thumb twister and listened to the muffled bell beyond the door. After a short wait, she decided no one was home and was just walking down the front steps when the door jerked open.

"Whatcha want? I'm not buyin' anything." Framed in the doorway was an old man leaning on an ornately carved cane that had a large onyx handle on one end and a larger rubber tip on the other.

"I'm not selling anything," Darcy said as she came back up the steps. "I just have a few questions I'd like to ask about the house over there."

Darcy watched the old man's face close down. "Don't have time to answer any more questions. You the police?"

"No. I work for the television station. Darcy Moreland." She held out her hand, but the man didn't move to take it. "And you are?"

"John Jacob Walker" he answered still eyeing her as if she were a salesman.

"Look, I know Ms. Romero and Gary Romero . . . and I just have a couple of questions to ask."

The old man's eyes brightened with recognition of the Romero name then slammed closed again. "Ask the Romeros then." He started to shut the door.

"I have, and I will, but some things are only seen by people who live here."

"Like what?"

"For instance, did you live here when Ms. Romero and her brother J. C. were over there?"

"Yup. Cora and I were new-wed then. This was our first and only house." The old man's eyes grew softer and looked past Darcy, then snapped back in focus. "J.C. was a little unruly, but Marie was a sweet little thing. She spent a lot of time with my Cora. Nice girl."

"In what way was J.C. unruly?"

"Too much money, no responsibility. Many's the time I heard him clanking up the steps half drunk and pounding on the door for poor Marie to let him in. Too bad about him dying so young though."

"How about the people who rented the house after J.C. went to California and Marie moved out? Did you know any of them?"

"A few," he motioned Darcy with his cane to sit on the porch swing. Darcy figured his old-fashioned chivalry coupled with the fact that she knew the Romeros, earned her the courtesy of a seat. Not a front parlor seat, but a seat none-the-less.

"Most of the renters were officers stationed at the Fort."

"You mean Warren Air Force Base?"

"No. I mean Fort D.A. Russel. Didn't have an Air Force back then. The Fort was used as a training center for a Quartermaster corps. Lots of young officers tried to get quarters in town if they could. Come to think of it, I think that's how Marie met her beau. Lived around here if I recall right."

"But then later, when it turned into an Air Force Base, did officers still live around here?"

"Sure. Off and on. I liked it better when Marie lived there though. She was good company for Cora when my wife was so ill."

Darcy glanced around for some potted geraniums or other sign of feminine influence. "So is your wife better now?"

The old man stared at her so long, Darcy felt the back of her neck quiver.

"No," he said finally. "She died a couple of years after Marie had to go live in that home. Some holy roller who lived in Marie's house for a while came over and tried to cure her, but my wife's Church of England. She didn't hold with non-traditional religions," John Jacob recited bleakly as if he accepted the hopelessness of death.

The warm autumn sun beat down on the cracked gray surface of the porch and some geese flew noisily overhead.

Darcy cleared her throat and stood. "I'm so sorry for your loss. Thank you for answering my questions." Darcy headed for the steps.

"Come back again. Not too hard talking to a pretty young lady now and then."

Darcy smiled. "Thank you very much Mr. Walker."

Her last view was of the old man on his front porch waving goodbye.

Darcy wasn't sure that side trip had been very productive, but John Jacob Walker seemed unusually sharp and willing to talk. She decided she would come back again when she had more time.

John Jacob watched Darcy go down his steps and over to her car. The image of her blurred and he stared at nothing and everything. He could remember that time in his life detailed and in color. He and Cora newlywed and so consumed with each other that the world might have ended, and they wouldn't have noticed.

He wiped a tear gathering in the corner of his eye. It was an exciting and terrifying time to be in love. There was the frantic fear of the war that loomed over them, and bravado that because life itself was so uncertain you lived every day at a high pitch. They had spent many evenings with the Romeros across the street. The Romero house was a gathering place of many young people flowing in and out of town. Always full of laughter and music as if they could keep war away.

When he thought about it, which was not very often, John regretted he had been deemed 4F because of flat feet. Cora, when he mentioned feeling so guilty about not being able to enlist, always said it was a blessing to her and all their friends to have him here watching out for people who had to leave loved ones behind. He hadn't really believed it, but it soothed his heart anyway. His head bobbed forward, and he slept reliving a time that was both simple and complex but had Cora in it, so it was perfect.

CHAPTER 8

Darcy braced herself for the inevitable confrontation with Adkins. The idea that he was trailing her and harassing her contacts was as irritating as a popcorn hull lodged in her teeth, and she intended to pry him loose and spit him out.

Zooming past the office manager, Wendy, Darcy grabbed the fistful of pink message slips, murmured a "Thanks," and headed straight for Zach Horton's office.

Zach was on the phone but motioned her into a chair by his desk.

"Yes, sir. I'm sure we can cover your ribbon cutting. When it gets a little closer, call me and we'll set up a remote feed. Thanks for calling and we'll see you soon." Zach hung up.

"They're opening a warehouse/distribution center next month." Zach smiled. "Sometimes I think Cheyenne is the pass-through capital of the continental United States. Everyone wants to have a distribution center here."

"Yeah, yeah. Semitrucks suck. I have a real problem here, Zach."

"More important than the destruction of civilization as we know it?"

"How would you feel about the destruction of Bryce Adkins?", Darcy asked.

"Personally, or professionally?", Zach smiled.

"Both, I guess."

"Personally, I'd be delighted to help you rearrange his body parts, but professionally, I'd feel compelled to resist the temptation."

"Uncle Arnold again?" Darcy sighed, bowing to the inevitable.

"All politics is local."

"Yeah, and all morons are connected. How does that work, Zach?"

"I could explain it to you, but it would waste time and wouldn't make you feel any better. So why are you stressed?"

"The bones investigation is mine. I called it in. I even stepped out of the way and let Bryce-the-Jerk do his standup non-story because I got that Uncle Arnold has you by the short ones . . ."

"Wow! You romped right into crude without a turn signal." Zach smiled around the remnant of a half smoked-stubbed-out-cigar.

"Damn it, Zach. I'm serious." Darcy turned away from him to look through the grime-smeared window.

"I can see you are. Why this new vehemence?" Zach leaned back, propping his feet on his desk.

Darcy wanted to throw a punch but hitting Zach wouldn't help. "He's following my trail and re-interviewing my sources."

"How did he find out who you were talking to?"

"I think he got into my computer."

"Proof?" Zach removed the stogie and put it carefully in an ashtray on his desk without looking at Darcy.

"No," she admitted. "But how else would he know? All my notes are on my laptop."

"Password protected?"

"What the hell are we? The CIA? I shouldn't have to password protect my notes from people who work here." She plopped into a chair in front of his desk.

"Are you naïve or just stupid?" Zach asked her. "This is a news gathering agency, Darcy. Highly competitive even in the boondocks of Cheyenne, Wyoming."

"So that makes it okay?"

"Nope." He picked up his cigar and replaced it between impossibly white teeth. "But it does give you a cheap lesson. Who did he interview?"

"Marie Romero. Her great-nephew was pretty steamed about it too. I don't think Romero would have minded except he hates Adkins almost as much as we do."

"Gary Romero is her great-nephew? Why were you talking to her?"

"She lived in the 'bones' house and I wanted to find out what, if anything, she knew. Turned out to be random. Now I don't know if she'll see me for a follow up."

"Don't waste too much time on this story. If the leads go soft, we'll have to drop it." Darcy opened her mouth to protest, but Zach held his hand up and ramrodded ahead. "I will tell Adkins it's your investigation and to stay out of your files. But for heaven's sake, Darcy, lock them up."

"Thanks, Zach." Darcy headed for the door.

"Keep me posted."

Darcy paused. "Newest post. I'm having dinner with Gary Romero when he finds the rental records."

Zach's right eyebrow shot to his dark brown hairline. "Hank know?"

"Nope. Why would it matter?"

"If I were Hank, it would matter to me," Darcy heard Zach mutter.

Deflated, Darcy returned to her cubbyhole. She had geared up for a skirmish that she couldn't indulge in until Adkins screwed up again. A clash with him was in her future. She was sure of it. She just didn't know when or how ugly.

She plunked into her antiquated desk chair with the wonky-springed seat that cupped her butt like an old lover. Lifting her feet to her desktop, she closed her eyes to assess. All-in-all, she was in good shape. Zach had pledged to back her so when Adkins got in her way again, she could drop-kick him to Nebraska.

A smile twitched the corners of her mouth as she imagined the carnage. Taking a deep breath, she gave herself a mental shake. Enough fun. Time to get to work.

She sat up again and scooped up the pink message slips and began to shuffle them. The most recent message was from Romero.

It just said, "Call." Typical guy message. She placed the slip high under her chin.

Next was a message from Dr. Villars at the University. Indisputably, the call back pile. She layered that also under her chin.

Abby had called about dinner tonight, and her friend, Liz Baker, had called about lunch sometime. This she relegated to right above her belt buckle in the sadly have-to-wait-for-later pile.

Next up was from her folks in Arizona. No doubt wondering if she was still alive and still adamant about not living in the family house while they wintered in Arizona. She loved the house where she grew up, but she would never feel like a grown up there. She placed the pink note over her heart and vowed to call them as soon as she returned the most important calls.

"An intriguing filing system. Can I help?"

Darcy's feet crashed to the floor, and the slips floated around her. Her heart thumped, and she could feel the heat of a junior-high blush rise from her neck to her cheeks. She took a deep breath as if trying to be patient.

"'Blessed is the man, who having nothing to say, abstains from giving wordy evidence of the fact.' George Eliot," she quoted.

Hank leaned negligently against her doorjamb. "Is that how you deal with everyone who offers to help you—or just me?"

He didn't wait for an answer. He stooped and picked up her messages from the floor.

"Gary Romero?"

Darcy snatched the notes from him. "Yeah. He said he'd give me the info on who rented the 'bones' house if I'd go to dinner with him."

"Nice bribe." He propped his black Levi covered butt on the edge of her desk, facing her, and folded his arms across his chest. "You going tonight?"

"I don't know. I haven't called him back yet." Darcy looked up. She felt like Hank was looming. Silly notion she thought. "Problem?"

"Nope." Hank stood and walked to the door. "I just didn't

know the going-rate. Pencil me in when you can, and I'll let you buy *me* dinner. I have information that might be worth a hamburger or two."

By the time Darcy could process what he'd said, he was gone. He couldn't be irritated about her having dinner with Romero . . . could he?

"I don't have time for testosterone-driven flare-ups right now," she muttered and picked up the phone.

Romero answered on the third ring.

"This is Darcy Moreland. You wanted me to call?"

"Yes," he paused. "Is everything okay? You sound a little annoyed."

"No. No. I'm fine. So, did you find the rental records?"

"Actually, we have a property manager who takes care of renting the property, doing repairs etc., but I have copies of all the rental agreements."

"Great! When could I get a copy?" Darcy tapped her pencil nervously on her desk.

"Well, I promised the first copy to the police. I don't want to shirk my civic duty—"

"Heaven forefend! Are you taking the guys in homicide to dinner, too?"

The dead air that followed made Darcy drop the pencil and sit straight. "Gary? You still there?"

"I was just running through my mind what I could have done to tick you off lately. I'm not coming up with anything."

"I'm sorry. I'm just generally cranky right now."

"I know a place that makes great Margaritas with enough tequila in them to overlook a nuclear attack. Interested?"

"Drooling as we speak. What time?"

"I'll drop the folder at the police station and come get you a little before five. Will that be okay?"

"Perfect. I'll see you soon."

She checked the time on her laptop and almost closed it before she remembered to password protect her files. She banged in "Yorick", assuming the oblique reference to the skull in *Hamlet* would keep Adkins out.

She grabbed her cell from her bag, speed-dialing Abby on her way out of the building. She got Abby's voice machine, so left a message that she was having dinner with Romero tonight, and that she'd fill her in on the details when she got home later.

Next up was Liz. By the time she'd reached the Algonquin Apartments, Darcy had set up a lunch date at their favorite pizza place on Wednesday.

Taking the stairs two at a time, Darcy told herself she'd call her folks after she'd showered.

"Oh Hell! I forgot about Villars," she muttered as she opened her door. "I'll call him first thing tomorrow." She tossed her bag on the huge brown sofa that took up most of her living room.

Recent images of Hank—hot kisses, strong hands, and tangled legs slipped into her mind.

"Get out of my head, Hank." She punched one of the pillows in passing. An hour later, Romero stood at her door, dressed in what her mother would call casual elegance: open collar, blue shirt with a tiny beige pinstripe, blue jeans faded in all the right places, and a tawny-beige suede jacket, and some foreign-looking leather boots, maybe snake. He was looking Antonio Banderas gorgeous.

His brown eyes roamed over her admiringly and she was glad she'd opted for a short, brown skirt that showed off her still-tanned legs, and a white scoop-necked shirt that hinted at the curves beneath.

"Very nice indeed," Romero said as he walked into the room. He handed her a large manila envelope.

"For me?"

"You sound surprised. That was our deal, wasn't it?"

Darcy slid the envelope onto her round bistro table. Part of her wanted to tear it open and read the names, but she glimpsed Romero's amused smile and caught herself.

"Yes," she said as she draped a light, fringed shawl over her shoulders, "that was the deal. I just thought we might treat it as more of a favor from one friend to another."

"As opposed to a business agreement?" He took a step to the

side of the door and let her pass.

"No. I mean it *is* business, but it's also friendly and helpful." Could she possibly sound more inane? "I mean—"

"You mean where are the Margaritas I promised you?"

"Precisely!"

Ensconced in a corner booth in one of the many Mexican restaurants in town, Darcy slipped her hand around an oversized goblet rimmed with salt.

"Do I drink this or swim in it?"

"Now there's a visual," Gary toasted her with his glass of two fingers of Stoli's and ice.

"Seriously, this takes two hands to lift."

"Saves the lag time waiting for a refill. Here, use my straw." He tossed her the small bar straw. "How's the investigation going?"

"Not really smoothly. I did get Zach to agree to get Adkins off the investigation though. Your Aunt Marie won't be bothered by him again." She took a large draw on the straw and savored the lemon/lime tang.

"Does that mean you're not going to bother her either?" His brown eyes bored into hers.

"Does my enchilada dinner depend on my answer?"

Romero leaned back, taking his drink with him. "It might."

Darcy couldn't see a hint of a smile. He was serious. She pushed her Margarita away.

"Well, Mr. Friendly left early, didn't he?" She straightened her shoulders and stiffened her spine. "I have never pretended to be anything but an investigative reporter. That's what I do. If my investigations imposes on friend's or acquaintance's lives, I'm sorry. In a town this size, my job is bound to become intrusive at times." Her hand reached for her purse that was hanging off the back of her chair.

Romero leaned toward her. "Dial down the righteous indignation, Darcy. I just wanted to get a feel for how far you were going to push this."

"As far as I have to to get some answers. Two people were buried in a crawl space almost sixty years apart. Don't you think they deserve some answers?"

"They're dead. Why would they care?" Romero leaned back and took another sip of vodka. His brown eyes dared her to disagree.

"Maybe I said that wrong. How can *we* not care?" Darcy paused, then stood to leave.

Romero stood as well. "Darcy, please. Sit down. We don't have to be adversaries. I will help you if I can. I promise."

Darcy took her seat again, but she didn't fully trust his quick reversal or his promise. Something felt dark and murky around the edges. For a brief flicker, she worried that he knew more than he was telling. She tried to dismiss the uneasy feeling.

"Okay," she said as she placed her napkin across her lap once more. "I presume you read the report about the renters."

"Yes, though as I said before, we have an agent who takes care of all the details."

"Do you have any thoughts about who the bones belong to?" Darcy fished out the lime floating on top of her drink and chewed the juice from the pulp and dropped the rind on her cocktail napkin.

"You made that look positively feral." Romero commented.

"Impressed?"

"Terrified."

"Don't change the subject. I'll do a follow-up check on the list myself, but I'm interested in your thoughts."

Romero didn't comment while the waitress placed steaming plates in front of them.

"I don't really have thoughts. More questions really. At the time of the more recent set of bones, the house was rented out to a documentary filmmaker who coincidentally disappeared before paying his last month's rent."

Darcy almost choked on her re-fried beans. "Do you think it could be him?"

"Him or someone he killed and buried there. Alternatively, it could be unrelated to the film guy at all. We sometimes get deadbeat renters."

"Doesn't your agent try to chase them down?"

"Hard to get other states to extradite for lost-rent-revenue issues." Romero smiled and drained the last of his drink.

"Who is your agent? Can I talk to him?" Darcy had already dug her pen and notebook from her purse.

"I thought you might want to call him." He rummaged in his inside top pocket and produced a business card.

"Norm Murdock. Property Manager. Mountain Plains Realty," Darcy read.

"I already told him to cooperate with you when you called." Romero signaled the waitress for a refill.

Darcy felt a light twinge of guilt for doubting him. "That is really nice of you, Gary. Thanks."

"All part of the plan."

"What plan?" Darcy sat back as the waitress took what was left of her Margarita and replaced it with a new one.

"The plan to seduce you, of course."

Darcy bobbed the hunk of lime in her glass to avoid looking at him. "Um, about that, Gary. I'm sort of involved—"

"Hank Nelson. Yeah, I know. But unless my sources are woefully inaccurate—"

"Sources? You have sources checking me out?" Darcy didn't know whether to be flattered or incensed. It felt a little creepy.

"Yes. I have sources for everything. I don't much like surprises, so if I'm interested in anything, or anyone . . ." He lifted his glass in her direction. "I always find out what I can about them."

"And what exactly did you find out about me?"

"Born and bred in Cheyenne. Mid-twenties. Graduate of the University of Wyoming with a B.A. in Journalism. This is only your second journalism job. Zach Horton is your boss and an old college friend—"

"How many fillings do I have?" Darcy felt herself drifting into indignation.

"That report is still pending," Romero didn't seem concerned at all by the jagged edge to her tone. "Would you like to tell me? It would save me some money."

"Oh, by all means. I think at last count, I had three." She scooted out from the booth. "Here's a newsflash, Mr. Romero, if you want to know anything else about me, ask." She tossed a ten onto the table. "For the drink."

She had walked halfway home before it occurred to her that she hadn't asked about the first set of bones and whether his family was living in the house at the time.

CHAPTER 9

Darcy stormed into her building angrier than the four-block walk could dissipate. She burst into Abby's apartment with a cursory knock and was greeted by Mac. His brown and tan eager face softened the edges of her aggravation.

Scooping him up, she scratched him behind the ears. "I should know by now that you're the only man I can trust." She nuzzled his fur and plopped onto the chintz sofa, holding him in her lap.

"I thought I heard you out here," Abby said as she ducked half out of her tiny kitchen. "That has got to be the shortest dinner ever."

"Never made it past the drinks."

"I'm just nuking some chicken and broccoli pasta. You're welcome to share."

"I'm not hungry, Abby."

"I'll bring it out anyway, and we can pick at it."

"I'm going to run upstairs and get the envelope Romero brought me tonight. Maybe there'll be something in it that will redeem this debacle of an evening."

"I'll wait for you." Abby set her round oak table with place mats and wine glasses.

By the time Darcy returned, a cold glass of Chardonnay waited, and a steaming bowl of pasta graced the middle of the table. Darcy's stomach growled.

"This evening has suddenly improved." Darcy sat and sipped the cool wine and skimmed through the list of renters.

Abby poured herself some wine and tore off a hunk of bread. "Anything pop out at you?"

"Not much information. Names and employment listed."

Abby snatched the paper from her hand and laid it face down on the table. "Eat your dinner. If something was that important, you would've seen it right away. Now talk to me. What happened with the dinner?"

Darcy gave her the Reader's Digest version, ending with, "It feels creepy knowing he's been checking me out. Like I'm part of a breeding program or something."

"That's a little overstated, don't you think?"

Darcy laughed and dumped a serving of pasta on her plate. "Yeah. It probably is. Thing is though, is he checking me out as a potential date or as someone he wants to maneuver away from this story?"

"Could be either, neither, or both. Don't jump to conclusions."

"You're right as usual. It reminds me of a guy I dated in K.C. He had me followed and let me know about it. Guy was super insecure." Darcy shivered at the memory. "Let's talk about something else." Darcy forked the creamy pasta into her mouth. "I think I'll go back and talk to John Jacob Walker again."

"The old guy who lives across the street from the house?"

"The same. Now that I have the list of renters, maybe he can give me some more specific information."

"Like what?"

"Like he mentioned some 'holy roller'—his words," Darcy hastened to assure Abby that she was not being derogatory. "Anyway, John Walker said some religious guy came over to try to cure his wife who was dying of colon cancer. He wanted to 'lay hands' on her, but even sick, the old gal was having none of it."

"Why would that matter?" Abby passed the baguette to Darcy after she broke off another chunk for herself.

"Because it looks like that guy was one of the renters listed at the 'bones' house when the most recent murder was committed."

Darcy sopped up the creamy sauce and stuffed the bread into her mouth.

"How do you know he was a religious—um—practitioner?"

"Romero's list includes employment. During the approximate time of the most recent set of bones, there were two men living at the address. One is listed as a cinematographer and the other as an ordained minister of the Church of the Resurrection. John Walker implied the man who came to see him was a Christian fundamentalist, and Romero said the cinematographer skipped out without paying the last month's rent."

"Do you think the victim was the Christian or the cinematographer?" Abby pushed back from the table. "Sounds like the title of a really bad 'B' movie. The Cinematographer and the Christian." Abby laughed as she cleared the table.

"I don't know yet." Darcy followed her out to the kitchen. "But I want to get a description from John Walker and see if it will point to one or the other."

"Well, it's a place to start."

The next morning Darcy presented herself at Mr. Walker's door. She amused herself by rocking back and forth on a couple of old, loose, boards on the porch to listen to them squeak. She had to ring twice and wait, but eventually the old man swung the door open wide.

"Welcome back, young lady." He greeted her with obvious pleasure. "Come in. Come in."

Darcy crossed into a long, dark foyer that smelled of old paste wax and grime with an underlying aroma of what she assumed was last night's tuna casserole.

"I'm sorry to bother you again, Mr. Walker—"

"Please call me John It's been a lifetime since a pretty young thing has called me something other than mister." He gripped his cane for support and wobbled into what Darcy thought was his front parlor. Darcy remembered her Grandmother had a front and back parlor in her home in Denver. The back parlor was for family, but the front parlor was for honored guests. She was flattered that John was treating her as a welcome guest. The room was decorated in faded chairs, mostly upholstered in what used to be bright chintz but had faded to soft pastels like an old photo.

"Okay, John. I have a couple of questions about the men who used to live across the street about five or six years ago that I hope you can help me."

"Be pleased to try. Sit. Sit." John gestured to an armchair that had originally been upholstered in dark blue velvet but was now muddy-colored and worn to the backing on the arms and the front of the seat.

Darcy perched on the edge of the chair, then reached into her huge tote and retrieved a small notebook. Flipping impatiently through several pages, she finally looked up.

"John, last time we talked you said one of the men who lived in the Romero house was a minister determined to lay hands on your wife and try to cure her. Can you remember how he even knew she was sick?"

John sank back into the bolsters of a lumpy sofa and scratched the gray stubble of his chin.

"Now that's a good question. I guess I never even thought about it before. Seemed like the whole neighborhood knew Cora was sick. I guess I just assumed one of the neighbors told him."

"How did he approach you? Were you talking generally, and the subject just came up?"

"Come to think of it, the man just came over and introduced himself as Caleb . . . no last name. I remember because I thought it was strange."

Darcy consulted her notes "His last name was listed as Smith, but that could be fake. Can you remember what he looked like?"

"I think he was about medium height and build . . . nothin' special. Kind of dark squinty eyes. Long hair and beard. Didn't much want him on the porch, I got to say, but you know how those things are. Man said he'd had some success at curin' people of cancer, and would I like him to try on Cora."

"So, is that when you asked Cora if she was interested?" Darcy tried to make short notes to herself to keep the chronology straight.

"Not straight away. Cora was sleepin' right then. He said he could pay us a little if he and his friend could film him layin' on his hands, as he called it. Said his friend was filmin' a documentary about his ministry."

John stood up abruptly. "Can I get you some water? I'm not used to talkin' so much and I could use some water."

"Um, no thank you, John. You go right ahead though." Darcy watched as he toddled out as if the floor was moving unsteadily beneath him. She checked her notes once more.

John dropped into the lumpy sofa when he returned; holding the jelly glass high in the air as if it would keep him from splashing the water out.

"John did you ever meet that . . ." she had to look at the name once more, ". . . Caleb's friend? The man who was filming the documentary?"

"Nope. Can't say that I did. Saw him a time or two though. Tall blond fellow. 'Bout 6 feet or more. Looked kind of gangly from far away."

"Did you notice when they moved out?"

"Police asked the same thing. Truth is, they never really moved in. I mean not in any real way. House was rented furnished and most everyone who moved in or out just had a few things to tote in a bag or a box. They left pretty soon after I told the preacher guy that Cora didn't want to be bothered."

"How long before someone else moved in, do you think?" Darcy glanced through the soiled lace sheers that drooped across the parlor window. She could see the unappealing rust-colored brick house across the way, crouched behind dark pines and mis-shapen bushes. The overhanging porch roof slanted slightly as if tilted by years of wet snow and wood rot.

Maybe it was her imagination, but it seemed there was a miasma of sadness surrounding the house. Some empty houses looked expectant, ready to be bought and begin life with a new family. The 'bones' house looked as if it were in mourning and about to crumble from the sheer weight of depression.

"'Course that was a long time ago." John took a deep sip of water to signal he had just finished a story.

"Oh, John, I'm sorry. My mind wandered for a moment. What were you saying?"

A tolerant smile of the old for the inattention of the young flashed across John's face. "Just the ramblings of an old man. I was just saying that the house used to be bursting with young people when the Romero kids lived there. Lots of parties. Whole neighborhood knew they were welcome."

"When was that exactly, John?" Darcy poised pen over paper, determined to focus on facts instead of fancy.

"Oh, I don't know." John's already cloudy eyes lost even more focus. "Early forties, I think. It was a charmed time. Even the war couldn't dampen our spirits. We were all so young then, ya see. I sometimes think I imagined how much excitement we had back then."

"Do you remember any stories about someone disappearing? Someone who partied at the Romero house?"

"It was the early part of the war. People came and went all the time. Some came to town and then shipped out with little or no notice. The railroad depot was clogged day and night with trains going to both coasts, packed to the roofs with soldiers and sailors being deployed or sent somewhere for more training."

"John, would you do a taped interview on the history of the Romero house for me? It would just be me asking essentially the same questions and my videographer, Bill Netters filming it?"

"Why?" John snapped him out the question.

"Because I'm investigating a story about the bones found in the house and you're the only neighbor I've found who has lived here during the time we assume both people were buried there."

John used his cane to struggle upright. "I'm not going to do anything to heap dirt on the Romeros."

Darcy scrambled up from the soft chair. "John, you misunderstand. I don't intend to smear the Romeros. I'm just trying to get a sense of how two people could have been left in the crawlspace of the house sixty years apart."

"I got no answers. I mind my own business." John sidled over toward the front door.

Darcy knew it would only be a matter of moments before John asked her to leave.

"John, listen. I feel strongly that this story should be covered responsibly. I'm not interested in sensationalism or scandal." Darcy watched his eyes squint just a little as if he were trying to gauge whether he should trust her.

"I won't lie and say I haven't got the time."

He somehow managed to look both charming and stern at the same time. He reminded her of her dad when she'd screwed up.

"It won't take much time in any case," Darcy hastened to reassure him. "Let me call Netters."

John walked back and sat. "Okay. But be warned. I don't hold with mudslinging or slander."

"Nor do I," Darcy said as she dialed Netters' number on her phone. She gave Netters the address. By the time she'd brewed two cups of tea for herself and John, Netters was there.

After short introductions, Darcy positioned John with the 'bones' house behind him, flicking the graying lace back from the window, and enclosing both John and the house in late afternoon light.

Arranging herself to the right of the frame, Darcy scooted the small mahogany side chair close enough to John, so he focused on her, not on Netters. She dropped her hand and silently signaled for the taping to begin.

"John Jacob Walker has seen a lot of history from his house in the old 18th street neighborhood he's called his home for over sixty years. You moved here when you and Cora were newlyweds, is that right?"

"Pert near. We'd been married for about six months before my Cora saw this little house and had to have it. I was a new clerk then at the old Stock Growers Bank. I was lucky that Mr. Marple would trust me enough to give me a mortgage."

"So you knew the Romeros who lived across the street?" Darcy shifted the mic as subtly as she could, trying to make John forget it was there.

"We were all young moderns. Hard to believe now, but this was a vital neighborhood full of hopeful and dedicated twenty-year-olds, sure we were going to save the world from tyranny." John laughed at himself. "We were sure full of ourselves back then. We called that 'piss and vinegar' in the old days."

"This would have been after the United States had entered World War II, is that correct?"

John took a sip of the Earl Grey tea Darcy had brewed for him. "Yes. We had a training center here at the Fort and new soldiers were coming to town from all over. Seemed like we'd burst at the seams, but we never did."

"What did young people do for fun back then?"

Darcy was trying to steer the conversation toward the parties at the Romeros.

"We had a real active U.S.O. here. Had regular dances for the men down at the Prairie Hotel. I think that's where Marie Romero met her beau."

"Marie Romero from across the street?"

"Yeah. She was a pretty little thing back then, and he was a handsome young officer." John was gazing back sixty years.

"What was Marie's friend's name? Do you remember?"

Darcy leaned a little forward and the hand holding the mic was sweating slightly. She couldn't believe her good luck. If John could come up with some substantive answers about who came in and out of the 'bones' house, she could help solve the mystery . . . maybe.

"Uh . . . Tom. Thomas McCaulley, I think." John squinted his eyes as if would help him see the past better. "He was a shiny, brand-new second lieutenant, if I remember rightly."

"What happened to Tom? Did he break Marie's heart?"

John blinked a couple of times as if coming back to himself. "Not in the way you're implying. Marie always told Cora how honorable Tom was and how patriotic. Come to find out later, he got shipped out for more training and then was killed in a fluke accident. He didn't even have a chance to fight. We didn't have the luxury of time. Things happened quickly back then. We were fighting a war you know." John's eyes narrowed at her as if she had been impertinent.

"I'm sorry, John. I keep forgetting. That must have taken a huge emotional toll on everyone. Did Marie and Tom at least have a chance to say goodbye?"

"No, that was the problem. I remember Marie came over to talk to my Cora that weekend. He was supposed to come by like he often did when he could break away, you see, and he didn't show up at the U.S.O. dance either. Marie was frantic because none of their mutual friends had seen him either."

Darcy nodded. She didn't want to interrupt the narrative. John was on a roll. Darcy was vaguely aware that Netters was shifting the shots by drifting around the tiny parlor.

"At first Marie thought he'd lost interest in her. She cried like her heart was broken. Cora reminded her that there could be a lot of reasons he hadn't come. I remember listening. There wasn't anywhere I could go except our bedroom, so I pretended to read the paper. Three days later, Marie came flying in with a note from Tom telling her he'd had to leave on the troop train heading to the West Coast that night and he'd write to her as soon as he could. He got his orders one Friday night and was gone. She was sad he'd gone, but happy that he'd thought of her."

"So, did he write her later giving her more information?" Darcy prodded.

"After a couple of weeks, she got a note from a mutual friend that told her Tom had been killed in some strange training accident. I think it was a jeep overturning or something."

"Did she try to verify that?"

Darcy felt her stomach tighten as she imagined young Marie hearing about Tom's death in such an impersonal way.

John shook his head sadly as if reliving it. "No. Part of the problem was that Marie had no standing. Tom wasn't her fiancé yet and the policy back then was not to share information about individual soldiers unless it they were family. She had no official standing with the government. She wasn't his wife or even a fiancé. They weren't about to release information to her."

"So that's when she withdrew from everything and moved up to Jackson's Hole."

"Yeah. I remember my Cora saying that death sometimes did that to people—carved out a hole in their heart that no one and nothing could fill."

John leaned his head back in his chair and swallowed a couple of times convulsively. Darcy inched forward.

"Are you thinking about Cora, John?"

John's milky blue eyes focused on her face.

"Cora, and Tom, C.J., and a whole potful of others. When you're my age, you know more people who've died than those who are still alive. Gets kinda lonely." Tears welled, but he didn't allow them to spill down his cheeks.

Darcy suddenly felt like an intruder mucking about in an old man's memories. She signaled Netters to stop taping and stood.

"Thank you so much for your help, John. I really appreciate it."

John didn't answer nor react when they left, softly closing the door behind them.

Netters cleared his throat and Darcy glanced at him out of the corner of her eye.

"Got to you, did he?"

"Reminded me of my Grandpa back in Iowa." Netters shifted his heavy camera bag from his shoulder onto his back. "See you back at the shop." He skittered down the steps and dashed to his truck.

Darcy smiled. She admitted to herself she was weary of the studied cynicism that passed for cosmopolitan sophistication these days. Reality TV with its phony tears and histrionics had numbed a whole generation who rarely saw authentic, honest emotion. She was oddly pleased she and Netters could still be moved.

She was so engrossed in her thoughts that she almost missed the bile-green slip that was tucked under her wiper. She got in her car and unfolded the paper.

GOD'S WAY IS THE ONLY WAY

Darcy looked around but saw no one who might have left the note. As she started the car, she tried to consider why anyone would leave a note like that.

Then she remembered the bumper sticker she'd put on her car as a joke: HONK IF YOU *ARE* JESUS. Someone didn't think it was funny evidently. She crumpled the paper and threw it into the already-trash-littered back seat.

CHAPTER 10

Darcy waved at Netters as he zoomed past her. She thought how content she was to be home and working for KCWY News as she pulled into traffic. She especially enjoyed working with Netters. He was fast, competent, and becoming an amusing collaborator.

Her iPhone app. buzzed from a dashboard. She looked at the ID push the answer button on her steering wheel.

"Hi Zach. I'm just on my way back. What's up?"

"Dr. Villars from the University called. He wants you to call Dr. Anita Garcia at Colorado State University. The number is 970-555-2143. I'll text it to you."

"And you're being my secretary because . . .?"

"Because Dr. Garcia is a forensic reconstructionist and if she has anything on the bones, you'll need my authorization to go to Fort Collins to talk to her."

"Weekly ratings come out, did they?" Darcy smiled as she pulled to a side street and parked under a brilliant, yellow-leafed aspen tree.

"I'm cut to the quick . . . but yes. We got a bump whenever we did a 'bones' story. How did the taping with Mr. Walker go?"

"Netters is on his way back right now. Have him start editing without me. I'll call Dr. Garcia and see if I can go there. I probably should contact Hank too. I'll text you if I'm heading south, okay?"

Zach hung up without comment, but Darcy was too pleased to care. She loved investigating the number-one-rated story. She liked Zach being so accommodating, but she really loved that Bryce Adkins must be grinding his teeth to dust in frustration.

She changed lanes, checked the text and told her phone to dial the number. She leaned back and enjoyed the mild fall sunshine while they patched her through to the right extension.

"Dr. Garcia, Forensic Reconstruction lab."

"Dr. Garcia. This is Darcy Moreland from KCWY News in Cheyenne. Dr. Villars gave me your number. I'm doing an investigation into the two sets of bones that were found here."

"Dr. Villars said you might call. You do understand Ms. Moreland, reconstruction is really just medical guesswork and artistic license. We can only approximate the features based on probabilities."

"I get that, but we have no idea who these men were, so any information you can add to the investigation would be great."

"I'm afraid I would have to get clearance from your police department to share any specific information with you. I believe Detective Hank Nelson would be the person to contact. Do you know him?"

"Oh yes," Darcy said and threw her small notebook on the seat beside her. "We're old friends . . ."

"Fine. As soon as you can get me the authorization, I'd be happy to share any findings with you."

"Thank you, doctor." Darcy thought fast. Concurrent with trying to figure out how to get Hank to agree, was the challenge of how best to tell the story. "Oh, and by the way Dr. Garcia, when I get the authorization, could we shoot some video with you? We'd only need a few minutes of your time."

"I guess that would be okay. I would have to insist on some prior notice though. This is a working lab, and we don't want to compromise any of our other investigations."

"I understand perfectly. We'd like to come tomorrow if possible. Can I just text you before we head out?"

"I think an hour would be enough notice for me to prepare," Dr. Garcia said.

That would be perfect. It only took about 45 minutes to drive down to Fort Collins. Darcy thought about her next move. She looked at her watch. It was three o'clock. By the time she got back to the newsroom and helped edit the John Walker piece it would be close to the 5:30 airtime.

She speed-dialed Hank's number.

"What do you need?"

At the sound of Hank's voice, Darcy felt her heart do the familiar thump, but she plowed on. "Not exactly a friendly way to answer."

"Not exactly feeling friendly. What do you need?"

"I was going to take you out for dinner tonight, but I'm having second thoughts." Bristling a little at his attitude, she sat up a little straighter.

"I tell you what, you tell me what you need, and I'll decide whether I want to have dinner with you or not."

"Forget it." Darcy waited a beat for him to relent, then gave in. "Dr. Anita Garcia."

There was silence on the other end.

"Hank?"

"Yes."

"I need your authorization—"

"I got the concept. I'm just trying to decide how much of a sucker I am."

"Did you change the subject?"

"Nope. I'd like to see you tonight, but I need to decide what level of dinner I should demand for a major consideration like this."

"Oh, for heaven's sake, Hank. Stop screwing with me."

"Deadly serious. I think access to the good doctor is worth a rib-eye. Don't you?"

"Yeah, yeah. I'll pick you up around 6:30 at the cop-shop, okay? And make sure you're packin.'"

"You want me to come armed? Quite a jump from 'not-friendly' to 'packin.'"

She laughed. "You know I mean bring the signed authorization. I'm going to drive down to see her tomorrow."

"I may come along and see what she's got so far."

Darcy chewed her bottom lip in a moment of indecision, "Okay by me. I'm bringing Netters and if you're there, I'll probably want a statement from you too."

"I'll see you at 6:30. I'll pick you up at your place and we'll begin negotiations."

Darcy heard him click off. "Goodbye, Hank," she said as if he were still on the line. "Can't wait to see you." She pressed the off button on the steering wheel.

By the time she reached the station, she was feeling smug. She could honestly tell Zach that she had a confirmed meeting with Dr. Garcia and might have a possible statement from the doctor as well as one from Det. Hank Nelson.

She was feeling so jaunty, she swung right past Bryce Adkins as he was heading out. She didn't even snarl at him even though she was fairly sure he called her a name under his breath. A chuckle worked its way up her throat. Pea-green jealousy from an enemy was the best.

A short stop would bring Zach up to speed on her way to find Netters.

The editing and voice-overs didn't take long to complete, since Netters had already made a start. They huddled close to the play-back screen and ran the video once more.

"Interesting commentary on the 'bones' house, even if it isn't hard news," Netters said as he punched back and forward on the video, editing small fascinating but irrelevant details from John Walker's recollections.

Darcy leaned back in her chair and linked her hands behind her head. "We may have caught a break. Dr. Anita Garcia is an expert at forensic reconstructions at CSU. She's been working on sculpting busts based on the skulls that Dr. Villars sent her."

Netters spun to face her. "You're shitting me! We'll get to see what these guys actually looked like?"

"Yup. All I have to do is get authorization from Hank and we're golden."

Netters' face drooped at the edges like a homeless Basset Hound. "He won't agree to that . . . will he?"

"We're having dinner tonight. I'll convince him or die trying. Get all packed up tonight and we'll head down to CSU in the morning. I'll clear it with Zach before I leave tonight."

"If I don't hear differently, I'll assume it's a go and pick you up in the van."

"Do we have to take a van? I always feel like a circus performer with 'KCWY News' emblazoned across the side."

Netters stood and popped the cassette from the machine. "Two points: one, you *are* a circus performer, and two, I can park anywhere on campus in that van." He saluted her cheerfully with the tape and left.

Darcy conceded the point about the parking. Lugging that camera long distances had to be a pain.

"I am *not* a circus performer," she shouted at the slowly closing glass-fronted door.

"Okay. You're not a circus performer. Good to know because I'm paying you to be a journalist."

Darcy jumped from her seat and slapped her hand over her hammering heart. "Zach Horton! Don't ever do that again. I about had a seizure." She plopped down on the small desk chair.

"Who're you kidding? Nothing scares you." He handed her a scribbled note on the station's letterhead. "Here is your authorization for the shoot. I gave Netters the requisition for the van. I need you both back by noon." Zach headed toward the door.

Darcy swiveled to face him. "You *do* understand I have to talk Hank into approving it, don't you?"

Zach stopped at the door, holding it open. "You said you were having dinner with him tonight."

"Yeah, but—"

"As your boss, I'm asking you to take one for the team. As your friend, I'm telling you to have fun." He slipped out the door and just missed being hit with an empty Starbuck's cup.

"Lilly-livered-un-reconstituted-chauvinist," she muttered as she slapped together her notes and stuffed them into her bag.

She drove home quickly. She wanted to look really good tonight. Rummaging through her closet she found some black jeans and a bright-red mohair sweater. If that outfit didn't shout "come and get me" it at least whispered, "The door is ajar".

She hoped she wasn't overestimating her influence with Hank. If it were a personal request, she was fairly sure he would agree to almost anything she asked for, but where their personal and professional lives intersected, experience told her it could go either way.

She had barely tucked the only credit card that still had some wiggle room on it into her glitzy red clutch when her doorbell rang. She ran her hands down the sides of her black jeans and checked her strappy three-inch heels that barely peeked out beneath her pants leg.

After one last tug on her red mohair sweater, Darcy swung open the door.

The look that flitted across Hank's face justified all the effort.

"Do you want me to drive too?" Darcy twirled her keys once around her finger.

Hank stopped the spin and tossed the keys into a basket by the door.

"Nope. Buying me a steak will be enough, thanks." He steered her out her door, closing it behind them.

"Hey! You just locked me out—"

"I still have the key you gave me last summer."

Silenced for a moment, Darcy concentrated on going down the steep oak stairway without catching her heel. Once she reached the lobby, she spun and held her palm up.

"Gimme."

"Really?" Hank cocked an eyebrow and his lips curved into a small grin.

"Yes, really. I gave that to you last summer for safety. I'm no longer in danger."

"Really?" Hank asked again and backed her up against the front door. Angling his hips to press against her, he brushed his lips slowly across hers.

Darcy refused to be disconcerted. She lifted her chin scowling into his impossibly blue eyes. "You tell me, Hank. You're the cop."

Hank laughed and took a step back. "That's Police Detective

Nelson to you, Ms. Moreland. And . . . no. You're not in danger . . . unless you want to be." He lifted a finger, tucked her hair behind her ear, and kissed her cheek softly.

Darcy felt a frizzle of excitement skitter down her spine. She shuddered and tried to regain her composure. "Let's go get that steak, shall we?" She reached behind her, turned the worn brass knob, and opened the door. The autumn chill she felt at her back was almost welcome.

The night was clear and dark enough to see stars twinkling in the thin air. Darcy inhaled as she walked down the steps to Hank's truck. She waited for him to unlock the passenger door and climbed in.

The blessedly short drive to the Cowhand Steak House was silent. Hank maneuvered easily into a space in front and came to help Darcy negotiate the large step down.

Inside, the restaurant smelled of onions and grilled meat. Country music competed with boisterous exchanges and the clank and clang of glasses and silverware.

Seated in a wooden booth, Darcy waited for her red wine, and played with the silverware wrapped in a napkin.

Hank leaned into her. "I'll begin. We need each other on this one. The investigation is stalled. We don't know who these bones belong to, and we need to try to get someone to ID them."

"So, making me buy you dinner was just a scam?" Darcy took the large, bowled glass from the waiter and took her first sip as had she pinned Hank with her stare.

Hank took a large gulp from his Coors draft. "Nope. I wanted to see you."

"So, you used the fact that I wanted to interview Dr. Garcia as a strategy to get a free steak? I know public servants aren't paid very well, but really Hank. All you had to do was ask."

"I've been on this bull before. If I'd asked you to dinner tonight, there'd be no hope in hell you'd come. My only chance was to make it seem necessary to your job."

"I am not that job-absorbed," Darcy jacked her jaw little then shifted her attention and a smile to the waiter and gave her order.

By the time the waiter left, Hank was half through his beer and wearing a roguish grin. "I just love pulling your chain. You get so wound up if anyone accuses you of being driven. It's not a sin you know."

"You make it sound like it is, and the truth is you'll never know if I would have accepted. Now you don't know if I'm here because I want to be, or because you tricked me."

"Oh, you want to be here, Darcy." Hank's blue eyes glinted dangerously. "And you should never lie to yourself. You can try to lie to me, but you should never lie to yourself. Show some respect for both of us." He took a long draw on his beer.

Darcy felt the heat of a blush on her cheeks. She played with the napkin corner.

Hank took pity on her. "Well that's enough foreplay."

Darcy's eyes shot up.

Hank laughed. "I meant we might want to talk about the case and what we each want. Have you learned anything new?"

Darcy filled him in on her interview with John Walker and added, "If you hadn't conned me into this date under false pretenses, you'd have seen it on the 5:30 news."

"I watched it before I picked you up. I always watch if I think you'll be on."

Darcy had to pause for the waiter to finish serving the food before she said, "Why Detective Nelson. Are you a fan?"

"I like to think of it as proactive self-defense. I never know what boiling pot you're stirring, and I like to keep ahead of the meltdown."

"Humph" Darcy chuckled and bit into a forkful of juicy filet.

"I was wondering if there was anything that ended up on the cutting room floor." Hank scooped up a forkful of smothered sweet potato.

"No. Pretty much the gist is he has lived there a long time and will probably be our best bet at identifying who those bones are. Walker was the only neighbor who had been there and knew the Romeros."

"So, you think the Romeros are involved in this somehow?"

"Don't you?" Darcy leaned toward him.

"I don't know yet." Hank raised his empty bottle and signaled the waiter for another round.

"Marie and C.J. lived in the house about the same time as the first set of bones," Darcy persisted.

"Maybe. Maybe not. Marie left for Jackson and C.J. left for California. The bones could belong to someone who rented the house right after they'd gone. We don't have an exact date for either set of bones. Just an approximate timeline."

"True," Darcy agreed reluctantly.

"You can't go on air with the reconstructions until we've asked Mr. Walker first. I want to get his take on the pictures before they end up on the news."

Hank looked stern, as if that would slow her down. "Only if you agree to stop and see him on the way back into town. Zach is expecting a story for the early evening news. And not that you care—but we're in a ratings war with Channel 8 from Casper."

Darcy slipped a bite of steak into her mouth, and smiled at the salty, smoked goodness.

"I can see how a ratings war might be more important than identifying two abandoned body." Hank said.

"Sarcasm again?" Darcy sent him a mock toast and drained the last mellow drop of her wine. "I won't feel guilty for trying to do my job. John Walker was my find, so you can just accommodate me."

"I could pull authorization for your interview tomorrow," Hank, threatened just as the waiter put down the new drinks.

"I know you don't mean that." She smiled, enjoying pulling his chain for a change. "These steaks are really good." Darcy took a small chunk and licked the rim of her mouth.

"So . . . tomorrow I'll drive into Fort Collins with you and send Netters ahead with the van. We can stop by John's on the way back and hope he can give us some good solid leads before I have to be back at the station. Okay?"

"Okay," Hank sighed deeply. "I know when I'm licked."

Darcy looked up. "Was that a crack?"

Hank laughed. "No just a re-occurring fantasy."

CHAPTER 11

BY THE TIME DARCY AND HANK got back to Darcy's place, the silence had grown heavy. Hank started to jump out of the truck, but Darcy stopped him.

"Hank, I think I'd better go in alone."

Hank closed the cab door and turned to her. He sucked a lung full of cool night air. "Okay, but can you tell me why?"

"Because I'm trying to be an adult here. I'm more tempted than you know."

Hank pulled her close and nipped at her neck. His large, warm hand traveled slowly down her back and cupped her butt. All Darcy wanted to do was curl into his arms, but she pushed him back.

"I don't want us to become that cliché. You know drinks, dinner, sex. Call me unsophisticated, but I never could see sex as an after-dinner mint."

Pulling her close again, Hank treated her to a soul-shattering assault on her mouth, complete with teasing raids of his tongue.

With a supreme act of will, Darcy pushed away once more. She held him back with her hand on his chest as she fumbled for the door handle. "I'm serious, Hank."

"Me too."

His eyes had turned from bright blue to a smoky silver gray.

Darcy jumped out of the truck and leaned in. Safe now, she smiled and said, "What time tomorrow?"

Hank sat back and grabbed the wheel, knuckles turning bloodless in his frustration. "You sure you can trust me to drive you down there?"

"Don't get sarcastic, Hank. Of course, I trust you. It *is* still illegal to transport someone over the border for sex, isn't it? How 'bout you pick me up about 8?"

Darcy didn't wait for an answer. She slammed the door shut and waved goodbye, then dashed up the steps to the front door of the Algonquin.

After about three beats before he put his truck in gear, Hank pulled slowly away from the curb.

Darcy closed the lobby door and leaned against it, breathing deeply. Hank muddled her senses like good champagne. By the time the bubbles tickled your nose the delicate wine slipped down your throat and made your toes curl. There was so much about Hank that made him practically addictive.

"Damn that man is dangerous," Darcy said softly as she knocked on Abby's door.

"Just me, Abby," she said as she pushed into the apartment.

Mac danced up to say hello, and she swooped him into her arms and nuzzled his fur. Darcy let out a sigh and plopped into her usual place on the sofa.

Abby bustled in from the kitchen with a bottle and two glasses. She filled one for Darcy and began to fill her own when she looked at Darcy closely.

"Did you run all the way home?" she asked. "You're a little flushed."

Darcy took an unhurried sip and smiled up at Abby. "Hank . . . um . . . got my blood up as they say. But I resisted." She took another sip smugly celebrating her victory over mindless lust.

"Really?" Abby sank into her favorite Chesterfield armchair. "Why?"

"Not the reaction I expected. I thought you'd be proud of me for resisting temptation." Darcy picked up the bottle from the table and held it to the light. "How much of this stuff have you already had?"

"That's a fresh bottle I'll have you know." Abby wiggled into her chair.

"Sorry. I didn't mean to insult you. I just thought you'd be on my side." Darcy kicked off her heels and slouched back into the sofa.

"I didn't know there *were* sides. I just thought . . . attractive young couple at the height of their—" Abby stopped herself and filled her mouth with wine when Darcy glared at her. Abby cleared her throat tentatively. "If you don't mind me asking, what's changed since this summer? You were well on your way to the top of Pleasure Mountain a couple of times, if I recall correctly."

Darcy shrugged. "Near death experiences bring out the risk taker in me . . . evidently." She shrugged philosophically.

Abby chuckled. "For heaven's sake, don't tell Hank that. You'll never be safe again."

"Speaking of death and dying . . ."

"I thought we were talking about sex." Abby pouted.

"Focus, Abby. Focus. I got a message from Dr. Villars that the skulls had been sent to a Dr. Anita Garcia at Colorado State University. It seems she does forensic reconstructions and Hank, Netters, and I are going down tomorrow morning. I am going to interview her and get pictures of the reconstructions. With any luck there might be someone who can recognize them."

"That would certainly be a step in the right direction." Abby drained her glass.

"John Walker is our best bet to ID the skulls. I hope his memory is as sharp as it seems to be." Darcy stretched and yawned. "C'mon Mac," she called with little energy and less conviction. "Damn! This being virtuous takes it out of me."

Mac was standing on his stubby back legs, blinking his dark brown eyes at her. Darcy lifted him and dragged herself to the door.

"I'll drop 'Himself' off before I leave if that's okay?"

"Only if you fill me in when you get back."

"Always," Darcy said through a yawn. "G'night."

Darcy woke early the next morning and had time to put on her brown slacks with the autumn leaves print, and jot down a series of questions for Dr. Garcia while she sipped her second cup of coffee.

She tried to cover the basics. She wanted to get some general information about forensic reconstruction, and then she wanted to know about her skulls.

She pondered the fact that thinking of them as "her skulls" should be creepy, but somehow wasn't.

Her phone buzzed, and she jumped.

"I'm out front." Hank said.

"Be right down." She tapped her phone off, grabbed her bag and notes, stuffed her feet into her brown suede ballet flats, tucked Mac under her arm, and raced down the stairs.

Pushing open Abby's door for Mac, she shouted, "I'll see you when I get back. Thanks."

By the time she had catapulted herself into the cab of Hank's truck, she was out of breath.

"Buckle up," Hank snarled.

"You don't sound very friendly." Darcy twisted to latch her belt.

"You want friendly, hang out with your dog." Hank pulled smoothly into traffic.

Darcy was silent for the short time it took to get to I-25. "It wasn't personal," she said.

Hank didn't even pretend to misunderstand what she was talking about. "I think that's what pissed me off. It wasn't personal."

"Huh?"

Hank shifted his eyes to her, then back to the highway. "I don't expect you to jump into bed with me just because I buy you a greasy steak—"

"I bought it, remember?" Darcy inserted. She smiled in his direction, but he was focused on driving.

"The point is I don't *expect* anything from you. I don't know what kind of guys you're used to, but I thought you knew me better than that."

"Sorry," Darcy choked out. She really was sorry. Not just because Hank was upset, but because she had lumped him into the category of guys, she knew didn't deserve to be called men. "Really, Hank. You're a good guy. I am just a little confused about us right now. I don't know if this is a budding relationship, or a more casual 'friends with benefits'. I need a little time and space to figure out."

Hank smiled and patted her knee reassuringly. "It's okay. No one died." He changed the subject. "What are you going to ask Dr. Garcia?"

"I think I'll just keep it pretty general. I'm kind of out of my league here. Biology isn't exactly my strong suit."

Hank broke into a predatory grin. "I could tutor you if you want."

Darcy laughed. "I'm pretty sure I'm not ready for graduate level course work, but I'll keep you in mind."

"That's all I ask." Hank turned up the radio.

By the time they took the Fort Collin's exit, they were comfortable with each other again.

The green lawns fronting the majestic sandstone buildings of the Colorado State University campus looked lush and welcoming. Hank pulled his truck right behind the KCWY van. Netters was unloading his equipment and bag from the side door.

Clipping her ID badge onto her jacket front Darcy strode ahead of the guys, following the direction signs to the forensic lab.

"Guess we follow the lady," Hank said as he picked up a folded tripod from the ground.

"Welcome to my world," Netters laughed as he hiked the heavy equipment bag over his shoulder.

Darcy held the door. The click of her heels echoed off the institutional tile covered floors and walls. The sensation of entering an enormous cave gave her pause, but she shook the feeling and strode forward.

Looking down the entry hallway, Darcy read the signs hanging over the doors at right angles. She spied the Forensic Anthropology sign three doors down and zipped into the office.

A twentyish-something young man was sitting behind a large oak desk. He stood when they came in.

"Hi. I'm Darcy Moreland. I'm an investigation journalist for KCWY News in Cheyenne. This is Bill Netters my videographer, and—"

Hank stepped forward hand outstretched. "Detective Hank Nelson with the Cheyenne Police Department. We're here to see Dr. Garcia. She knows we're coming."

"Ah . . . yes sir. I'll call down to the lab right away." The young man punched in the extension quickly and smiled reassuringly to the trio in front of him.

"I was getting to you," Darcy hissed in Hank's ear.

"My investigation, Ms. Moreland. You're just eye candy." He grinned at her bright red flush.

"Dr. Garcia will be right up," young man said. "Would you like something to drink? Soda, coffee, water?"

"Nope," Netters said as he gently deposited the equipment bag by the cracked brown leather sofa and sank into its deep cushions.

"No thanks," Hank said and leaned against the doorjamb.

"I could really use some water if it wouldn't be too much trouble," Darcy smiled at the young man who looked more like a California surfer than an Anthropology graduate student.

"Sure thing." He dashed out the door so fast, Hank had to shift out of his way.

Darcy rounded on Hank. "Now listen here, Buster—"

"That's Detective Buster to you, Ms. Moreland."

"This is my story."

"Only because I gave you authorization to be here. Do I need to withdraw it?"

Darcy opened her mouth to reply, but the grad student had returned with her water.

"Have they come to blows yet?" said a trim brunette in a white lab coat.

Netters stood and hefted his bag again. "They're still at the spitting and scratching phase. Bill Netters," he held out his free hand. "Dr. Anita Garcia?"

Dr. Garcia chuckled and shook his hand. "I'll show you the way."

Darcy was fuming. Her hands were now full, and she hated being caught being less than professional. It was Hank's fault, she was sure. She wasn't infuriated enough to screw up the assignment though, so she took a deep breath and a sip of water as she followed Dr. Garcia.

The lab was a short jog down a five-step stair and through two stainless steel doors. Inside the lab, steel tables dotted the room with various skeletal remains scattered and tagged.

Dr. Garcia strode to the table furthest into the room. When she swung around to face Hank and Darcy, she smiled.

Darcy was impressed. She was petite and gave the impression of barely controlled energy. Her small hands reminded Darcy of a child's except she wore a heavy gold band on her left hand. The dark brown eyes that crinkled at the corners and the streaks of gray through her hair, spoke of a life well into its second half.

"I'm pretty sure I can tell which is the reporter and which is the cop . . ."

"Detective," Darcy and Hank said together, then laughed.

"Ah—so no war—just a skirmish?" she raised an eyebrow at Netters who smiled and nodded. "Okay, let me see if I can help everyone get what they need.

"Detective, I suspect that in the course of the taping we will answer most of your questions, but just in case, here is the written report with copies of the reconstruction photos for dispersal. She turned to Darcy. "Ms. Moreland, I presume you will want some basic information about the process and some specific information about these remains."

"That would be great. If we need to, we can always edit it," Darcy said.

"Young man," Dr. Garcia turned to Netters. "You can set up over here to avoid the glare from those windows."

Netters nodded and began unpacking his gear.

"Ms. Moreland, you will probably be most comfortable on the stool, and I'm going to stand on a platform behind this table. If I don't, I'll look just like another of these heads."

Everyone laughed at her self-deprecating humor and the stiffness in the room relaxed a couple of notches.

"Whenever you're ready." Dr. Garcia rested her hands in front of her. There was a sheet draped over what looked like a continuous lump running down the middle of the slab.

Netters handed the mic to Darcy. "Women and elephants never forget. Dorothy Parker" Darcy said to check the level. Netters began the count and ended by silently pointing to Darcy.

"I am standing in the Forensic Anthropology Reconstruction lab here on the campus of Colorado State University with Dr. Anita Garcia who has taken custody of the skulls from the remains unearthed from the crawl space beneath a Cheyenne home. Dr. Garcia, could you explain to us a little about the procedure of forensic reconstruction?"

"Of course. When identification of remains is impossible through regular means, forensic reconstruction is often the last resort. It's really a combination of art and geometry."

Dr. Garcia folded the sheet back carefully revealing a skull on a stand that had what looked like plastic push pins studded all over the surface. Two blue glass eyeballs stared out from the eyeholes in the skull.

"The skull must be placed on a moveable stand at the Frankfort Horizontal Position where the eye socket and top of the ear canal are in line. That's part of the geometry. These are called tissue markers, which are glued on the skull. The depths of the markers are based on averages determined by race, age, and gender. Once the markers are placed, a forensic reconstruction artist begins adding a clay layer over the skull. The reconstruction artist will use whatever information they can from the forensic anthropologist."

"That would be Dr. Villars at the University of Wyoming, is that correct?"

"Yes, that's right. Unfortunately, he was unable to give us much information beyond gender and approximate age of each of these skulls. This is where the art comes in."

Dr. Garcia pulled the sheet back revealing two finished reconstructed skulls complete with wigs, one dark-haired, and one fair-haired. The dark-haired bust looked the younger of the two. His hair was styled in the close-crop of the 1940's. The fair-haired bust looked considerably older, but the wig they put on him was longer and tapered.

"Were you able to determine anything more about these two men?" Darcy asked.

"Not much, I'm afraid. Neither had any old injuries that would have affected their appearance before they died. All injuries that were apparent on the skulls were part of the cause of death in both men. I can tell you that the younger man was probably English/Welsh extraction while the older man was most likely of Norse/German extraction. We base these determinations on the ethnic-specific averages and facial bone structures. Based on Dr. Villars's findings we tried to fashion hairstyles for the time these men were thought to have been alive."

"Is there anything else you can tell us?" Darcy asked.

"Only to remind you this is just an educated guess, not scientific fact. When we do reconstructions, we have very little information to go on, so you must look at them as approximations."

"Thank you, Dr. Garcia. This is Darcy Moreland reporting to you from the Forensic Anthropology Reconstruction Lab on the Colorado State University campus in Fort Collins." Darcy gave Netters the sign to cut, then she turned to Dr. Garcia.

"Thank you so much. That was exactly what we needed."

"You're welcome. If you think of any more questions later, don't hesitate to call me." Dr. Garcia looked at her watch. "I'm sorry to have to rush off like this, but I have a class to teach. Detective Nelson, do you have everything you need?"

Hank said as he glanced at the written report. "Yes, ma'am. Thanks."

They watched Dr. Garcia walk out of the lab.

"Wow. She is really fascinating, Darcy said as she moved Hank to the stool behind the heads. Netter's got into position and gave Darcy the silent count. Darcy straighten toward the camera.

"also with us today is the lead Detective for this case, Detective Hank Nelson." Darcy canted her shoulders to look at Hank. Hank nodded in acknowledgement.

"Detective Nelson, have you ever had to use Forensic Reconstruction before?"

Hank eyed her . "Not since I was at the academy. They did give us a flyby introduction to it, but at the time it was a fairly new field. For it to be helpful, you have to have access to someone as knowledgeable and talented as Dr. Garcia."

"Did Dr. Garcia give you any information that you think might be helpful?"

Hank held up the pictures. "The knowledge about ethnicity is a help. We can also put this into our facial recognition program and perhaps get verification about these two men. As always in cases like these citizens can be extremely helpful. If these pictures jog anyone's memory, please call the hotline or contact me directly. We will continue to follow any leads that will give us more information."

"Thank you, Detective Nelson." Darcy turned back to the camera and Netters switched from a two shot to a modified closeup. "This is Darcy Moreland reporting for KWCY. We will continue to look for answers." Darcy signaled to cut.

And they were finished.

"See Hank, not so bad. We are starting to get the hang of this. Win win." Darcy looked at her watch. "Barely 10 o'clock. That was quick and clean."

"I'll see you back at the station," Netters said as he packed up his camera.

"We have to check with John before I get back," Darcy said. "With any luck he'll recognize the picture of one or the other . . . maybe even both."

Hank followed Darcy back to the truck.

"It is okay if we stop by John's with the pictures, isn't it?" Darcy asked as she snapped her seat belt.

"As long as you understand that I may have to ask you to keep any response he gives us off the record for a little while."

"Why?"

"Because the memory of an old man is not always reliable, so we'll need to check out what he tells us—if anything—before we release any details to the public."

"That makes sense. OTR until you say otherwise."

"Off the record?"

"Yup." Darcy flashed him a smile.

The weather was warm for early fall and the bright blue sky was almost cloudless. Traffic was light, and the highway stretched ahead with open vistas. They passed the Old Fort, a rock formation on both sides of the highway that looked like piles of sand-colored hardened lava.

"I wonder why they closed this down as a rest area?" Darcy said.

"Didn't want the responsibility, I guess. Too much risk of some-one climbing on the rocks and falling."

"It's a shame though. I always thought it was fun in a spooky kind of way."

"I'll bring you out for a picnic someday."

"You pack it, and you're on."

Exiting I-25 onto Lincolnway, Hank drove up to 18th and pulled to the front of John Walker's house. The windows were dark and there was no one on the porch.

"He may be out," Hank said as he opened the door of his truck.

"I don't think so. I don't think he goes anywhere much." Darcy ran up on the porch and twisted the knob on the old Victorian bell.

There was no answer. She peered through the glass in the door. Leaning in to get a better look, the door gave way.

Hank caught her before she fell and then pushed her behind him.

"Hey!" Darcy protested.

"Be quiet and stay behind me." Hank scowled at her and then peered into the living room. The heavy curtain made the room dark and shadowy.

"Mr. Walker. It's Detective Nelson and Darcy Moreland. Are you here?" They crept forward.

The first thing that hit her was the metallic smell of blood. She slapped her hand over her mouth and nose to keep from gagging, but a muffled scream escaped.

John Jacob Walker lay sprawled on the floor in a dark puddle of blood. His face was covered with a kitchen towel, but Darcy recognized John's signature rainbow suspenders. A butcher knife jammed in his chest.

Hank squatted down and felt for a pulse. He looked up at Darcy and shook his head, then pulled out his phone and called it in.

Darcy crept closer and saw John's hand was clutching a green piece of paper. She stooped to reach for it, but Hank intercepted her.

"Don't touch anything until the crime unit shows up."

Hank and Darcy when outside and sat on the porch bench. Hank had his arm draped across her shoulders to keep her from shivering. Darcy couldn't hold her tears back. "This is all my fault. If I hadn't stirred up a hornet's nest, this would never have happened."

Hank dug in his back pocket and gave her a handkerchief. "Don't beat yourself up. You were doing your job. I know it's cold comfort, but you are doing a service for the whole community. It is actually worthwhile."

Darcy dabbed at her cheeks. "You don't always think so."

"Not when you get in my way, no. But when we work as a team, we can do some important things."

"But Hank, poor Mr. Walker didn't deserve to die just because he talked to me. I should have set up safeguards for him. Altered his voice and black out his face. It never occurred to me that this would happen."

"Sudden death is always a shock, Darcy. You are not responsible for every crackpot out there. You may think the word is mightier than a butcher knife, but in this case you'd be wrong."

Darcy chuckled at his mangling of the quote and rewarded Hank with a tremulous smile.

The investigation unit appeared. Hank and Darcy followed them back in. After the team took pictures, they gave Hank a set of gloves, so he could retrieve the note. He un-crumpled it and held it up for Darcy to see. It read:

Testis falsus non erit qui loquitur perbit.

"What does it say, Hank?"

"I think it's Latin."

"Let me look at it by the window. I had two years of Latin in Catholic high school." She pulled his arm closer being careful not to touch the paper.

"'*Falus*' I think means false, '*testis*' I think means testimony, but I don't remember enough vocabulary to decipher the rest." Darcy's face suddenly lost all color.

"Don't go getting queasy on me." Hank put his arm around her waist to steady her and seated her on a nearby chair.

"It's not just that Hank. I got a note on the same green paper after the first time I talked to John. It wasn't in Latin though. I just thought some crank left it, so I just threw it in my back seat."

CHAPTER 12

Stunned by the implications, Darcy and Hank didn't move for a moment in silence.

"If you received a note on similar paper, you could be in danger." Hank said.

"The thought had occurred to me." Darcy looked up at him. "But why? None of this makes any sense. John Walker was a kind old man who never hurt anyone . . . and I'm . . . I'm pretty ordinary. It gives me the creeps that someone was watching this house."

Hank spun around and told the head of the crime unit he'd be right back, then he hoisted Darcy from her chair.

"C'mon. We're going to try to find your note." He propelled her out the door so fast she couldn't argue if she'd wanted to.

It took only minutes for Hank to pull up next to Darcy's Audi and jump out.

"Keys?" he asked perfunctorily.

"Just a second . . ." Darcy dug into the depths of her bag. She handed them over. Hank pushed the button twice and had the back door thrown open before Darcy could draw her next breath.

"Good Lord, Darcy. Don't you ever clean out your car?" Hank said as he picked up and tossed food wrappers, notes from assignments and old beverage cups.

Under a box of half-eaten fries, Hank spied a green piece of paper and dragged it from the debris by one corner. Holding it in the sunlight, he read, "GOD'S WAY IS THE ONLY WAY." It was in the same scribbled scrawl as the note at John Walkers.

"See why I thought it was just some crank?" Darcy said.

"Yeah," Hank said. "What are you going to do now?"

"I need to call Zach and get a mobile crew over to John's."

Hank moved back to his truck. "Are you going to do the report?"

"I think so."

Do me a favor," Hank said as he handed her back the keys and then climbed into his truck. "Make the report general and don't mention either of these notes. Okay?"

"Sure. That's reasonable, but will you call me when they get a translation of the Latin one?"

"Yes . . . oh and Darcy?"

"What?"

"Watch your back. I don't know why John was killed or why you got this note, but I think we're dealing with a very irrational human being. Be careful."

"I will. I promise."

Hank drove off and Darcy watched him go before she dialed Zach.

"I need a mobile unit at John Walker's house on 18th."

"Why? Was he able to identify who the bones were from the reconstructions?" Zach's voice sounded excited.

"He's dead," Darcy said. She couldn't help that her voice sounded so flat. She was terrified to look at the truth of what she was saying. If she thought about it, she'd fall apart.

"Dead? Did he have a heart attack or something? "Zach asked.

"No. Hank and I found him in his living room, stabbed through the chest . . . so yes, I guess it was a heart attack of sorts." Darcy sat in her backseat, no longer able to stand and talk.

"Are you okay? Do you want to go home? I could send someone else out there to do the report."

"I'm fine. I'll do it. Send Netters. I don't have to tell him how or what to do."

"You got it." Zach paused. "Darcy, I'm sorry. I know you liked the old guy. It showed in your interview."

"Yeah, I did, Zach. He was a nice old man who didn't deserve to die this way."

"If you need to take the afternoon off after you do the report, I'd understand."

"Thanks, Zach." Darcy tapped her phone off. She knew she wouldn't, couldn't, take the afternoon off. She needed to tell as much of the details as Hank would let her. She needed to make sure the public was informed and mobilized. If this guy was as nuts as Hank seemed to think, who knew who might be next? She felt a shiver crawl down her spine.

After a short call to Abby's to tell her she had to do another story, Darcy drove back to John Walker's house and waited for Netters.

Thankfully, when Netters appeared, he didn't ask her any questions about John Walker's death.

"Where do you want to set up?" he said over his shoulder as he pulled out his camera.

Darcy glanced around and spied a large cottonwood tree to the left of the house. "Over there."

Darcy finished off her sparse notes, trying to make the report concise but effective. Netters handed her the mic and made some minor adjustments to his lens.

"Ready?" he asked.

Darcy nodded and waited for his countdown.

"John Jacob Walker, the subject of an earlier report from this reporter, was found slain at his home today. The cause of death has not yet been established by the Medical Examiner, but stabbing is the unofficial cause.

Police Detective Hank Nelson and I discovered the body when we had stopped to ask Mr. Walker about some forensic material from the 'bones' house across the street.

The Police choose not to speculate at this time whether this is a random break in with robbery as the motive or if it is in some way related to the unusual discoveries in his neighbor's home.

As usual, the police request that anyone with information about this crime contact the Cheyenne Police Department or utilize their anonymous tip line.

Mr. Walker was a longtime resident of this quaint established neighborhood. His death is a large loss to this community.

This is Darcy Moreland reporting for KCWY News."

Darcy stopped speaking and slumped, the mic dangling at her side. Netters rushed to take it from her, leading her to sit on the porch steps.

Keeping his focus on packing up the camera equipment, Netters squatted nearby.

"Kind of a shock, huh?"

Dropping her head to her hands Darcy answered a little above a whisper. "Yeah. A shock."

"Do you think it was a coincidence? Some kids maybe thinking an old man would make a good target."

Darcy looked up, her mouth an angry slash. "Not for one damned second. John was stabbed through the heart in a vicious attempt to silence our only credible witness." Tears welled up on the edges of her narrowed eyes.

"The bastards left a note on his body written in Latin! In Latin, damn it! Like they'd planned the murder ahead."

"What did it say?" Netters plopped to the lawn at her feet.

"Hank's going to get it translated. All I know is that whoever it was had been watching the house. I got a note on the same paper right after I'd talked to John the first time."

"You're shitting me!" Netters rose to his haunches and looked around to see anyone watching from a parked car. "Was yours in Latin?"

"No. Plain English . . . well sort of. It said, 'God's way is the only way.' I thought it was some crank offended by my bumper sticker."

"What does the bumper sticker say?"

"Honk if you *are* Jesus."

Netters snorted. "It's sarcastic, but not that offensive. I've seen worse."

Darcy stood brushed off the back of her pants and hiked her bag onto her shoulder. "One man's humor is another man's insult." She walked toward her car.

"I'll take the video to the station. Why don't you go home?"

Stopping and turning, Darcy looked at him. "And do what? Try to guess who of the neighbors and hundreds of people who drive by daily would kill a nice old man in cold blood? I'll go crazy if I don't do something."

"Right. I'll meet you in the editing room."

Sighing deeply, Darcy dashed away the tears that had finally spilled down her cheeks.

JUGGLING SACKS FROM THE CLOSE-BY sub shop, Darcy squeezed into the small editing room.

"I come bearing bribes. Turkey and Swiss on whole wheat," she plunked the sack in front of Netters, "and an unsweetened iced tea." She stabbed the straw though the hole in the lid.

"Not that I'm suspicious, but what do I have to do for you?"

"I thought once we edited the report, we shot today . . .," Darcy methodically unwrapped her Italian chicken sandwich on a Chapatti roll.

"Spit it out. I may be easy, but I ain't cheap. What do you want me to do?" Netters hadn't even unfolded the sandwich from the red-checked paper.

"Unless Zach assigns us to something else. I thought we could look at the video we shot at John's house. I started thinking we shot it in front of the window. Maybe we can see something."

Netters tore the paper off the overstuffed sandwich. "Count me in!" He slurped some tea as if in punctuation.

It took a short time to edit the report on John Walker's death. When Darcy handed it over to the news director Tom Hutchins, he stopped her from rushing back to the editing bay.

"Zach said to come see him when you finished this." Tom said. "He told me to save some time for a follow up report."

"About what?" Darcy snapped.

Tom held his up his hands. "Hey, don't shoot the messenger. I'm just the director, not the station manager."

"Sorry, Tom. I think I'm wrapped a little too tight right now."

"Yea I heard. It sucks, Darcy. I'm sorry about the old guy."

"Me too, Tom. Me too."

She made a right turn and strode purposefully to Zach's office. Knocking perfunctorily on his door, she didn't wait for an answer before she went in.

"What now, boss? A sidebar on unregistered butcher knives?" She dropped into one of the chairs in front of Zach's desk.

Zach glanced away from his screen and glared. "Aren't you the one who said she had to keep busy?"

"Please don't put me on pot-hole-patrol." She looked so bleak; Zach laughed.

"It's a little better than that. Bryce Adkins was in here earlier champing at the bit to go interview Marie Romero about Walker's death—"

Darcy shot up. "I'll strangle the little squint with my bare hands! That's *my* story, Zach. I don't want that snot-nosed son-of-a—"

"Whoa! I told him that. Though give the devil his due, it was a good idea. Do you think she'll talk to you?"

"Before she'd talk to him." Darcy sat again, pulling her phone from her pocket. She smiled reassuringly at Zach, while she waited for Marie to pick up.

"Hi. Ms. Romero? This is Darcy Moreland from the TV station." She nodded.

"Yes, that's right the young woman who talked to you earlier. I'm calling because I have some sad news about one of your neighbors." Darcy bit her lower lip, hesitant to blurt it out.

"I'm sorry to tell you that John Jacob Walker was found earlier today. He had been stabbed to death. Yes, ma'am. I'm sure it was him. I was the one who talked to him earlier about your old house." Darcy waited. There was a profound silence on the other end.

Darcy looked at Zach's sympathetic face, took a deep breath and dove right in. "The thing is, Ms. Romero, I'd like to get a statement from you since you were such long-time friends. Would that be possible?" Darcy held her crossed fingers up and Zach nodded.

Darcy finally signaled with a thumbs up. "Thank you very much, Ms. Romero. May we come over in about fifteen minutes? Okay, we'll see you in a little while. Goodbye."

Darcy headed for the door. "We're on our way." She stopped and looked at Zach. "I will admit to you Adkins made a good call, but if you ever quote me . . ." she thought for a second, "I'll lace your PB&J with sand. Okay?"

"Got it," Zach said.

DARCY AND NETTERS ARRIVED at Sage Hill Assisted Living Community, breezed past the reception desk, and took the elevator to the second floor.

Marie Romero answered the door almost immediately.

"I am sorry to disturb you, Ms. Romero." Darcy said. "This is my videographer Bill Netters."

Marie smiled and motioned them to sit by the fire and sat in the opposite chair.

"Would it be okay if I set up across from you?" Netters asked.

"I suppose that would be fine. Do you need me to close the curtains?" Marie scooted to the front of the white linen wing backed chair as if preparing to rise.

"No Ma'am. This will be fine. Darcy, can we get a level for Ms. Romero?"

Taking the mic, Darcy held it in front of Marie. "Just say something in your normal tone of voice."

"The weather is getting chilly out there," Marie said.

Netters nodded, and Darcy began:

"Ms. Marie Romero was a longtime neighbor and friend of the deceased, Mr. John Jacob Walker.

"Ms. Romero, how did you know Mr. Walker?"

"He was newly married when he and Cora moved into the house across the street from us. It must be close to seventy years ago now." Marie shook her head as if finding that information amazing.

"Were you close for all that time?" Darcy asked.

"Heaven's no. I mean I moved away, and then moved back. His wife Cora died. I moved here to Sage Hill. I guess you could say we were Christmas card friends for most of those years."

"But when they first moved into the neighborhood, you saw each other often?"

"Oh yes. We were all young you see. My brother J.C. loved to throw parties and John and Cora were always invited. They were great fun."

Tears welled in Marie's sherry-colored eyes.

"Ms. Romero do you know of anyone who might have wanted to kill Mr. Walker? Did he have any enemies?"

"Not any that I knew of." Marie said, and chuckled softly. "He always used to joke that his worst enemy was creeping senility. Said he did crossword puzzles to keep it at bay."

Marie dabbed at her moist eyes with a lace-hemmed handkerchief. "He was a kind-hearted man who never hurt anyone in his life. He didn't deserve to die like that."

"I agree, Ms. Romero. Thank you for your time."

Darcy signaled to cut. Rising to leave, Darcy turned back to Marie.

"I hope that helps alert others in the neighborhood about the danger. At the very least, I think you humanized John and I hope it will encourage someone to call the police if they have any information. Thank you again." Darcy moved toward the door.

Marie rose to show them out. "One question, Ms. Moreland."

"Yes?" Darcy stepped back and let Netters pass in front of her and out the door.

"How has the investigation about the bones been going? Have you discovered any more information?"

"Ironically, we were going over to ask John if he could recognize either man from a recreation that Dr. Garcia had done for the Police Department here. That's how we found him."

"What is a recreation?" Marie asked.

"The report will be on the news tonight, but basically it is a clay sculpture based on the skull. It can only be an approximation, but sometimes they can be a pretty close representation of what the man looked like when he was alive. I had to leave them at the station, or I would show them to you now."

"I will watch with enormous interest." Marie smiled as she closed the door.

Once Netters and Darcy got back to the station, they locked

themselves into the editing bay, splicing the video they'd shot at John Walker's place along with the footage of Marie Romero.

"This should keep them off our backs for a while," Netters said.

"I think it is a good report. I have to admit, going to Marie Romero's was a good idea." Darcy peered at the screen. "I'll take this to Tom; you cue up that interview with John Jacob."

"I'm on it." Netters said, already sorting through the video tapes.

By the time Darcy had returned, Netters was cuing up the tape. They ran it through once, backed it up, and ran it again. Nothing jumped out at them.

"Try it once more in slow motion. Focus on the street out the windows, both behind John and behind me," Darcy said.

At first, neither saw anything unusual, but as the interview progressed, Netters sat up straight and punched the pause button.

"What?" Darcy asked.

"That's the second pass for that white Chevy van. Look." He rewound and played it again.

"It looks like the same van." Darcy squinted her eyes to see if it helped, "But honestly, white Chevy vans are all over the place. How can we be sure this is the same one?"

Netters hit the forward button and stopped on another view of the van as it turned the corner behind Darcy. Netters stopped and enlarged the frame.

"I can't see its license plate," Darcy moaned. "Why is it dark like that?"

"Because it's fitted with a film that makes it hard-to-impossible to photograph or to read."

"Why would a regular repair van have that?"

"Why indeed," Netters smirked. "There she is. Third time around the block and now parked right across the street from your car."

"Netters, Look! That guy in black jeans and hoodie got out and put that note under my wiper. Can you get a look at his face?"

Netters zoomed in, but the detail was lost, and the hood obscured any distinguishing characteristics.

"Damn!" Darcy sputtered in frustration.

"At least we've identified the vehicle they were in. I'll see if I can pull some decent stills off, and you can give them to Hank."

"Great. Maybe they can do that BOLO thing they do."

"Don't get too excited. We don't know for sure that the guy who put the note on your car was responsible for murdering John."

"But the paper and the writing were the same. I know it's just circumstantial right now . . . but if it looks like a duck, and quacks like a duck . . . Besides, at least I feel like we're doing something."

Darcy propped her chin in her hands and watched as Netters pulled several shots of the van and the man off, and scanned them into a photo shop program.

In minutes, they had pictures of the van from several angles and the man from front and back.

"I hope they catch you and wring you out," Darcy said to the man in the picture.

CHAPTER 13

BRINGING ABBY UP TO SPEED on the investigation was always time-consuming. Darcy never seemed to have the answers to all of Abby's questions. The upside was Abby always had wine and sometimes her questions were a big help.

Knocking on the door, Darcy heard the cheerful sound of her dog Mac barking. "Just me," she shouted out as she eased the door open. Mac scampered and yapped at her feet, and she finally took pity on him and picked him up, simultaneously toeing off her shoes and dropping her bag by the door.

She was beat, physically, and emotionally. She just hadn't realized it before.

"I presume you'd like a taste of this really nice Zin I got at the liquor store," Abby said as she brought the dark bottle and two large goblets.

Darcy opened her mouth to protest, but Abby jumped right in. "Don't you wrinkle your nose, young lady. This is a wonderful red. Not at all tannic. You need to branch out. Woman does not live on Pinot Grigio alone." She poured a small dollop into each glass. "If you don't like it, I'll drink it, but I'm betting you will." Abby sat took a fortifying sip and closed her eyes in appreciation.

"Honestly, Abby," Darcy sipped tentatively, "you act like wine is the panacea of life. Hey. This isn't half bad." Darcy took a deeper taste.

"Damned with faint praise," Abby shook her head in disgust. "Okay. Give me a run-down. I haven't had time to watch the news today." She squirmed in her favorite chair until comfortable.

"We got a great report on the reconstruction forensics, and Dr. Garcia gave us some pictures to take back. I have to say, it gave me the willies to look at their faces. Somehow it was easier when they were just bones." Darcy said.

"As if a layer of reality was added, huh?" Abby leaned forward on her elbows.

"I guess. Anyway, the busts looked so real, and the photographs Dr. Garcia gave use were so clear, I just know we will find someone who knew these men." Darcy gulped the last of her wine and held her glass out for more.

Abby obliged. "What happened?"

"When Hank and I went to show the pictures to John Walker, we found him stabbed to death in his living room."

"Good Lord! What a terrible shock dear. Are you okay?" Abby reached across to pat Darcy's knee.

"Yeah, but it was grisly. Whoever killed him left a note in Latin. Hank's getting it translated, but I had gotten a note earlier this week on the same paper."

"You got a note? In Latin?"

"No, it was oblique . . . fundamentalist Christian thingy. Something about God's ways . . . something, something, something. I threw it in my backseat, thinking it was a joke."

"Clearly not." Abby sipped her wine thoughtfully. "Does this mean you're in danger too?"

"Hank thinks it might mean they were watching the house at least. Anyway, Netters and I pulled some shots of the guy who put the note on my car. We hope Hank can get someone to ID him." Darcy held her glass out not drinking.

"Not that I'm not sympathetic, but you need some food before you suck down anymore Zin." Abby picked up the bottle and disappeared into the kitchen.

"How about some leftover lemon chicken and rice?" Abby shouted from the kitchen.

"Fine." Darcy put her glass down on the small table snugged up to the side of the settee and grabbed a magazine off the table and leafed through it. Her eyes didn't even focus on the bright, glossy pictures. She was filling the quiet with distractions. Mac jumped up on the sofa next to her and rested his furry head in her lap.

"You always know how to make me feel better," she said aloud as she stroked between Mac's ears.

"Well it's only leftover food and pretty good wine, but it's a start," Darcy stood abruptly and Mac scooted onto the floor.

Abby laughed as she set the plates down. "Oh. You were talking to Mac, not me."

"You too, Abby." Darcy went over and hugged her tight. "Having you and Mac to come home to saves my sanity."

Pushing her toward her place at the table, Abby said, "Well, sit. Eat."

Darcy heaped her plate with brown rice, mushrooms, and topped it with half a breast fillet.

"My mom is much less on my case now that I told her I eat here a lot." Darcy smiled. "She worries."

"She should. You don't eat well." Abby got up and switched the TV on. "Hope you don't mind." She scooted into her chair again. "If it bothers you, I'll turn it off." She held up the remote in a good faith pledge.

They ate silently and watched the news. When Darcy's report came on, Abby started to fill the glasses again, but Darcy put her hand over hers.

"I'll stop pouring. I can tell you want to keep your head clear." Abby said.

Darcy watched with a sense of detachment. The shots of the ambulance and the black body bag that held John Walker's remains, her description of his death, all left her unmoved. It was as if she had packed the horror of finding the body in a small box in her head labeled "Do Not Open."

There was a short voice-over where she heard herself explain that Marie Romero agreed to talk to them on camera. The interview followed.

"Darcy! You didn't tell me you went to see Marie today."

"I guess I forgot to tell you. It was a busy day. Shh. Here's the report on the reconstructions."

Both Abby and Darcy leaned in. The close ups of the recreations and the explanations of Dr. Garcia flickered across Abby's 19-inch screen. Abby clicked the off button as soon as the report finished.

"Who the hell could give a damn about the weather or sports after that?" Abby said. "Quite a challenging day."

"Yeah." Darcy stood up and began carrying dishes into the kitchen. "I think I'll go upstairs and run a tub. I hate to eat and run . . ."

"Here. Take this." She thrust the half-full bottle into Darcy's hand.

"Don't mind if I do," Darcy smiled. "Come on Mac. Make your goodbyes."

Abby lifted him and accepted a moist lick on the cheek before putting him down. She slung her arm around Darcy and walked her to the door.

"Those reports were well done, Darcy. If anyone has any information about John Walker's murder or the two men buried in the 'bones' house, they will call Hank. You've done all you could do for now."

"It doesn't feel like it's enough," Darcy gave her a quick hug and a weak smile. "But it will have to do. Thanks for everything, Abby."

Compared to Abby's comfortably overstuffed, almost fluffy apartment, Darcy felt her space had all the appeal of a hospital waiting room. She threw her shoes and bag in the corner of the living room and placed the bottle and glass on the small bistro table by the kitchen.

Stripping down as she went toward her tiny bathroom; Darcy stuffed her clothes into an already-full hamper then leaned over the ball and claw tub and ran some hot water. Lacing some lavender bath salts over the surface, she breathed in the relaxing scent. She stretched and popped her back.

"Not for you, young man. This tub is for me." Darcy pointed to the door and Mac wandered toward the door, then curled up on the floor.

He looked so dejected Darcy had to laugh. She crouched down by him and scratched behind his ears. "Thanks for the laugh, bud. I needed it today."

She finished stripping, then climbed into the hot tub. The cast iron kept the tempeture of the water warm and the capacity was perfect for a neck deep, bone-melting soak. She stayed in until her fingers puckered, then reluctantly wrapped a soft white bath sheet around her body and padded out to the bottle she had left on the table.

With her half full glass of Zin in her right hand and scrunching up the trailing ends of the bath sheet in her left hand, she gingerly negotiated a path to the brown velvet sofa in the middle of her living room. She took a deep gulp of wine, licked her purple stained lips, and leaned her head back against the softness of the sofa. Darcy closed her eyes.

She awakened with a start at her home phone ringing. It almost never rang. She only kept a landline to please her folks who were sure that cell phones were unreliable.

In her foggy recoil, she almost tossed her empty glass in the air, but saved it from crashing to the floor. She crawled across the surface of the couch to retrieve the phone, mostly to stop the maddening ringing.

"Hello!" she practically bellowed into the phone.

"Gary Romero," the curt voice over the phone said. "I want to see you. I'll be there in 5 minutes."

Darcy looked at the now disconnected line. "He didn't sound pleased," she said to Mac as she dashed to her bedroom to dress.

She barely had time to slip into some jeans and t-shirt before she heard what she was coming to identify as the quintessential-Romero-rap. She certainly hoped her solid oak door could survive.

She swung the door open, and Romero swooped in.

"Darcy, this has to stop," he roared at her.

"I agree. You cannot continue to batter on my door like the hounds from hell."

"Don't be stupid," he growled at her.

"You first," Darcy said with a sass she didn't really feel. Romero was a good-sized man and right now, he was red-eyed pissed.

Romero ran his hand through his dark black hair and took a deep breath. "May I sit down?"

"Sure. I prefer that to you standing over me and glowering like that." She waited until he sat on the ladder-backed chair by the door.

She stood above him and put her hands on her hips. "Let me guess. You're ticked because I interviewed your Aunt Marie about John Walker's death. Is that it? For your information, Mr. Romero, she agreed to be interviewed, and although she *is* in her golden years, she *isn't* in her dotage. And besides—"

"My aunt had a massive stroke this evening," he interrupted Darcy's rant, his voice tired and defeated.

"Oh my God, Gary." Darcy dropped to sit on the overstuffed arm of the sofa across from him. "Is she okay?"

Romero looked up at her. "Of course she's not okay," he over enunciated as if it would help him maintain control. "And I blame you."

"Me?" Darcy popped off her perch. "Now wait just a damn minute. She was fine when I left her earlier this afternoon."

"The nurse at the home said she ate an early supper because she wanted to see the evening news." Romero stood, glared at her in accusation, stood, and began to pace. "One of the young aids was with her when she stroked. Luckily, she initiated emergency protocols." He finished his restless stride, staring her down. "She stroked watching your report on those damn bones. Lindy said my aunt gasped and then couldn't seem to inhale. When she tried to speak, it came out all garbled."

"Gary, I can't tell you how sorry I am—"

"Save it. I'm telling you to stay away from her. Don't go anywhere near her. Do you understand?" He took a step forward and Darcy defiantly didn't back up.

"Save it. I didn't do anything to cause that stroke and you know it. You're just angry and scared and want to take it out on somebody."

"If you hadn't been stirring up old memories—"

"You can back that mule right down the trail, mister. She is living in an assisted community because she had a stroke before. She moved there way before I met her." Darcy raised her chin and glared. She was relying on the innate chivalry of a Western Gentleman not to punch her in the jaw.

Romero didn't disappoint. He grabbed his hat and headed for the door. "Stay away from her." He slapped his hat on his head and stormed out the door, leaving it open in his wake.

"At least he didn't slam it," she said to Mac as she softly closed it.

Despite her previous bravado, Darcy felt traumatized. It was all too much for one day—talking to Dr. Garcia. finding John's body and now Marie having a stroke. Regardless of what she said to Romero, there did seem to be a connection to the bones. But what?

John was murdered because he could have identified at least one of the recreations. Darcy was certain of it.

But what could have caused Marie's stroke? Did she recognize one or both of the men? Was seeing a life-sized bust of someone long dead and forgotten have caused her already vulnerable system to collapse?

Darcy felt guilty. She didn't need Gary Romero to tell her that she'd stirred up a snake pit that even she didn't understand. She fervently wished she had never started this story.

"No I don't," she said aloud. "Whatever malevolence is out there, I'm going to root it out and smash it into bits." She strode toward her bedroom. "C'mon Mac. Keep me company."

The next morning her bravery had vanished and left in its place a raging headache. She felt like she'd been bludgeoned with a ball-peen hammer. She dragged herself over to the sink to make some coffee, but the sound of running water was so painful, she only filled half the pot.

The resulting brew was closer to espresso than coffee, but she gulped it down, swallowing several aspirins with the strong swill.

She had no sense of time, but a corner of her un-pickled brain registered the sound of her cell buzzing in the depths of her bag. Tempted to let voice mail pick up, she sat and stared at her bag, trying to uncross her eyes. When Mac began barking, she admitted defeat and dug her phone out. She accepted the call just to stop the whanging it was causing in her head.

"Darcy? This is Hank. Do you have a couple of minutes this morning?"

"Um. How alive do you need me to be? Abby fed me some poisoned Zin last night and my head is about ready to fall off my neck and roll across the floor."

Hank chuckled. "I do need you to focus. How 'bout I go by The Taco Stand and get you a couple of breakfast burritos? Would that help?"

Darcy choked back a whimper. "Oh Hank. I would love you forever. You'd be saving my life!"

"Good. That works for me." Hank said then hung up.

Darcy tried to make her fuzzy brain decide whether he meant he intended for her to love him, or whether he intended to save her life. At this precise moment, she didn't care what the answer was as long as he produced the burritos.

The aspirin and coffee finally blurred enough of her headache to allow her to get into some jeans and a soft denim shirt. Now that she was awake, she was uncomfortably conscious of the seeping chill coming from the old wooden window frames. She pulled on some wooly socks for good measure.

By the time Hank arrived with the burritos, she had managed to brew a new pot of coffee and set out some plates.

She practically pulled him into the room, grabbing the sack from his hand. "Sit," she commanded him as she unfolded the bag and sniffed at the contents. "Oh man. I am starving."

She portioned out two burritos each on the plates. Her stomach rumbled and her mouth did a saliva dump that only this particular breakfast could produce.

Hank chewed his food in his quiet deliberate way, while Darcy nearly inhaled hers. She was done and patting her distended belly, long before Hank attacked his second burrito.

"Don't you ever get indigestion, eating so fast?" Hank smiled at her.

"Nope. Got my cast iron constitution from my dad. We used to race to see who could finish first." Darcy laughed. "My mom hated it."

Hank sipped his coffee and peered over the top of his cup. "Feeling better now?"

"Much better than I have any right to expect. Why?"

"Because I have some disturbing news for you."

"If it's about Marie Romero having a stroke, don't bother. Romero barged in here last night and told me to stay the hell away from his aunt."

"No I hadn't heard. How is she doing, do you know?"

"No. And I'm not likely to find out either. Romero is blaming me and the bones story for causing his aunt's stroke. I have to admit I feel guilty about both John's death and Marie's stroke."

"That's just your Catholic guilt talking. The investigation would have been ongoing whether you were doing a story on it or not."

"Yeah, but John wouldn't have been killed because I interviewed him, and Marie wouldn't have had such a strong reaction to the recreation story if it hadn't been on the nightly news."

"Is that what Romero told you?" Hank put his warm hand on Darcy's.

"Pretty close. He said she was watching the story about the reconstructions when she stroked." Darcy wiped a small tear that had eased out from the corner of her eye with the sleeve of her sweatshirt.

"She could have keeled over watching Saturday Morning Cartoons."

"But she didn't, Hank. That's the point."

Hank reached into his shirt pocket and pulled out the small spiral topped notebook he always carried. He flipped through the pages and then stopped.

"I hate to dump this on you today, but you said you wanted to know."

"Know what?"

"The translation of the Latin note we found with John. Now before I tell you, you need to know this is off the record. Okay?"

"Yeah. Sure." Darcy tried to peek around the edges, but Hank pulled it to his chest like it was a winning poker hand.

"I mean it Darcy. I won't have you compromising the investigation just so you can get a story."

"I've got it, Hank. What did it mean?"

"It was cobbled together from two Biblical passages near as we can tell, from Proverbs and Zechariah. Loosely translated it reads:

A false witness will not go unpunished, and he who speaks lies shall perish, and be cast the weight of lead upon the mouth thereof.

Darcy listened and tried to make sense of the quotation. "Are they saying that John lied about something? And what was that bit about lead in his mouth?"

"The ME found melted solder had been poured into his mouth."

Darcy winced at the image of molten lead being dumped into John's mouth.

"Cold comfort, but the lead was poured in *post mortem*. More as a symbolic gesture than anything."

"Oh God, Hank! How barbaric."

"Yeah." He stood and pulled Darcy to him in a clumsy hug. "That's why you're going to be placed in protective custody until we find these maniacs."

CHAPTER 14

SHE TRIED TO STAND UP and pushed hard against his chest, but he held her hands tightly, pinning her in place.

"Hank, be reasonable. I can't do my job locked down and surveilled. He chuckled at her. "Ten points for a good work ethic. Zero points for common sense." He pinned her to the wall gently with his body. "Not that I'm not enjoying this full body contact, but I need you to stop wiggling and listen to me."

She stilled. She felt his "pleasure" press hard against her. She felt her face flush deep red but didn't want to consider why. If she once admitted how he made her feel hot all over and melted her knees, she was afraid he'd use her weakness for him to control her. To give him his due though since last summer when Mac and Abby were kidnapped he had been her rock. He was just as scared for their safety as she was.

"Okay. I'm listening."

He backed away but still held her at arm's length. "All we know is that whoever murdered John Walker is also responsible for the note you found on your car."

"Is that your best guess or is there some proof?"

"A little of both to be honest." He dropped his hands from her arms and ran them through his hair. "The writing is connected. We're sure of that. Same paper, same writer." He flopped onto the sofa. She followed him and sat tucking her feet under her.

"So, what's the problem? I mean other than I am evidently on the mailing list."

"We can't be sure that the person who wrote the notes was actually responsible for the murders."

"Murders? As in more than one? You said murders. Who else was killed?"

She leaned toward him, wanting desperately to shake the answer from him. She tucked her hands under her butt instead. She was fairly sure he wouldn't respond well to emotional eruptions, but her heart was pounding.

He reached inside the pocket of his coat and pulled out a scrap of paper in an evidence bag bag and handed it to her. His tightened jaw was the only evidence he was braced for her reaction.

"It's just a copy of the note," he explained.

The writing was faded, but the scrawl looked identical to John Walker's note and hers. Again, it was in Latin, and she tried to decipher it.

Et qui blasphemaverit nomen domini morte moritaur lapidibus opprimet eum omnis multitudo sive ille civis seu peregrinus fuerit qui blasphemaverit nomen Domini morte moriatur

Torturously sounding out the words one at a time, she finally looked up at Hank. "This is way beyond my high school Latin. 'Blaspheme' is obvious and 'morte' is death, the rest of it . . ."

He pulled out his spiral-topped notebook from a shirt pocket. He flipped several pages and then began to read his notes. "It says: 'And he that blasphemeth the name of the Lord, he shall surely be put to death, all the congregation shall certainly stone him: as well the stranger, as he that is born of the land, when he blasphemeth the name, shall be put to death.' It is Leviticus 24:16."

He passed his notebook to her, and she scanned the Biblical quotation printed out meticulously. She read it twice silently.

"Well that explains those smooth stones you found by the body." Her voice shook, but she had to ask. "Where did you get the note?" She handed it back. Her hand trembled, so she stuffed it under her butt again.

"It was with the newest set of bones. Tucked into the last layer of the sheet that was his shroud. Obviously, it became more important when linked to John Walker's note," He grew quiet.

"Go ahead and say it—and to mine. You think the guy who left me that note is the same one who murdered Mr. Jones and John Walker."

"No. I think the guy you caught on video tucking that note on your car was just the messenger. We may be dealing with a fundamentalist cult executing people who don't follow the letter of Old Testament law. Because of your nosing around, I think you may have been targeted."

"Well that's just crazy ridiculous!" She sprung up and began pacing.

He watched her in silence, finally he said, "Really? You really want to dismiss this because of frustrated temper?"

She stopped in front of him. "I am not dismissing anything. And I am *not* in a temper." She leaned down. "Which, by the way, is an insulting and patronizing thing to say."

He reached up and yanked her into his lap. "If you're not dismissing it, what was all that pacing about?"

"Frustration." She smiled. "I was trying to think of how many Old Testament laws I've broken lately."

"What did you come up with?"

She squirmed suggestively. "Lust, I think. Whatever the rules are about not being lustful, I'm pretty sure I've broken some of them."

"Which ones?"

"Do *not* tell me you don't remember." She twisted in his lap to straddle him.

"As entertaining as this is, the real issue is how to keep you safe."

"Protective custody is out." She pushed on his muscled chest and tried to stand.

He yanked her back down. Taking her chin in his hand, he forced her to look at him. "Okay. I could move in."

"Think again," she said, but her mouth twitched into a smile. "Abby would be scandalized."

He grinned back. "I doubt that." He turned slightly and retrieved what looked like a necklace from his pocket and slipped it smoothly over her head.

"What's this?" She lifted it up. It was a pendant an inch square with a red button in the middle. The chain was a sturdy bead chain like they used on military dog tags.

She looked at it closely. She started to push the button in the middle, but He stopped her.

"Don't press that unless you need help," he said sternly.

"What happens? Some kind of alarm?"

He nodded. "A silent one that goes directly to the station."

"It looks like . . . like . . . Hank tell me this is *not* one of those 'I've fallen, and I can't get up!' necklaces."

"Same principle except it sends an alarm and has GPS tracking as well."

She slipped it off her neck and stood in one fluid motion. "Thanks, but no thanks." She handed it to him. "I don't like the idea that you can track me like a lost dog or something."

"I can always have you fitted with a Martha Stewart ankle bracelet instead, but rumor has it they're not very comfortable."

"Hank Nelson! Have you lost your ever-lovin' mind? I am not a criminal, and I won't be treated like one."

He stood towering over her. "I gave you several choices Darcy. Pick one. This is non-negotiable."

Facing him for a moment, she stretched out her palm for the necklace. Instead of dropping it into her hand however, He gently slipped it over her head.

"Don't take this off even in the shower. If you get scared or you hear something, don't wait to investigate. Push the button. Understand?"

"I've got it." Darcy sounded surly even to her ears. She heaved a deep sigh and pulled him back onto the sofa. "Hank I'm sorry. I know you're just trying to keep me safe, and I appreciate it, but honestly even if you're right about these being cult killings, why would they bother with me?"

He pulled her close, so her head rested on his chest. "They

would bother with you because you are trying to get to the truth about some murders. Add to that, you are an annoyingly assertive young lady—a subculture not appreciated much in cultist communities—and you could easily be branded as a blasphemer and bearer of false witness."

She snuggled closer enjoying the warmth of his arms. "Don't forget loose woman." She giggled.

"Yuck it up. These people don't tolerate anyone they consider an enemy. They believe in capital punishment of the most barbaric kind, and if you're not on their 'kill to silence' list yet you soon will be."

"I think that's one of the nicest things you've ever said to me. She pushed up to kiss him exuberantly on the mouth. "My dad always said you could judge a man by his enemies." She smiled up at him.

He grabbed her upper arms and shook lightly her once. "This is not a game, Darcy."

Wrapping her arms around his neck, she kissed him again. "I know it's serious, and I do appreciate that you want to keep me safe. If they are determined to try to kill me, I don't think I can stop them even with this new jewelry."

"Yeah well, humor me."

"Okay" She snuggled back in his arms.

He nuzzled her neck. "I hate to look a gift horse in the mouth, but why are you being so cooperative?" He ran his hand up and down her back.

"Mmmm," she sighed, "That feels good." She lifted her feet off the floor and draped them on the empty end of the sofa.

His hand drifted lower, then snaked under her loose denim shirt. With one deft pinch, he unhooked her bra.

She laughed. "How long did it take to perfect that move?"

Chuckling, he said, "What else do junior high boys have to do?"

His warm, slightly roughened palm eased under her bra and drifted to her front, surrounding her breast. She felt a deep, soft glow begin to build, and she canted her shoulders slightly to give him better access.

"How's the hangover?" He asked as he nuzzled close to her ear.

"Hangover?"

"Never mind." He kissed her deeply, turning her gently until she lay halfway under him and inserted his knee between her legs.

He began to slowly unbutton her shirt. She slipped her hands into the top of his jeans and let her fingers tease.

He sucked a lungful of air and stopped unbuttoning her shirt.

"Pay attention to what you're doing, Mr. Nelson." She laughed, undoing his fly, and cupping him with both hands.

"It's Detective Nelson if you're going to go all formal on me," gasped out, "but somehow this doesn't feel like the time for it." He lowered his head and latched his mouth around her breast. She arched in appreciation but continued her caress.

"Darcy," he managed to rasp out. "If this isn't going anywhere, we need to stop. I can't take too much more."

Pulling her hands from his pants, she began running her palms up under his faded t-shirt.

"I'm feeling very into protective policemen this morning." She drew her hands slowly down his chest, plunging back into his open jeans.

He tugged her hands free and held them together between them. "If this is just gratitude, contribute to the Policeman's Protective Association."

She clasped him once more and began to rub with progressively more friction.

"I'm serious, Darcy. Are you sure you want to do this?"

"Yes, I'm sure." Her whiskey colored eyes widened and fixed on his smoky blue ones.

"Well then," Hank stood and grabbed her hand. "I am a grown man and I need a bed." He dragged her toward the bedroom.

"Do you need time to take a pill?" she teased.

He looked at the pronounced bulge in his jeans. "Not tonight." He swung her in an arc, and she landed, sprawling, in the middle of her unmade brass bed.

"Hold on."

She barely had time to grasp the bars above her head before he was dragging her jeans off her body. She smiled up at him as he struggled free of his own jeans.

"What you lack in finesse, you make up for in sheer exuberance," she quipped. She quickly reached into her bedside table and palmed a foil wrapped condom.

Wrenching his t-shirt off, he stared down at her. "You ain't seen nothin' yet."

She laughed as he pounced on the bed and wrestled her free of the remainder of her clothes. Sprawled beneath him, she wrapped her arms around his neck and pulled him close for a deep, wet kiss.

He burrowed deep into her neck and nibbled briefly on her ear before returning to her mouth.

She closed her eyes and drifted with his kisses that were softer now and yet more compelling. She felt his hands run up her sides, leaving a heat in their wake like a lava spill. When she felt his hands drift back down again, her body arched and pressed against the length of him.

She felt a conflicted need for him to go faster yet she reveled in the softer, slower pace he was setting. When he flicked her nipple with his tongue, she felt passion boil into a scream, but the sound was swallowed by his kiss.

"Hank . . . Oh Hank . . ." she heard herself whisper on a gasp.

Kissing down her cheek, he simultaneously captured her butt and pulled her close, so she could feel his hard desire for her.

"Hmmm?" He hummed vaguely against the soft curve of her jaw.

"I want . . . I want . . ."

"What do you want?" He worked his way from her neck to her flat stomach and rimmed her navel teasingly with his tongue. "I can't wait to hear."

She arched again. A frustrated wild cry caught in her throat. She grabbed fistfuls of his dark hair and yanked his head up, so she could see his eyes. Burnished silver, she thought. They looked like bluish burnished silver.

"Can we move this along a little faster?" She tried to sound less desperate and more in control. She ended the request with a hollow sounding chuckle.

He smiled at her. It was a wicked little boy smile. "No," he said succinctly, then dropped his head and began to work his way inexorably lower.

Skipping her center where she quivered with a warm, throbbing, ache, he swerved to her inner thighs, laving them with his tongue and driving her wild with his warm breath.

"Hank! Damn it!"

"Shh. Working here." The breath of his whispered response had her arching and thrashing until he pressed her hips deeply into the mattress. He continued his attention to her legs, ducking behind each knee and teasing the soft flesh with small nips. As he kissed down her calves, she groaned.

"Patience, my love. Patience." He laughed softly as he stroked the inside sole of her foot.

"Tickles!" She kicked out, but he grabbed her ankles and stilled them.

"Just lie very still and be a good girl."

Before she could damn him to several dark, deep levels of hell, his hands began to slip up her legs and the warm honey of passion flooding her senses again.

By the time he'd reached where she wanted him most, she was wet and ready for him. He dipped his tongue, tickling and licking her sensitive nub.

She arched and shrieked, feeling the insides of her thighs quiver with the rhythm of her panting breath.

"Oh God! Oh my God!"

He loomed above her grinning with mischief. "Flattering, but inaccurate."

She tried to swat at him but missed. He griped her arms and rolled her on top of him. He threw his arms out to his sides.

"I can't resist anymore. Take me."

She straddled him, letting her moist, warm center cradle him as if reminding him where he needed to go.

"I really should make you beg. It would only be fair."

Folding his arms under his head, he smiled up at her. "How disgustingly maudlin do I need to get before you take care of my baser needs?"

She she wiggled on top of him, eliciting an irritated huff before his strong hands bracketed her hips and held her still.

"Begging is one thing, but teasing won't be tolerated."

"What's good for the goose is good for the gander," Darcy taunted as she ran her hands up his chest and tweaked his nipples with her teeth. Straddling him, she watched his eyes as she leisurely tore the foil with her teeth. Taking her time, she slowly drew the condom down the full length of him, delighting in teasing his sensitive ridge.

Before she could get a breath, he'd tossed her under him and slipped into her.

She bucked in protest. "Hey! Not fair!"

He withdrew to her sensitive edge then surged into her again. "Do you really want to argue right now?" He pulled back and plunged once more.

All she could manage was a squeak in answer.

The pace grew fevered. Neither was capable of speaking. As the heat grew, pulsed, and coiled through her blood, she felt swathed in passionate heat, building until the mutual eruption left them both sweat soaked and panting in the dappled lace filtered sunlight.

CHAPTER 15

DARCY STRETCHED LIKE A CONTENTED CAT. She rolled on her side so she could see Hank and play with the dark, thick hair that curled slightly on his neck.

"Isn't this a bit long for regulations?" She tugged on a lock.

"Hmmm?" He asked.

The usual hard planes of his face were softened now, and the furrows in his forehead smoothed out. Darcy smiled when he opened one eye and cautiously peeked at her.

"Problem?"

"Nope. I'm just thinking unkempt is a good look for you."

"The look you're enjoying is me satiated . . . my freshly f—"

Darcy covered covered his mouth. "Don't you dare reduce what just happened between us to the same level as gulping down a burger and fries!"

A deep chuckle rumbled up from his chest. "Actually, I was just playing with the words. I could text you with FFF, and you'd know exactly what I meant."

"What's the last F for?"

"Face, you deviant. What did you think it stood for?"

"Fool?"

Hank rolled on top of her and looked fierce. "You're going to pay for that." He held her hands immobile above her head and leaned down to kiss her.

Darcy's cell buzzed on her night table. She arched her back, bucked, and rolled out from underneath him, enough to grab the phone answer it. "Sorry," she mouthed to Hank.

"What?" she said. "I wasn't scheduled for anything this morning."

Darcy listened. "That son-of-a-bitch! I'll be right there." She turned the phone off and scrambled out from under Hank. "Bryce Adkins—that degenerate—that sneaky venomous twit—is in Zach's office right now convincing him that I need to be pulled from this story because I'm no longer unbiased. He told Zach about my note and that it was the same as John Walker's." She hopped around the room, trying to pull on her jeans.

"And that means . . .?"

She paused to pull her t-shirt over her face." That means you have a problem, if true. That means you have a direct leak to that slime ball from your department."

"I guess this is the end of the delightful after-glow time." Hank swung out of bed and retrieved his jeans.

Darcy jammed her arms into her favorite denim jacket. "Find it and plug it, Hank." She flung her bag over her shoulder and slammed out the door.

"Not my favorite way to start a day," Hank said to the now empty apartment.

The short drive didn't improve Darcy's mood. By the time she roared into Zach's office, she was almost beyond coherent thought. She rounded on Bryce Adkins like an avenging angel. Adkins backed away. She continued to close the distance until she'd pinned him to the wall without even touching him.

"You sorry excuse for massive hair gel and cheap after-shave. What makes you think you can snake my story out from under me?"

"Now calm down, Darcy." Adkins tried to square his shoulders.

"Ms. Moreland to you. You aren't a colleague. You aren't a reporter." She leaned in until he slumped a little against the wall. "And you are definitely sophomore-stupid to tell me to calm down and hope to live."

"Okay, Darcy." Zach came from behind his desk. "You've vented your spleen and Adkins is all ears. Aren't you?" Zach looked pointedly at him.

"Sure," Adkins replied grudgingly.

Darcy wasn't through. She spun to face Zach. "And how dare you listen to this village idiot? This is my story from beginning to end and you know it!"

"It is whoever's story I say it is . . . and *you* know it!" Zach snapped back.

Raising her hands in surrender, Darcy sat in front of Zach's desk clamping her mouth shut.

"Fine," Zach said as he rounded his desk and sat. "Adkins."

Bryce sulkily dropped into the other chair like a grounded 16-year-old.

Zach scowled. "This is a news-gathering agency. If your objectivity has been compromised, Darcy, maybe Adkins should take over."

"I'd damned well like to know where this little squint got his information." Darcy glared at him.

"None of your damn business. I don't have to reveal my sources," Adkins shot back.

"Enough, both of you. Now, Darcy, try to see it from Adkins' point of view—"

"I'd love to, but I can't get my head that far up my—"

"Finish that thought, and you will not only be off this story, but you'll be also on involuntary leave. Understand?"

Not trusting herself to speak, Darcy nodded. Adkins smirked.

"Is it true that you got a similar note?" Zach asked.

Darcy squirmed. "Yes."

"And when were you going to tell me?"

"When you needed to know. It's just a coincidence. It wasn't even a threatening note."

"Ask her if the police didn't tell her to wear an alarm pendant in case the murderer tries to get her," Adkins gloated.

Zach raised a questioning brow, and Darcy nodded.

"Is that a real possibility?" Zach canted his hip on the edge of his desk.

"No. Hank is just being paranoid."

"I'm starting to feel a little creeping paranoia myself." Zach tapped his pencil on his desk. "Adkins, you can wipe that smile off your face. I'm leaving Darcy on the story."

"But—" Adkins rose from his seat.

"She's made the contacts and done the research." Zach shifted his focus to Darcy. "But if you so much as feel the hairs rise on the back of your neck, I want to know about it. Is that clear?"

"Crystal, boss. Thanks." Darcy got up to leave.

"You can't do that! I'll call my uncle," Adkins whined.

Darcy couldn't resist. She turned at the door and said, "Ya know Bryce, I don't know what you're taking to make you so insufferable, but it's working." She caught Zach's glare. "Leaving now, boss."

She closed the door behind her and leaned on it as she sucked in a deep breath.

Netters came around the corner. "Well?"

"Dodged the bullet this time. Thanks for the call." They began walking together past the editing bay, toward her office.

"Sure. Just dumb luck—and Adkins' big mouth—that I heard about it."

"We have got to find that leak. I told Hank to look for into it on his end." Darcy pushed through the door. "Is Adkins still screwing that receptionist at the police station?"

"Hell, I don't know. The thought of it makes my skin crawl." Netters shuddered. Darcy laughed.

"Have we had any hits on the reconstruction story?" She pushed into her crowded cage of an office.

"Just a few kook calls last time I checked. Wendy is keeping the list out front. Do you want me to go get it?"

"I'd appreciate it. Maybe something will jump out at us." Darcy sat and opened her e-mail file.

She skimmed and scanned, did a couple of short notes, inter-office memos, and a personal response to her friend Liz Baker inviting her to lunch.

She was just about to close when a note caught her eye. It was from an e-mail address entitled: cameraseye@gmail.com.

Hi,

This is about the story you did on the reconstruction of skulls they found in that house.

I don't know the one guy, but the other one I think I met when he opened a bank account. I used to be an accounts manager at Cheyenne Federal Bank. The reason I remembered him was he deposited a check from the Synergy Film Festival for an award in documentary films.

He was nice enough to talk to me. I told him I was a big docu-fan and that I had tried my hand at some modest attempts. He offered to look at my work and give me some feedback, but when I tried to call him later that week, there was no answer. I just figured it was his way of blowing me off.

I could be wrong, but I think his name was Shawn Dobson.

Hope this helps.

Jess Bowen

Darcy sucked in her breath. This was a break; at least she hoped it was. She dashed off a note and asked for contact information. Bowen answered almost immediately. They agreed to meet in the reading room of the library the next day.

Darcy dutifully copied the correspondence to Hank and closed her e-mail.

Netters had been reading over her shoulder as she read and answered the e-mail. "Wow! Synergy Film Festival is legit. If he won an award from them, he must be really talented."

"Not anymore he's not," she Googled the name, Shawn Dobson.

Lots of articles popped up. "Shawn Dobson must be a popular name."

"Try that one." Netters pointed to an article about a film called *Faith, Hope and Judgment.*

Darcy clicked it open to find a brief summary of a documentary by Shawn Dobson based on the rise of religious extremist cults in America.

"Looks like a fit, unless this Shawn Dobson is still alive." She punched the "*link this page*" option and wrote a small note to Hank: "Can you check through Synergy Film Festival or something and see if this guy is still alive? Let me know."

Almost instantly, she got a reply. "Pizza and beer at Abby's tonight?"

"I'll check and call you later," she shot off, and then closed her screen.

She found Netters' grin semi-insulting. "What?"

"Just cozy. It's nice when you can combine business with pleasure."

Darcy glared at him and began stuffing notes into her bag.

"You going to tell Zach about this lead?" Netters began stringing her paper clips into a chain.

Darcy snatched them from him. "Knock it off. Can't you go irritate someone else?"

"Probably, but why? Are you going to tell Zach . . . or can I?"

"I think we'd better wait and see if it pans out. If this Bowen character is a reliable source and Hank can find out about the existence or extinction of Dobson, then we'll have the basis for a story."

"Do you want me to go with you to meet this guy tomorrow?"

Darcy headed for the door when she turned back. "That might be good. One video-nerd to another." Slinging her bag over her shoulder, "Meet me at nine in the Capitol Room at the library. Bring the coffee. Latte, low fat, Venti. "

Darcy was thinking of the details she was going to tell Abby, but just as she entered the apartment, Abby waylaid her.

"Don't get comfortable. We're going to the hospital."

Abby, uncharacteristically decked out in a dress with a tailored jacket, was holding a potted purple mum.

"What happened, Abby? Who's in the hospital?" Darcy, occupied with listing Abby's friends in her head, almost missed the answer.

"Marie Romero. We're going to see Marie Romero if they'll let us in."

Darcy felt the color drain from her extremities, and cold set in. "I can't do that, Abby. I practically caused her stroke in the first place, and that was just my news report. Can you imagine what will happen to that poor lady when I appear in her hospital room?"

"Nonsense. You are no more responsible for her stroke than the weatherman is responsible for the weather."

"Yeah, well, tell that to Gary Romero. He gave me strict instructions to stay away from his great-aunt."

"I can't recall a time when strict instructions from anyone ever interfered with what you wanted to do. Don't tell me you're frightened of Romero."

A direct hit. Abby knew her former student well. Darcy was tempted to slap her hands over her heart in a parody of being shot, but she really was frightened. Not of Romero really, but of causing Marie any more distress. That reconstruction report recalled something that was traumatic enough to have triggered her stroke.

"I just think I should stay away from her while she's recuperating."

Abby shoved the heavy plant into her arms, effectively pushing her from the apartment into the hall.

"Bothers you so much, *you* give her the plant." She locked her door. "C'mon. We'll take your car." Abby held the lobby door open.

Darcy sighed. She recognized Abby's stubborn streak as an echo of her own, as problematic as that might be.

The drive to the hospital was blessedly brief and for the most part, silent.

"Hmph," Abby snorted as they turned into the attached parking structure.

"What?" Darcy squinted in the darkness of the garage.

"Did you see that sign for valet parking back there?"

"Uhh, no. I'm looking for a parking place."

"The way medical costs are going up, it's somehow fitting to put in valet parking like a high-priced hotel."

They slid into an empty space, she turned to her friend. "Are you going to be terminally cranky? Cuz if you are, you can go up alone." Darcy said.

"Nope. You're not getting off that easy. Come around here and take this plant will, you? I think it's dripping."

By the time they'd made their way into the elevator, Darcy's nerves were frayed.

"Are you sure this is a good idea?" She watched the numbers change above her head.

"When I called, they told me she could have visitors. We're visiting. Stop working yourself up into a froth. Ah, here we are."

The doors swooshed open, and they followed the number plaques to Marie's room.

It was a large private room decorated with bright blues and greens and boasting a huge window. The windowsill was already cluttered with plants and flower arrangements that testified to her extended family and many friends. The television droned softly in the background.

Marie was propped in the bed, her white hair combed but falling loose on her shoulders. Someone had brought her a gown from home. The soft blue color did nothing to brighten Marie's pale face. Her brown eyes watered, and she used her left hand awkwardly to dab at them.

Abby and Darcy approached the bed.

"Hi, Ms. Romero. Remember me?" Darcy asked as she leaned close.

Marie opened and closed her mouth as if trying to speak. She tossed her head, and real tears filled her eyes.

Darcy glared at Abby who was gingerly placing the mum plant among the other lavish flowers. "Damn it, Abby! I told you this was a bad idea."

Darcy felt a firm tug on her sleeve and looked down to find Marie's left hand pulling at her.

"What is it?" she asked and then did a mental head slap. "I mean, uh, do you want us to leave?"

Marie shook her head "No."

Relieved, but still concerned, Darcy asked, "Do you want us to call your nurse?"

Again, Marie shook her head. Darcy looked to Abby to help.

"Hi, Marie. I'm Abby McNeil, Darcy's friend. I came to visit you with her once."

Marie closed her eyes, sighed deeply, then opened them again.

"You're having trouble nodding your head, but your memory

is fine. Is that it?" Abby prompted.

Again, Marie blinked.

"My friend Sarah had the same problem when she had a stroke last year." Abby beamed at her. "Not to worry, it soon went away. She is as good as a newly-minted penny now."

Marie answered with a lopsided smile and dabbed a small dribble from the side of her mouth.

"We don't want to tire you. Your great-nephew Gary was kind enough to tell Darcy about your unfortunate difficulty, and we just wanted to wish you well." Abby smiled first at Marie and then at Darcy.

"Uhm, about that. You might not want to mention our visit to Gary." Darcy stopped when the realization of what she'd just said penetrated. She let slip a nervous, self-deprecating chuckle.

Marie smiled at her obvious distress.

"She doesn't have much experience with victims of stroke," Abby jumped in to explain. "The truth is Gary was a bit put-out with our Darcy. He seemed to think it was her fault that you had a stroke."

Darcy swerved away from the bed in a short circle. "Ah, for heaven's sake, Abby. Don't bother her with that. I don't care what Romero thinks."

Marie lifted her eyebrows in doubt or inquiry. Darcy couldn't be sure which.

"Uh . . . I mean . . . I don't mean to be rude. I of course care about Gary's feelings . . ."

She stumbled to a stop when she saw Marie smile.

"Oh. You're wondering why he blames me?"

Marie blinked.

"He thinks you were watching my report on the reconstructions that Dr. Garcia did on those skulls and . . ." Darcy interrupted herself. "I just feel awful!" Tears welled up in her eyes.

Marie reached across to pat Darcy's arm with her good hand. She shook her head slightly.

"You mean, 'No, you weren't watching the report' or 'No, it didn't cause your stroke'?" Darcy asked.

"For heaven's sake don't ask her two questions at a time." Abby leaned closer to Marie. "Did you see someone you recognized in Darcy's report, dear?"

Marie's eyes filled, but she blinked slowly and deliberately.

Darcy gasped, then covered her mouth. This could be it. This could solve at least one of the identity mysteries. She couldn't believe the luck.

"Was it someone you knew when you lived in the house?" Abby

Marie blinked once more, and tears spilled down her pale cheeks.

"Abby, stop. Stop. It's upsetting her. This can all wait until she feels better."

"It'll wait a damn sight longer than that," said a gruff voice from the doorway.

Startled, Darcy swerved around. Romero was looming in the doorway, looking thunderous.

Abby jumped into action. She drew herself up to her full 4'3" and inserted herself between Romero and Darcy.

"Now, Mr. Romero, don't blame Darcy for this. I made her come with me. She really didn't want to."

Romero looked over the top of Abby's head directly at Darcy. "You should've gone with your first instinct, Ms. Moreland."

"Look, I'm sorry . . ."

Just then, the substantial water sipper that had been resting on the bed table crashed to the floor.

Darcy was closest, so she bent to pick it up. As she started to replace it, Romero crossed the room and grabbed it from her hand.

"Go away and leave my aunt alone. Is that clear enough?"

Romero loomed menacingly close to Darcy. She swallowed and tried to answer. She couldn't push any sound out, so she just nodded.

"Good. Now please leave." He replaced the sipper on the table with barely restrained force.

Darcy turned to go, but when she glanced beyond Romero's massive torso, she saw Marie. The beautiful old woman was shaking her head emphatically.

Darcy was fairly sure she knew what Marie meant. Marie had a tale to tell and was willing to tell it. Darcy nodded in response and left.

CHAPTER 16

Marie Romero laid in her hospital bed and considered her nephew looming over her. She was sorry for causing him to worry, but his smothering protectiveness was driving her over the edge. Worse, she couldn't tell him.

"I'm sorry you were disturbed, Auntie," Romero said softly.

Marie shook her head in emphatic denial.

Romero blinked in confusion. "Do you mean you don't' think I'm sorry?" He waited for her to answer. Marie shook her head and softly patted his hand that was gripping the side bar.

He tried again. "Do you mean they weren't bothering you?"

Marie both blinked her eyes and nodded her head.

"You had a stroke because Darcy Moreland keeps interfering in your life. I don't know what you saw in that report that upset you, but I am determined to keep her out of our lives."

Aunt Marie lifted her comforting hand and Pulled herself up as far as she could. She looked her nephew in the eye, shook her head and gestured for him to go.

Romero sighed. He recognized that cold stare she had often used on him when he was a kid and had done something indisputably awful. "Okay, I'll go." He hated that he sounded like a kid in trouble. She was the only woman on earth that could do that to him.

MARIE RELAXED BACK, CLOSED HER EYES, and let the memories flow.

Cheyenne had mostly been a ranching and railroad town when the country entered the second world war. Fort D.A. Russel was renamed as Fort Francis E. Warren after one of Wyoming's Senators in the '20s. After the Declaration of war on December 8, 1941, the whole country mobilized. The fort became a training garrison capable of holding 20,000 men.

Marie had barely graduated from high school when she applied for a teaching license. She and had passed her teaching exam which tested subject mastery and was waiting to be assigned to a school. Her brother C.J. thought she was crazy. Their family had a huge ranch out of town and had buckets of money. She didn't need a job.

It was an exciting time for her. She and her friends set up a U.S.O. that held dances for the trainees from the fort in the Prairie Hotel ballroom. That was where she had met Second Lieutenant Thomas McCaulley a a pretty slick dancer. The girls weren't allowed to monopolize any one soldier for the night, but when she began to dance with another, Tom would cut in and finish the dance. It got so nobody else even bothered to try anymore.

Marie smiled crookedly at the recollection. A small tear rolled down her cheek. Tom had been unusually handsome. But it was his kindness she remembered most. He would hang around and help with the cleanup. Then he'd politely ask to walk her home. It was cold most evenings, but she never felt it. Several times they got caught in a snowstorm and Tom would pull her close and cover her with his heavy overcoat. While she was snuggled so close to him, he said, "Marie, if I wanted to ask for your hand, who would I ask?"

She felt her face grow hot with a blush. "I guess either of my brothers."

"Who is the one you live with here in town?"

"Oh. That's C.J., but my older brother Robert is still out at the ranch, and rarely comes into town." Marie whispered, unwilling to break the spell. Her heart beat faster.

They talked about everything except the war. They thought if they didn't mention it, it wouldn't be real. But it was real.

Winter slid gently into Spring. Marie and two of her friends walked to the hotel to set up for another dance. As usual, they brewed a large pot of coffee, and set out some day-old doughnuts on a buffet table by the wall. Marie stood behind the table and filled the coffee cups leant to them by the hotel. Her eyes were constantly roaming, but on this night, Tom didn't come. She waited the whole night, thinking he had gotten hung up at work.

When Tom wasn't there to monopolize her company, she danced every dance with a new partner. She never let her glance drift away from the front doors for long. Tom never came. The evening dragged on. She remembered that the soldiers she danced with had been exceptionally kind and attentive. They had varying aptitudes for dancing, but they all had lots of enthusiasm. The thing that struck her was that they were barely out of the school room themselves. We were sending our brightest and our best to that ongoing war across the globe. Marie remembered. She tried not to think of how many of those boys never returned to their homes.

She remembered walking home with her friends in the soft spring night. "Maybe he called my home and left a message," she said to her friends. She kept that hope alive until she unlocked her front door. She went right to the alcove that held the heavy black Bakelite phone and picked up the message pad right beside it. She squinted at it in the dim light. No message.

"He will call tomorrow," she said as she climbed stoically up the stairs to her room. Because she was the only girl in the Romero family, the decorator who designed her room went a little overboard with pink ruffles everywhere. Marie couldn't, wouldn't tell him she hated pink and ruffles. Accepting all the frills as a kind gesture from her brothers, she got used to them.

She got ready for bed. She laid her robe and slippers by her bed. She half expecting him to come to her home this evening and explain. She tried to read *For Whom the Bell Tolls*, by Ernest Hemingway, but it was too close to what the country was going on now. The planning and blowing bridges up. The loss and the fear. She put the book back down and turned off the light. The night crawled on. She listened for every sound, but eventually fell asleep. She slept fitfully.

The next morning she came down for breakfast. C.J. sat at the table with his head in his hands.

She took his coffee cup and refilled it. "That's what you get when you spend your nights drinking and gambling." C.J. mumbled a reply then dropped his head to the table cradling it in his folded arms.

She decided she would have to talk to her brother Robert about C.J.'s bad choices.

She was reluctant to do that because she was sure Robert would make C.J. come back to the ranch. If C.J. had to leave town, Robert would insist that she come too. She could not live here alone even when Mrs. Carter came each day to cook and clean and cook for them, she refused to spend the night. She had her own family to care for. Robert would never agree to his sister being alone in the house at night. It wouldn't help, she knew, to tell him that C.J. was rarely home at night as it was.

She sighed heavily and poured herself a cup of coffee. She walked by C.J. to the phone to check if any messages had been taken. Nothing.

As the day wore on, she became worried that something horrible had happened. Tom had given her a telephone number for his apartment, but she was not comfortable using it. His two roommates might think she was forward.

After breakfast, Marie crossed the street to talk to her neighbor, Mrs. Walker. Cora was only a little older than Marie, but she was a newlywed and maybe she could give her advice. She knocked on the door and Cora answered.

"My you're up and about early this morning," Cora smiled so Marie could know she wasn't annoyed at the interruption.

Marie entered cautiously. "Is John still here? I would hate to intrude."

Cora linked her arm with Marie's. "Don't be silly. John is fiddling with something in the garage. Even if he weren't he would be pleased to see you. He always says he loves being surrounded by beautiful ladies." Cora laughed and made Marie sit on a kitchen chair while she finished up the dishes.

"At least let me help. It will give me something to do with my hands and calm my nerves."

Cora turned around at this strange comment and handed her a dish towel. "What's going on that you are nervous?"

"Oh it's just silly."

Maybe not," replied Cora when she handed Marie the plate she'd washed.

"Do you remember Tom McCaulley?"

"Of course I do. You act like I'm in my dotage. What about him?"

Marie told Cora everything about the hint Tom had given her about asking her brother for her hand,

Cora got excited. "That is wonderful! I really like your young man. So what's the problem?"

"He didn't come to the dance last night. I thought he might have called, but there was no message when I got home. I even asked Mrs. Carter this morning but she was distracted by a small rug that was missing from the front parlor. I said maybe C.J. sent it out to be cleaned. She shrugged and went back into the kitchen."

"Marie," Cora said. "There are a dozen reasons he had to miss the dance. Remember, this is wartime and as a young officer he is likely to be kept terribly busy. He will probably come by or call you the first chance he gets."

"I am afraid he regrets hinting that he wanted to marry me and is embarrassed," Marie said softly. Her eyes sparkled with unshed tears.

"Oh for heaven's sake." Cora put her fists on her hips and faced Marie. "Of all the silly things to worry about. Has Tom done anything to make you believe he's a coward?"

Marie felt like she'd been hit by a brick. "No. Never." She said and hung her head.

"Of course not," Cora said. "I guarantee you'll hear from him soon and you'll have a good laugh at yourself."

"I suppose you're right," Marie agreed. She handed the dish towel back to her friend. "Thank you for listening."

"Anytime. You'll see. It will all work out." Cora said. "Let me know if you hear anything."

Marie smiled and hugged her friend. Somehow wartime had made every little thing seem overly important, she thought.

Marie tried to pretend everything was normal. She met with friends, and went shopping and lunching, and worrying. She had heard nothing from Tom. She didn't know whether to be hurt, angry, or afraid.

One day she returned home, and Mrs. Carter met her at the door. "Your young man called," she said. She handed Marie the notepad where she had taken a message. Marie clutched the notebook to her heart and ran up the stairs wanting to read the note in private. She finally worked up the courage to read it:

"Please tell Miss Romero that I am deeply sorry that I haven't been able to contact her. I received orders to transfer to a training center in Texas. We left on the night train, and I have been busy training new recruits. Tell her I will write her as soon as I possibly can."

Marie laughed and cried and ran down the stairs and across the street to tell Cora.

"I told you the there was something that stopped him from coming." Cora hugged her with enthusiasm.

Marie said, "I feel so relieved. Not knowing was the worst. I'm sad he had to go to Texas but at least I know he hasn't forgotten me."

Three days later she got a call from someone who said he was one of Tom's friends. He said Tom had given him Marie's number in case something happened to him. He said Tom told him she was incredibly special to him but since they hadn't yet married, she wouldn't be contacted officially. The friend said he was sorry to have to tell her that Tom had been killed in a training accident, an overturned jeep or some such thing. He knew she would want to know. Marie's good breeding kicked in enough for her thank Tom's friend and hang up the phone. She just stood there, frozen. Part of Marie died that day.

Marie lay in the hospital bed and sobbed into her handkerchief.

CHAPTER 17

"WELL, THAT WAS RUDE," Abby said as they waited for the hospital elevator.

"Yeah, but not unexpected. Romero is certain that my stirring up the past is what caused his aunt's stroke." Darcy pushed the button again, trying to hurry the elevator along,

Abby snorted in disgust. "If her health is that fragile, Mr. Gary Romero should stir his stumps and move her in with him, so he can watch her."

Giving Abby a shoulder hug, she laughed. "Thanks for the support, but to be fair, I don't think she would allow that. Beneath that fragile appearance, I have the feeling Marie could be difficult if crossed. I kind of like that about her."

The elevator doors opened with a swoosh and a chime. Once isolated and the elevator began its decent, Darcy smiled.

"What? Do you know something?" Abby demanded.

"Just that if I can manage to see Marie without her watchdog nephew, I think she's got some information she wants to share."

"How can you be sure? She can't talk."

"No, but she looked determined to tell me something. I think if we wait a little longer, she may well recover enough to answer some questions. My money's on Marie. She's really tough."

On the short ride home, she filled Abby in on Jess Bowen and Shawn Dobson.

"Hank's checking to see if Dobson is still alive. Oh! I forgot to tell you. He's bringing pizza and beer to your place tonight. Is that okay?"

"Sure. I'm dying to know what he found out." Abby snapped off her seat belt as they pulled up in for the Algonquin. "I think I'll take a nap right now though. Want to be fresh for the 'hunt.'"

Darcy trailed her up the wide concrete steps of the building. "This isn't a game, Abby. These guys are serious."

Stopping by her door, Abby turned and gently ran her hand up Darcy's arm. "I know that sweetie. It just helps me not be so frightened for you if I pretend it's a lark. You understand, don't you?"

"Sure," Darcy hugged her tightly. "Go enjoy your nap. I may try to get one in too."

Abby smiled and swung into her apartment. Mac scampered at their feet.

Darcy bundled him up, and kissed Abby quickly on the cheek. The soft fragrance of baby talc and Chanel Number 5, Abby's signature scent, made Darcy smile. "We'll come down around five. Okay?"

"Lovely, dear." Abby closed the door, obviously anxious for her nap.

Mac looked up at her questioningly.

"Yes, I'm home early." She started up the stairs to her place. She put Mac down and he dutifully followed, half-hopping, half-lurching up the 12 steps to the second floor.

She tossed her bag just inside the door and heeled off her shoes. Stripping clothes off as she went, she paused in the bathroom and began to run a hot tub embellished with Jasmine Nights Bubble Bath.

Snagging her favorite thick, white terrycloth robe off the back of the bathroom door, she dutifully stuffed her dirty clothes in the hamper before padding to the refrigerator. She lifted out a half bottle of chardonnay and poured a half a glass into a heavy glass goblet she'd brought back from some spring break in Mexico. That was a great trip if she remembered it accurately.

She toasted Mac, who had curled up in the corner on his cedar chip bed. "Here's to peeing in the bushes!" She sipped the cod wine. "This is pretty good."

"Be back in a little while, bud. I need to soak off this grubby day."

Slipping off her robe, she positioned her green wine glass atop the lidded hamper where she could reach it from the bath. She stepped into the froth of bubbles and sucked her breath in as she slid into the hot water in the deep cast iron ball and claw tub.

"Oh, my heavens!" she whispered on the steamy air. Resting her head on the rolled back of the tub, she grasped her wine and took a sip, being careful not to let the hot water lap up too far and warm her wine.

She reviewed her day, starting with Hank bringing her a warm breakfast burrito and red-hot sex. Great cure for a hangover. She took another sip of the crisp wine and let it drain slowly down the back of her throat. Grinning full on, she sank lower.

What a perfect way to begin a day, if Adkins hadn't ruined it, she reminded herself. She fiddled with the alarm pendant that rested between her now incredibly pink breasts. It was sweet of Hank to be concerned about her, but he should be more concerned about Adkins and where he was getting his information.

She thought of her meeting with Jess Bowen from the bank tomorrow. Great break. If it really was Shawn Dobson and they could connect him to the award-winning film about religious extremism. It was a link and helped explain the Bible verses, and the stones found with his body. She made a mental note to bring the forensic recreation picture with her to the library when she met Jess.

Marie was also a great break. She wanted to tell her something about one of those skulls. She was sure of it. She got why Romero felt he was protecting his aunt, but he didn't need to be such a jerk about it. The last of the cool wine slithered down her throat and the heat of the bath untied whatever tense muscles in her neck the wine didn't reach.

She felt almost human. By the time she emerged through a cloud of steam, her body was lobster red.

She snuggled her robe around her slim body and curled up on the window seat. Pulling back the light cotton café curtains, she rested against an overstuffed pillow and burrowed her feet beneath an afghan her grandmother had knitted for her.

Her window looked out on 18th Street. The late afternoon traffic was picking up as the westward sun slanted through the autumn colored leaves and sparkled off the asphalt.

Except for the looming winter, fall was her favorite season. The crisp, cool air sliced into her lungs, and the smell of dried leaves and mulled cider always made her feel cozy and restful.

She loved the occasional hustle of the street. It was lightly trafficked for most of the day, but morning and evening, it was a conduit for workers in the downtown area, mostly airmen from the base, bankers, lawyers, and CPAs. Pickup trucks and motorcycles, and utility vans heading east signaled the winding down of the day.

Rolling her shoulders, trying to keep her neck loose she glanced at Mac who was eyeing her. "Well come on up, mutt." She smiled at him. He didn't wait for a second invitation. Generally banned from all furniture, this was a real treat. He wiggled, squirmed, and finally nested in her lap, pressing his cold nose to the equally-cold window.

She pulled him back and used the sleeve of her robe to wipe the steam and smear that marred her view.

As the glass un-fogged, her eye was pulled to a white utility van parked behind her blue Audi on the street. She shivered involuntarily. "Don't be stupid," she said aloud, knowing she was using her voice in the empty apartment to exorcize her anxiety. "White Chevy utility vans are commonplace. There must be thousands of them all over town." Still, she tried to see if she could make out the license plate or any distinguishing characteristics.

As she watched a figure clothed in black jeans with ragged cuffs and wearing a faded black hoodie jumped out of the van. He pressed his tall, angular body close to the side of the van and waited for the light to stop the flow of traffic for a moment.

She watched in fascination as the hooded figure snapped open the door of her car.

"Shit! I thought I locked that damn door!"

The man didn't take long. She could see him reach into his sweatshirt pocket and take something out which he placed on the driver's seat.

By now, her forehead was pressed firmly against the window trying to see what he'd left, but it was no use. She was too far up, and the angle was bad.

She held her breath as she watched the man return to his van and pull out into the clogged traffic. She thought for a moment that he might have planted a bomb. Her stomach clenched, then turned over as she braced herself for the explosion that didn't come. When she sucked in some air, half breath-fueled relief and half-fueled rage.

"Get off, Mac." She nudged him to the floor, forcing herself to be gentle with him. It wasn't his fault after all.

She flew to her bedroom and dug out a pair of worn gray sweatpants with PINK plastered across the butt and a long-sleeved t-shirt. She was still wiggling into her clothes when she dashed back to her living room and slipped into some discarded flip-flops by the door.

As she scrounged in her bag for her keys, she thought of calling Hank, then decided against it. She could almost feel that alarm pendent burn into her chest.

"This isn't really an emergency. I don't even know what he left." She spied Mac eyeing her. "You stay and guard the apartment. I'll only be a minute." Mac barked once as if he understood.

She plunged down the steps and out the front door but forced herself to slow down as she approached her car. Leaning down to peer in, she could just make out a lump on the driver's seat, but the gray dusky light wouldn't let her see clearly.

She opened the door easily and cursed herself for being so careless. The interior light winked on.

A black, baseball sized river rock rested in the middle of the seat.

"What the hell?" Her hand shot out to lift it off the seat, but she stopped herself. What if it had fingerprints on it? Why would someone leave a stone in her car? Stone?

She shivered, and her heart began to pound. One of the bodies had been stoned to death. One of the notes had specified stoning. Darcy's knees buckled under her, and she grabbed the open door for support.

A black BMW whizzed by her. The driver leaned heavily on his horn. The shock of the sound cleared her head, and she slammed the door closed and pushed the lock button on her key fob.

She clamped her jaw tight and strained to walk slowly up the steps. Once in the lobby, she wanted desperately to scurry into the safety of Abby's apartment, but it was just a dumb rock, she assured herself as she climbed up to her apartment.

Mac's bark of hello made her smile. Picking him up, she kissed the top of his head between his ears. She felt the cord of terror unwind.

"It was just a stupid rock, Mac. Means nothing. Just someone's idea of a joke." She was still terrified but talking aloud to Mac was a self-soothing ritual that helped. She nuzzled him against the side of her face, and he licked her cheek. Funny how his unconditional love calmed her. She set him on the window seat.

"Guard my car while I go change, okay?" Mac spun twice and plopped down to stare out the window as if following her command.

She chuckled and felt world's better. Digging in the back of her closet shelves, she discovered her favorite fuzzy pink sweater. Pulled free, shaken out, and fluffed up it brought memories of crackling fires and slipper socks.

Might be rushing the season a bit, she thought, but she needed to focus on good things. No more bones or stones tonight, she told herself emphatically.

The sweater nestled and clung softly to her skin, and she began to feel her mood lift to the level it had been before the unwarranted intrusion had shattered her sense of peace. Slipping into some comfortable gray slacks, she ran a brush through her long blond hair.

She had just slathered on her preferred pink gloss when the phone rang. She jumped a foot, then laughed at herself.

"Hello?"

"It's me. I couldn't nap. You want to come down?" Abby chirped.

"Sure. I'm almost ready. Be down in a sec."

She decided to brush Mac before they went to Abby's, more because she felt guilty for not spending more time with him, than any hope that Mac's brown and honey colored fur would ever look well groomed.

"Well, mutt," she dropped him back on the floor, "that's the best I can do for you. Let's go see Abby."

She was almost cheerful when Abby opened the door.

"This looks great." She gazed around Abby's cozy apartment. Tall, pillared candles twinkled next to a nest of squat ones of varying sizes. Plates were laid out on a tablecloth-covered table along with heavy gray pottery steins.

"Fancy," Darcy lifted the solid mug. "Where did you get these?"

Abby smiled. "I helped steal them from a restaurant in Munich at the height of Oktoberfest. My friend Kari is a master clearing the table of 'souvenirs', and she's really good about sharing her expertise."

She laughed. "And your little black soul likes the irony of feeding a police detective beer from a stolen mug. True?"

Abby's blue eyes snapped and twinkled, but she shrugged noncommittally.

The doorbell buzzed and for some reason, seeing Hank come through the door with a pizza box and a six-pack made her nervous. Unflinching, she admitted to herself that she wasn't looking forward to telling him about her visitor. She decided to put it off for as long as she could.

"Is there anything in the world that smells better than hot pizza?" Abby took the box and flipped it open.

He placed the beer next to it on the table. "I didn't know what you guys liked, so it's half meat lovers and half tomato and basil."

"Perfect on both choices," Abby gushed.

Hank's eyes landed on the beer mugs. He lifted one expressive eyebrow. "Hofbräuhaus?"

Abby had the grace to blush. "How did you know?"

Hank laughed. "I've got a set too. I probably wouldn't have, but they made it such a challenge to try to get away with it, I couldn't resist."

Darcy twisted off one of the beers and poured it into a chilled mug. She toasted, "Here's to my two favorite thieves."

Plates piled high, beers poured and the three of them settled in at the table. The room grew quiet while they ate.

"This hits the spot. Thank you, Hank." Abby smiled at him.

"Not a problem," he smiled up at Abby. Turning to Darcy he said, "You've been kind of quiet."

"Who me? No one was talking. Why pick on me?" She winced inside recognizing how defensive she sounded.

Both Abby and Hank gawked at her. She got up, took her beer, and flopped on the sofa. She pulled Mac into her lap as if for protection. Hank and Abby followed her in. Abby took her usual place in her Chesterfield chair and Hank sat close on the settee.

"Give." Hank's blue eyes were riveted on her.

"Give what?" She took a sip and put her mug on the coffee table in front of her.

"You're holding something back and I want to know what it is."

"It's nothing." She wanted to squirm but sat still through sheer force of will.

Hank nodded slightly at Abby. "This 'nothing' is what exactly?"

Darcy's eyes darted from one to the other. "Look. I came home, had a little wine and a hot bath and I was sitting in my window seat just watching the traffic and . . ." Her voice dribbled off.

"And . . ." Abby prompted.

Darcy shot her a steel-edged glare. "And I saw a white utility van park behind my car on the street. At first, I didn't think anything of it. I mean you know how many white utility vans there are out there."

"Get on with it."

"Alright! Damn, Hank, you make me feel like a criminal."

"Sometimes there is extraordinarily little difference between a reluctant witness and a perp. If I were you, I'd talk fast before I have to pull out the bright lights and the thumb screws."

"I bet you crack them up at the cop shop."

Hank narrowed his eyes and his jaw clamped tight.

"Okay. Okay. No big deal. This guy in a black hoodie got out of a white utility van and put a rock in my car and then drove off. Satisfied?"

Hank sat unresponsive. His blue eyes had turned dark cobalt, and he looked like he was trying to choose his response carefully.

"Did the rock have any writing on it?" Abby asked.

"No, but it was a message just the same, wasn't it, Darcy?"

"I don't know. Maybe . . ."

Hank's voice grew low. "Do you have the rock? May I look at it?"

"I left it in my car. I didn't touch it."

"A small shred of common sense."

"You don't need to be insulting. I didn't do anything."

"Exactly. You didn't call me as soon as you saw the guy. Why is that?"

Darcy stood up and grabbed her beer from the table. She took a gulp without looking back at him. "There was no point. I went down and saw it was just a rock and I knew you were coming over . . ." She felt him behind her before she saw him.

Hank swung her around, cupped her face in his hands, and forced her to look at him.

"You went down to check it?" Hank bit off every word.

"Uh yeah. Wouldn't you? I thought it was weird."

"What is weird is that a basically intelligent woman involved in a complex investigation that has already proved fatal for one, possibly two poor souls, would leave her car doors unlocked. You already got one note. What are you waiting for, an engraved invitation?"

"Okay. So, I left my door unlocked. Is that illegal?"

Hank ignored her sarcasm. "Added to that, you go down to investigate. What did I tell you *not* to do?" He didn't wait for the answer. "I told you to press that panic button if anything even looked suspicious."

She took her beer and sat at the table with one leg curled beneath her. Hank just watched her, shook his head, and followed her, turned his chair to face her.

"Darcy, these guys are dangerous. You did get the connection between the stone and the note on the body, didn't you?"

"What note? What stone? Which body?" Abby stared back and forth.

Darcy looked up. "One of the set of bones was buried with a note that said he was stoned by the congregation and there were stones lying around that looked like the river rock in my car," she looked at Hank. "Did I get it right or is there something I missed?"

Hank grabbed his phone autodialed a number, muttered several terse commands, and flicked it off again.

"The crime lab will retrieve the stone. You did lock the door this time."

She dug her keys from her pocket and slapped them into his hand.

CHAPTER 18

Darcy and Abby watched from the window as a patrol car pulled up and checked with Hank. A gloved police officer retrieved the stone, dropped it into a plastic bag and left.

"That's that," Darcy said with hollow bravado and poured herself more beer.

"Hank's not really angry at you, dear." Abby sat back down in her chair.

"I know. I'm not used to looking for sinister motives from all sides. It may be normal behavior for Hank but being paranoid is not my style."

The ladies sat in companionable silence until Hank strode in and handed Darcy's keys back.

"We'll dust the rock for prints, but it's probably a waste of time." He swigged the dregs of his beer, fixing Darcy with a stare. "Is there anything else you'd like to share with me?"

"Did I tell you about Jess Bowen?"

"No. But I'm certain you're about to." He crossed back to the table and opened another beer. "Abby?"

"No thanks. I can't drink beer fast. Carbonation you know. Who's Jess Bowen?" she asked Darcy.

"I got an e-mail from him today about one of the re-construction pictures. He thinks he recognizes a guy named Shawn Dobson who opened an account at the bank Bowen works for. I was going to ask if they have ever run a missing person check for him."

"I can look into that. Does this Bowen still work for the bank?" Hank was writing notes to himself in his spiral-topped notebook.

"I don't know. I didn't exactly grill him. I did agree to meet him tomorrow in the Capitol Room in the library. I'll ask him then."

"*We'll* ask." Hank snapped his notebook closed and stuffed it into his shirt pocket.

"You are not invited, Detective Nelson. I wasn't even going to talk to you about this until I checked this Jess Bowen out. I didn't want to waste your time."

Hank sat next to her. "Really? You're going to meet with a lead in an ongoing homicide case alone—"

Darcy cut him off. "Netters is coming. He's bringing the coffee."

Hank upended his beer, left his mug on the table.

"Tell him I take mine black, high octane. Abby, as always a pleasure." He smiled at Abby then turned to Darcy. "What time tomorrow?"

"9:00," she answered without thinking. "But if you come, you let me do the questioning. I don't want you scaring the hell out of him. Okay?"

"How 'bout I just scare the hell out of you?" He was out the door before she could form an answer.

On the way up to her apartment, Darcy caught herself grinding her teeth in frustration. She hated when Hank took over like that.

Her conscience admitted in a barely audible voice that she appreciated him when he was protecting her . . . most times. Thing was, she wanted to pick the times. His insistence on butting into her life, particularly when she was trying to do her job, was annoying and embarrassing.

She opened her door and Mac scampered in ahead of her. After putting on some sweats and socks, she curled up in the corner of her sofa and flipped open her laptop.

She scanned her e-mails, most of which were routine. She saw one from Jess Bowen confirming their meet tomorrow, which reminded her to shoot off a note to Netters about Hank's coffee order and added that he might want to bring a generic one for Bowen as well.

Closing her laptop, she padded off to bed. Her last thoughts were a jumble of black-hooded men, river rocks, an imaginary Jess Bowen, and the infuriated Hank Nelson.

Morning sun poured in through her east-facing windows. Darcy stretched and yawned. She looked at the alarm on her bedside table. A part of her brain registered that it hadn't gone off, that it was now 8:30, and that she was going to be late.

"Shit!" she shouted on her way to the bathroom. Toothbrush clamped between her teeth, she hopped on one leg to the dresser and pulled out a confection of a a satin thong, lacy bra and a baby blue V-necked sweater. She tried to brush her teeth and slip into her black dress slacks at the same time, narrowly avoiding dribbling a blob of toothpaste on her clean clothes. She rubbed the green splotch on her floor with her big toe, mentally vowing to clean it up later.

She was zipped, clipped, glossed and out the door in under 15 minutes. She called Abby on her way to the library.

"Abby? Sorry. Did I wake you up?"

"No. I'm up. Just reading the paper."

"I had to leave in a rush this morning. I forgot to set my alarm. Could you check on Mac sometime today? I'm not sure how long I'll be gone."

"No problem, dear."

"Thanks. You're a big help."

She clicked her phone off and shuddered, wondering what single mothers did when they forgot to set the alarm. "Thank God for Abby." She whispered her sincere prayer just as she swung into the parking lot of the library.

The Capitol Room was on the third floor and by the time the elevator doors swished open, Darcy felt more in command of herself. The reading room faced the state capital with expansive windows. Furnished with tables, straight-backed chairs, easy chairs, and lamps, it blended style and comfort.

Technically designated a silent reading area, but Darcy was sure no one would be there to be disturbed since it wasn't used often during the week. The three men gathered around an oblong table by the window. They weren't looking in her direction, so she took a moment to study Jess Bowen.

He had sandy brown hair worn a little long. He sported a long-sleeved shirt without a jacket, but his tie was a conservative stripe, and his loafers boasted a shine. It appeared to Darcy that Mr. Bowen was still an employee at the bank or working in an office somewhere. She pushed open the glass doors.

"Hi boys, waiting for me?" Three pairs of eyes swiveled toward her. Bowen's were brown she noticed. He stood and walked toward her. Darcy guessed he stood about 5'8" to 5'10".

"Hi. I'm Jess Bowen. I recognize you from TV." He shook her hand a nice firm grip.

"Please sit down, Mr. Bowen," Darcy said as she slipped into the remaining spot. She picked up the one unclaimed cup and took a sip. "Yum! Sorry I'm late. Alarm problems. Incompetent programmer." She laughed and rummaged in her bag for her notes. "I presume you've all introduced yourselves?"

Bowen nodded. Hank and Netters both mumbled answers that she took for assent.

"We appreciate you taking the time to help us. This is a copy of the forensic reconstruction of the most recent skeletal remains found." She slipped the 8x10 across the table. "Does this look like the gentleman you talked to at the bank?"

Bowen studied the picture carefully. "Except that a sculpture or a painting is idealized by its very nature. Yes. That looks remarkably like Shawn Dobson."

"What can you tell us about Mr. Dobson, Mr. Bowen?" Hank asked. Darcy shot him a frosty look.

Bowen looked between Hank and Darcy. "Is there a problem?"

"No. Detective Nelson is here unofficially because he asked to be. Strictly speaking you don't have to answer his questions unless you want to." Darcy smiled sweetly across the table at Hank. His eyes narrowed a fraction.

"Oh, I don't mind. I'm happy to help. I think it's terrible if that was his body in that basement. He seemed like such a nice guy. He was a gifted filmmaker, too." Jess took a swig of coffee.

Netter's eyes lit up. "No joke, man. I Googled him last night and uploaded his latest film for Synergy on fundamentalist fanaticism. I didn't get a chance to watch the whole thing, but it scared me so bad, my hair started to fall out!" Netters laughed and ran his hand through his receding buzz cut.

Bowen laughed. "Yeah. I thought it was spooky that he pixilated the faces. I don't know what these people look like, but I know they're out there and they're crazy. They were so casual about Old Testament justice."

"I thought using that *Film Noir* technique was brilliant!" Netters blathered on. "The grainy black and white made it feel like it was happening in the 20's or 30's, except then you'd catch things that slapped you back to the here and now. Inspired!"

Darcy knew that once they started talking film geek, she would never get them back on track again "Okay. Okay. We can get into this a little later, but for now we're trying to get a handle on who this guy was." Darcy smiled to take the sting out of her words.

"Like I told you in my e-mail, he came into the bank to open an account. We started talking, and I found out he was a filmmaker . . . which is kind of a dream of mine."

"Do you still work at the bank?" Darcy slipped in the question before Hank could.

"Been there for eight years come September. Why?"

"Could you check to see if there has been any activity on Dobson's account in the last six years?"

"I could get a warrant if you need one," Hank contributed.

Bowen smiled, "I don't think a warrant will be necessary. I can check after I get back to the bank. If you need any specific information about the account though, I will need some authorization."

"When you met Dobson, did he seem nervous at all?" Darcy leaned in. "Did he tell you anything about the extremists he was filming?"

"Not nervous exactly, but he did say he had to find a way to disappear for a little while. He said it wouldn't take long for this guy

Caleb to find out about the documentary. I do remember he told me to keep his account open, and he'd be back for it. I guess I didn't think anything about it then."

"Do you recall anyone else trying to access his account?" Hank asked.

"No, but they could have if they had his access code or debit card. I'll check."

"Thank you, Mr. Bowen. You've been a big help. At least we have some other areas to investigate now." Darcy stood and offered him her hand.

"You can call me Jess, Ms. Moreland. I'm a big fan." Bowen smiled at Darcy.

"You should talk to Netters here. He's the one that makes me look good." Darcy winked back at him.

"That's the truth," Netters said.

"I've got a little time." Bowen sat down and in minutes, the two men were knee-deep in techno jargon over the influence of 3D printing and virtual reality. They didn't even notice Hank and Darcy leave.

"You always flirt with guys you interview?" Hank asked in the elevator.

"Absolutely." Darcy grinned up at him. She loved it when he got all bristly and she could see no reason not to pull his chain. Amused, she watched him clamp down his irritation.

He was silent until they exited the library. "Headed to the station?"

"I think so. I don't think I have enough from Bowen to do a story yet, but I have other things I'm looking at."

Hank walked her to her car. As she turned to get in, he stopped her and pulled her close for a deep kiss.

"Be careful," he murmured in her ear.

Turning her head slightly, she kissed him on the cheek. "Always," she said and slipped into her car.

IT WAS EARLY IN THE MORNING. The cool air of autumn was bracing. The fresh pine scent of the evergreens that surrounded the campsite invigorated him. Caleb sat on a flat rock and watched his followers go about their assigned tasks. They looked listless to the point of robotic. This would never do. He needed them full of the fervor of God.

Caleb stood and rearranged his once white, rough cotton robe around his skeletal frame. He stepped up on the flat rock and waited. A hush came over the encampment. All eyes were on him.

"My brothers and sisters," Caleb glanced around, and they gathered around. Even the children were drawn inexorably to him.

"It has been too long since we have battled the evil that surrounds us." He heard murmurs of agreement from his flock. "We must go out into the world again and flush out sinners from the gutters of society wherever they are."

He waited as the listless cheer faded. "I know we have been too absorbed with worldly tasks." He gestured with his bony, nob knuckled hand toward the laundry hanging from the limbs of surrounding trees and flowing in a circle to include the large communal pot always kept warm over red coals and filled with whatever they could trap or shoot, to a woman nursing her child nearby.

"We must not live for this world but for the Divine. We have been chosen to execute God's justice."

"The way of the Lord is a refuge for the blameless, but it is the ruin of those who do evil." So sayeth Proverbs.

He observed the eyes of his followers begin to gleam with anticipation.

"Evildoers will bow down in the presence of the good, and the wicked at the gates of the righteous. God tells us again in Proverbs." He scrutinized his people as they nodded their heads in agreement.

"And where do we find these evildoers and godless people?"

"In the Other!" the crowd exclaimed in unison.

"Exactly. In the Evil One's world that is full of corruption and deceit. Where friends turn to foes to disrupt the work of the Lord. Where lies are told as truths and truths are painted as lies. I tell you that the God who destroyed Sodom and Gamora because the world became so steeped in sin, is watching us. He is asking us to be the winnowers, sifting the chaff from the wheat. If we are not successful in our work all mankind will be destroyed by the hand of a Just God."

Shouts of "Amen" rippled through the crowd. Caleb saw they were swaying rhythmically as they formed an impenetrable wall united in their passion.

DARCY SPENT THE REST OF THE MORNING cleaning up some paperwork and submitting vouchers. Focused on the minutia, she almost didn't hear her phone alert her she had a message; a text from Maria Romero.

Come C me. Am home.

Darcy closed her computer remembering to lock it and dashed out the door. She shouted to Wendy the office manager, that she was following a lead, and she'd check in later. She didn't wait for a reply.

Not a patient driver, Darcy found it particularly annoying to fight traffic all the way to Sage Hill where Maria lived. She was there in 15 minutes.

Another 5 found her at Maria's door. It was open a crack, so Darcy peeked in.

"Marie," she called out. "It's Darcy." She pushed the door wide and saw Marie sitting at a table strewn with old photographs.

Marie looked up and waved her in. Darcy closed the door and sat at the table where Marie gestured her to look at the pictures scattered over the surface of the table.

They were yellowed, and some rolled up at the edges as if they had been thrown in a drawer somewhere. Darcy examined them closely.

One showed a handsome man standing next to a beautiful woman with black hair. The young man was in a uniform and the young woman was dressed in the style of the 1940's. Darcy looked up.

Maria's smile was a little crooked on one side, but it lit up her sparkling brown eyes. She nodded, then tapped her chest.

"This is a picture of you and Tom?" Darcy asked.

Marie nodded. Tears welled up, and she handed Darcy a closeup picture of Lieutenant Thomas McCaulley. Darcy's stomach took a jolt. It was very clearly a picture of the first man buried in the 'bones' house.

"Marie," Darcy choked out. "Tom was buried in your basement?"

The tears flowed freely then as Marie nodded and dabbed at her eyes with a lace-trimmed handkerchief.

"What happened? Do you know?"

Marie shook her head, then pointed to Darcy.

"You want me to find out?"

Marie nodded vigorously, grabbed Darcy's hand, and pressed it to her chest over her heart. Her eyes implored Darcy's help.

"I'll try, Marie. I really will. You do realize that someone in your family might be implicated in his death. Are you willing to risk that?"

Marie dropped her hand. Her face grew hard, and she nodded emphatically.

"Your great-nephew Gary isn't going to like this you know."

Marie smiled softly at the mention of her nephew. She tapped her chest again.

"You'll take care of Gary?" Darcy asked. She doubted this frail old woman would have any luck convincing her nephew to allow such an intrusion into his family history, but she didn't want to argue.

"I will let you know if I find anything." Darcy stood to leave.

Marie nodded, rose, and pulled Darcy into a gentle one-armed hug.

Minutes later, Darcy scrubbed her own tears away on the elevator ride to the first floor. What a lovely lady Marie Romero was, and how courageous.

On the drive back, she called Zach and filled him in on her conversations with both Jess Bowen and Marie. "So, it looks like we're really getting close to identifying both sets of bones. That doesn't solve the 'why' though."

"Do you have any leads on that angle?"

"We're waiting for Bowen to get back to us about Dobson's account, and Marie is going to try to convince her nephew Gary Romero to cooperate, while I keep digging. "

"It's a start, I guess." Zach sounded frustrated.

"We could run a 'progress' story, Boss. You know, 'Here's what we know so far.' Do you want to do that?"

"Can you check with Hank and make sure we won't muck up his investigation?"

"Sure. I'll swing by on my way back. I'll let you know."

The short detour didn't take long, but Hank wasn't in. She scribbled a note to him about a progress story at this point and told him to call her. Just to be safe, she tried to call his cell, but it bumped her to voice mail, so she backed it up with a text. One of these should reach him.

Her first stop when she got back at the station, was to track Netters down. She found him in the editing bay, uploading Dobson's film. He was so intent on the monitor; he didn't hear her come in.

The pictures were a little grainy and wobbly. It reminded Darcy of *The Blair Witch Project*. The voice-over was a raspy whisper and it distressed Darcy to realize this was most likely the voice of the man who was the second set of bones.

"Caleb is the undisputed leader of this fiercely loyal band of believers. He is a terrifying mix of cult leader, evangelist, survivalist, and mass murderer. Like most megalomaniacs, Caleb welcomes my filming him for posterity and is unaware that I'm shooting two different films.

Originally from Texas, Caleb and his group has been wandering nomadically for the past several years. Caleb likens himself to Moses and tells his followers that he will settle them in a secure place to await the final conflagration that is to come.

In the meantime, he schools them with Old Testament severity, and harangues them about purging non-believers and sinners from their midst, as well as the world outside."

Darcy stared at the images that flickered across the monitor.

"Wow! He looks like those old pictures of John Brown with all that wild hair and long beard, doesn't he?"

Netters jumped and almost fell out of his chair.

"For the love of God, Darcy, don't sneak up on me like that!"

"Sorry. Sorry." She slipped into the seat next to him. "Why are all the faces blurred except Caleb's?" Darcy leaned forward for a closer look.

"Because Dobson says in his introduction most of his followers are mentally weak and can't discriminate between right and wrong when it comes to Caleb's teachings."

"But aren't they responsible for killing people? At least for killing Dobson?"

Netters clicked off the screen. "Most likely. The irony here is that they were almost certainly ordered to stone Dobson, and he was the only person who stood for them."

"Why did you turn it off?" She reached forward to the switch, but Netters grabbed her hand and stopped her.

"I can't watch anymore. This is my second time through. Trust me. You don't want to see the rest of this. It is horrifying."

"Why? What does it show?"

"The brutal amputation of a hand of a follower accused of stealing. I've never seen anything like it."

"Are you sure it wasn't just . . . you know . . . mugging for the camera?"

"No. Trust me. Her screams were real. It was a community endeavor. A few men held her hand flat against a tree stump and the crowd cheered at each fall of the ax. It took a long time and several whacks. It reminded me of the stories about incompetent executioners who took several tries before the heads came off.

I'm sure Hank needs to see this. Maybe he can tell where they are from the film. Hard to get much details about setting because Dobson was centered on the brutality of the act.

Netters left her in the editing room. "I'm going to take a break. Tell Zach I'll be back after lunch, assuming I can eat anything and keep it down."

CHAPTER 19

Darcy watched Netters leave. She stared at the blank monitor for several minutes. Better to grapple with the devil you know than the devil you don't know, she said to herself. She took a deep breath and switched on the monitor. The video was still cued up to the same place Netters left it.

She stared at the images. Except for Caleb, who looked like a caricature of a zealous Moses, the people in the film were extraordinary in their ordinariness, all of them dressed in conservative clothes ranging from Army gray-green to chamois gray-yellow. The obvious goal was to blend in. Darcy rolled the video back to the beginning and watched in horror at the young woman's hand was hacked off.

Because the faces were pixilated, Darcy couldn't get a read on the general emotional temperament following the brutal amputation. There was no change in the body language except all adopted a military stance during the amputation and then calmly broke ranks.

"They're just wandering around like it's a company picnic. What's up with that?" she said aloud and leaned closer to the monitor.

"Yeah, Hank," Netters said into the phone. "I have it loaded up on my computer here." Darcy jumped when he walked into the room. Her heart beat a manic tattoo and she had to breathe deeply or pass out.

"Scary, huh?" he said to Darcy.

He smiled at Darcy and continued his conversation. "Yeah. I'll make sure she stays put."

Darcy rounded on him. "I thought you were going to lunch."

Netters shrugged, fished a candy bar from his pocket.

"Good job going healthy," Darcy said. "Who will you make sure stays put?"

Netters reached across her and put the monitor on standby. "Hank said to stay at the station until he gets here." Netters made a show of picking up the papers and debris cluttering the small workspace, so he didn't have to look at her.

Darcy glanced pointedly at the dark screen, then back at Netters.

"You guys are acting like I'm four years old. If you won't let me watch the film here, I'll watch it later." She gathered up her bag and headed for the door.

Netters tried to block her exit.

"What are you going to do? Wrestle me to the ground?" Darcy looked up at him.

Netters glimpsed fleetingly around to see if someone could help. There was no one.

"Move."

He took one step to the side. "Ah, hell." Netters dropped into his chair and flipped the computer back on directing it to another file. Darcy barged out the door.

Desperately needing to be active, Darcy escaped to her office and began to type up notes for a voice-over interview of Jess Bowen, then checked her messages to see what Zach wanted to do about her story, but he hadn't answered her yet.

She was uneasy about doing a regular on-camera interview with Jess. She didn't want him to end up dead like John Walker.

These Caleb-Wackos operated on a different set of dogmas than she could comprehend. They cut off a woman's hand for pilfering flour, stoned Dobson for blasphemy, and slit poor John's throat for allegedly giving false witness. Darcy shivered.

She decided to block Jess' face out and disguise his voice. She wasn't taking any chances.

She called Wendy and told her she needed to talk to Zach when he had a minute, then continued to sketch in her notes.

She struggled to organize the details of the story, as she understood them without coloring them with emotion. She began with the 'bones' house, the broodingly dark home that hid its secrets so well for years. She listed the skeletal remains of "Mr. Jones and Mr. Smith" and sketched in some details from her story on the anthropology lab and what they could tell about the bones. Then she listed some details from Dr. Garcia and her reconstruction sculptures.

Next came John Jacob's death and the Biblical quote in Latin. She wrote a short note about Marie Romero identifying the oldest set of bones as her fiancé of sixty years ago.

Next, Jess Bowen and his description of Shawn Dobson, an award-winning documentary filmmaker who was doing an exposé of fundamentalist churches and religious cults, jotting a reminder in the margin to check with Hank whether she could reveal about the documentary notes.

She skimmed over her notes looking for the holes . . . what she didn't know and couldn't speculate about.

First, she didn't know how or why Thomas McCaulley died. If, as she suspected, it was someone in the Romero family, she was fairly sure she'd get no help from Gary Romero. She wondered how many stumbling blocks he'd put in her way—didn't matter. She had promised Marie she'd find out.

Second, she was sure the religious cult was responsible for Dobson and Walker's death, but how did they find the proof? And who could the police charge with it? If Caleb sent his "followers" to do the executions, he could be charged with conspiracy to commit murder, but that would necessitate one or more of the cult members turning on their leader. That wasn't likely. Well, that was Hank's problem.

Darcy let out a frustrated sigh and threw her pencil down, just as Zach walked in.

"Problems?" He picked up her notes and perched on the edge of her desk to read them.

It was silent in her small office. She watched Zach pull out the purple pen he used to write notes on copy and circled a half dozen places on her page.

He handed it back. "I only foresee several lawsuits and/or police gag orders on your notes. Most of what you've got about the whys and hows of the bones is conjecture and circumstantial. I think the only piece I would feel comfortable with is the Jess Bowen ID of Shawn Dobson."

"What about Marie confirming one of the reconstructions was her fiancé?"

"If you think for one moment that Gary Romero is going to let that stand, you're an idiot. He'll sue us down to our shoe soles claiming Marie had diminished capacity and as her guardian he wasn't present at the interview and had forbidden you to bother her. Then he'd move right along to liable since you would be implying that someone in his family was responsible for one of the bodies . . ."

"Ok, Ok. I got it. Gary Romero is going to have to admit to it sooner than later. Marie had pictures and she's getting better every day." Scanning the circled items, she agreed to the deletions until she could find out more information, but wasn't happy about it.

"I'm not going to make Jess a target. We'll have to film him blacked out and disguise his voice." Darcy propped her feet on the corner of her desk and tilted her chair back.

"I think filming may be a little premature. Why don't you just do a stand up by the 'bones' house and say that the one set of bones has been tentatively identified as Shawn Dobson. Be sure to clear that with Hank first though."

"That would be nice for a change." Hank's lanky frame filled the doorway. Darcy's head twisted around always amazed how the sound of his voice could make her insides smile.

"Well, I'll leave you two to your negotiations," Zach said as he stood and walked to the door. "Nice to see you again Hank," he said in passing. Hank nodded.

Darcy was too tired to put up even a nominal argument. She handed him the marked-up notes.

Hank stood above her and scanned the paper. "And the purple circles are . . .?"

"The points Zach thinks makes us vulnerable to litigation."

"Have to agree. I also agree with your conclusions, but it is all circumstantial. Except . . ."

Darcy dropped her feet to the floor and leaned toward him. "Except?" She snatched at the word as if it was a life preserver.

"Lose that hopeful tone. It isn't much. I did check on Shawn Dobson. His sister who still lives in Chicago, listed him as a missing person six years ago. I called her and told her we thought we'd found his remains but would like to be sure. She's sending us his dental records for comparison."

"That's great, Hank. So, we can be sure that Jess Bowen got it right?"

"I think you can classify it as a lead in an on-going investigation if you want."

"What about Marie identifying her fiancé's picture? I saw an old photo of Thomas McCaulley, and I think it's him too."

He shifted his stance to lean against her desk. "I think we'd better hold on to that information for a bit."

"Don't tell me Detective Hank Nelson is scared of the Family Romero." She grinned impudently up at him.

"Not even a little, but I do think there is a more compassionate way to pry information out of Gary Romero than implying on the 5 o'clock news that someone in his family is a murderer."

"What?"

"That would be telling, and then I'd have to shoot you." Hank grinned back at her. He tossed the list on the desk as he stood to leave.

"Just to clarify about Dobson, I can say we have a tentative identification in an ongoing investigation, right?"

"Right."

Darcy grimaced. "Makes me sound like a politician."

"Whatever it takes to keep you out of trouble. Speaking of which, watch your back. I'm getting nervous about that cult coming after you, especially after I watched parts of the video Netters sent me. Do you still have that GPS I gave you?"

"Yup, it lies safe and warm between my breasts." Darcy couldn't resist taunting, "You do remember my breasts don't you Detective?"

Chuckling as he leaned down to kiss her, he hooked a finger into the top of her shirt and peered down. "You are an evil, wicked girl, and the angels will not save you when I make you pay for that."

"I can't wait," she quipped. "Tonight work for you?"

"I'll call you," he said and left.

Darcy packed up her notes, grabbed her bag and went in search of Netters.

Predictably, he was still in the editing bay. She pushed the door open. "C'mon. We're going to do a short update in front of the 'bones' house."

Netters shut down the computer and grabbed his camera bag that was never far from him.

In five minutes, Darcy stood on the buckling sidewalk in front of the 'bones' house. Directly across the street, she saw the yellow crime scene tape still surrounding John Jacob Walker's house.

She positioned herself so the shot would frame the house without making it look like the small gothic-shaped window was sprouting from her head. Netters was in place.

She nodded. "Don't look at me in that tone of voice." —Dorothy Parker" she said into the mic to check levels. Netters did a count, and she started.

"This is Darcy Moreland reporting once more in front of the house where recently two sets of bones were found buried. We have learned one set has been tentatively identified. Authorities are awaiting confirmation through dental records provided by his family to make a positive confirmation. The investigation is ongoing, so as usual, the police are asking anyone with information to contact them. We will continue to report details as they become available."

She signaled a cut, and Netters began packing up his camera.

"Would you mind taking the video back to the station?" She asked Netters.

"No, but I don't think you should be wandering off by yourself."

"Heaven save me! I am not 'wandering off' like a child at the zoo. I'm going home to do some laundry and maybe, just maybe, if I feel really bold, I might walk my dog. Okay?"

"Hey, don't jump down my throat. You didn't see the whole film." Netters headed for his truck.

"Yeah. Because you guys won't let me," Darcy muttered to herself.

Soon she was driving off toward her apartment building. She opened her sunroof and delighted in the loud music from her stereo and the crisp Autumn breeze that ruffled her long hair. She took a side trip around her neighborhood and the nearby park to look at the colored leaves and to try to decompress a little. By the time she got home, her spirits were slightly revived.

Dutifully locking her car as per Hank's instructions, she dashed up the front steps and pushed open the heavy wooden door. Surprised a little at the warm sense of homecoming she always felt, knowing that whatever insanity was going on outside this place, just steps away she had her friend Abby and her dog Mac waiting to enfold her in normalcy.

She pushed open Abby's door. "It's just me," she hollered out. Mac was already dancing around at her feet. Tucking him like a football under her arm, she wandered into the kitchen to find Abby with her sink full of hand laundering and up to her elbows in suds.

"Why don't you just send that stuff to the cleaners?" Darcy propped her hips against the gray linoleum countertop in the tiny kitchen.

Abby glanced over her shoulder and smiled. "Because some of us live on a pension and don't have a glamorous job at a TV station."

Darcy let go of an unladylike snort. "Yeah. Glamorous." She deposited a wiggling Mac to the floor and opened the refrigerator. Taking a bottled water, she twisted the top.

"Want one?"

"Not now." Abby drained the soapy water and filled the sink with rinse water. "What did you do today?"

Darcy repositioned one of the chairs at the dining room table and straddled it, so she could watch Abby in the kitchen. It took little time to fill Abby in on the day's events. "And so, the upshot was I did a short no names update story on the Shawn Dodson ID and didn't mention Marie Romero at all."

"Probably best," Abby said as she carefully squeezed the water from a delicate blouse and draped it over a laundry drying rack. "I know patience goes against your hard-wiring, Darcy," Abby got herself some water and joined Darcy at the table. "But in this case, I think it will be less hurtful."

"Seems to be the consensus." She swigged more beer.

"It sounds like there's little doubt that the religious cult is responsible for at least two deaths proving it is Hank's job. As for Marie Romero and her unfortunate fiancé, I'm sure you'll think of a way to deal with any information with discretion."

"Thanks for your faith," she got up, replaced her chair, and threw her water bottle in Abby's trash and bin. "You've inspired me. I'm going to go do my laundry."

"Do you want to come for dinner?"

Darcy stopped at the door. "I think I'm going to take Mac for a walk after I get a couple of loads done. How about I walk over to Carl's Junior and get us a bag?"

"Okay by me. See you soon." Abby went back into the kitchen whistling a disjointed tune.

An hour later, Darcy dropped off two small loads of folded laundry in her bedroom then rummaged in the front closet for Mac's leash.

Pulling it out triumphantly, she held it in the air. "Who wants to go for a walk?"

Mac ran around her and barked excitedly.

The weather was perfect for walking. The late day sun beat down, but the slight breeze kept her comfortable in just her Aran sweater.

She loved her neighborhood with its older houses trying to fight off the encroachment of miscellaneous businesses and fast-food places. Some had been recently rehabilitated, and others remained empty like the 'bones' house.

Darcy let her mind play with the thought of the endless stream of people living in these houses, the laughter, the small dramas, the large life disasters. She imagined children playing in well-kept yards. Neighbors walking home from town, women laden with parcels wrapped in brown paper and string, men tipping their hats as they passed.

She let out a sigh. Life in the past and from this distance seemed remarkably uncomplicated. She wasn't as naïve as all that. She knew the truth. Every generation had devils to wrestle.

Mac and she were wandering more than walking. Up one block, over two, back on another route. She was enjoying looking at the houses as she strolled. Unlike the newer houses up north of the city, each of these houses was unique. One might have a small turret and Victorian gingerbread while another might be Tudor or Neoclassical.

She was intrigued by a house that seemed to go on forever and suspected that an addition had been attached to the original structure.

"Let's go check it out, boy," she said to Mac and pulled gently on his leash.

They ducked down a back alley and looked over the fences to see the yards, some pristine, others overgrown. Intent on looking at the curious addition that went up and out with seemingly no real plan, Darcy didn't see the white van that turned into the alley until Mac began to bark.

Heart pounding, Darcy told herself that it was just a service van, probably a plumber or something. She pulled Mac close and pressed her back against a high weather-beaten wooden fence to allow the van to pass.

The van slowed to a crawl and drove past her. She let out a relieved sigh.

The van stopped. The rear doors burst open. Two men dressed alike in black hoodies and ragged jeans jumped out and grabbed her shoulders roughly.

Darcy lurched to the side and broke the hold of one of her assailants. She struck a glancing blow with the heel of her hand to the jaw of the man on her left before he spun her around and slammed her face up against the fence. The jolt to her cheek shot a vicious pain pain to her whole head. She saw stars and felt weak. She tried to kick her attacker who held her flat against the fence, but he was bigger and had a long reach.

Mac was barking and pulling on the leash. She let go of Mac and tried to press the button on the medallion that Hank had given her, but she couldn't tell in her panic if she had pushed it or just grazed it. The man pulled her right arm straight back from her body and applied bone crushing force on her wrist, pushing her fingers back at a right angle to her arm.

The sharp pain radiated up into her shoulder and she winced as her cheek scraped across the rough wood surface. In slow motion, her dazed mind tried to process what was happening.

She kept hearing Mac barking. The guy on her right kicked out at him. Seeing her dog attacked ramped up Darcy's adrenaline.

"Leave him alone!" She twisted and tried to kick out, only dimly aware of her shoulder screaming pain.

When they smacked her face into the fence once more, she thought she heard the crunch of bone echo through her head, and she screamed. They stuffed her mouth with an oily piece of cloth and duct taped over it.

Twisting both her arms behind her, they bound her wrists with more duct tape and began wrestling her to the back of the van. Writhing and thrashing, she kicked out wildly, as they jerked her off her feet and flung through the open doors of the van.

The impact sent a jolt through her whole body. She struggled to sit up. Just as she tucked her legs beneath her, she saw one of the men kick Mac into the air. Mac yelped, bounced off the fence, and then just laid there. She threw back her head and tried to howl, but all she could manage was a strangled cry. That was the last thing she saw before they slammed the doors closed.

CHAPTER 20

A SHARP RIGHT TURN THREW HER ON her side, over the three wooden van ridges in the bed of the van. They ran the length of the bed of the van, exacerbating her battered hip. More painful, was the terror that Mac was dead and she would probably follow him soon.

Darcy tried to tamp down her desperation. She wrenched her body to sit up again and pivoted horizontally bracing herself in a tight corner of the van so turns wouldn't continue to topple her.

She forced her brain away from her terror which was unproductive and focused on solutions. Surveying her surroundings, she noted there were no windows in the back doors. So much for signaling other motorists.

No tools of any kind either. She scanned the sides, looking for a tear or sharp edge she could use to cut the duct tape. No luck.

She twisted her wrists but couldn't move them at all. She flexed her fingers to try to keep the circulation going.

The vibrations in the bed of the van helped her guess how fast they were going. Highway speeds she decided.

Where could they be taking her? Her heart began to pound. She breathed deeply through her nose which helped calm her heartbeat, but the panic was still there.

Another turn. Darcy tried to imagine a map in her head and estimate the time they'd been traveling. Nothing came through the haze of fear. She kicked her heels in frustration.

Accepting the inevitable, she leaned back against the corner and tried to conserve her strength.

She kept replaying in her mind that guy kicking Mac, his yelp of pain as he flew against the fence. He was such a brave little dog, but he couldn't possibly have lived through that. He didn't deserve to die that way. Hot tears rolled down her face, and she attempted to dry them on her shoulder.

She desperately tried for emotional indifference. She let her thoughts wander. She hummed tunelessly to herself.

Another turn accompanied a slowdown, the crunch of gravel and another turn. The van traveled leisurely turning and turning in an intricate pattern Darcy couldn't track.

Finally, they stopped. Darcy flinched when she heard the side van doors slam and again when they threw open the back doors.

The man who had kicked Mac crawled in to get her and she lashed out with her foot, catching him square in the nose.

"Shit!" he screamed and tried to stanch the flow of blood.

A disembodied voice boomed outside of her sightlines. "Brother William, you will do penance for improper language."

"Yes, Father Caleb." he replied meekly and backed out of the van.

Her second abductor crawled in. Darcy thrashed and kicked, but the other man was prepared. He captured her legs in a bruising grip and pulled her out. She landed with a puff of dust on the hard ground.

The sharp pain knifed up her back and down her legs. It also stopped breath and for a moment. She almost gave up.

When they yanked her to her feet, her will to live resurfaced. Darcy tried to scream. She found herself face-to-face with Father Caleb. Up close he was as mesmerizing a snake poised to strike. The small part of Dobson's video she had seen had not captured the intense eyes and the charismatic aura of a fanatic.

He stood around six-foot, with weatherworn, deeply wrinkled

skin, like a pair of work boots that had been left out on the porch too long.

He had to be at least mid-forty or more. His gray hair hung in greasy hanks that drooped into an equally droopy beard. He smiled at her, a yellow flash of predatory teeth, the two canines pointed and longer than the rest. He wore a soiled, threadbare, gray/white robe that looked stolen from a choir or a graduation, years ago.

Darcy recoiled as Father Caleb came closer and peered into her face.

He smiled broadly at her muffled scream. He viciously ripped the tape from her mouth to get a better look at her. "Not an unattractive sinner, but a sinner none the less. We are not without mercy, Ms. Moreland," he said as he removed the cloth from her mouth and dropped it. "But you are a purveyor of false witness and must therefore pay the ultimate price to save your immortal soul."

Darcy ran her tongue around her mouth trying to erase the dryness created by the gag and the terror. At last, when she trusted her voice not to break, she said, "I have never knowingly given false witness in my life. If you feel you or your people," she turned her body to look at the gathered followers of about forty or so including children, "have been unjustly maligned I apologize. If you would like to clarify what you believe to be true—"

He backhanded her across her face. She almost fainted from the pain. His beefy hand managed to connect with the same cheek she had banged against the fence when they took her.

"I *know* the truth, you heathen. I don't *believe* something is true." Father Caleb thundered. Darcy leaned back to avoid his fetid breath. "God Almighty has condemned you. Would you bargain with your Lord? Have you no shame?" He shoved her violently into a wall of people. "Prepare her," he declared and stormed off.

Strong hands grabbed her arms on both sides and pulled her forward toward an outcropping of rounded red rocks.

She recognized this place. She was deep in the Medicine Bow National Forest in Vedauwoo. She looked at the shabby makeshift camp as they passed.

Silently, the men and women produced several lengths of sheeting and dropped them in a pile at Darcy's feet.

Remembering John Jacob's slit throat, she looked down at the sheets and back up at the people.

Father Caleb ritualistically cleaned his hands in a bucket of water hanging from a branch. He stopped and walked to her.

"Oh, I see you are familiar with Old Testament scriptures. You wonder why we are preparing to stone you rather than send you to hell like your friend Mr. Walker." He gestured to one of his followers for a towel. He didn't look away from Darcy but yanked the tattered rag from the woman and dried his hands.

"Simple really." Another flash of yellowed teeth. "We are stoning you because you are also a harlot." He bent forward until his forehead almost touched hers.

"Think you that we were not watching, harlot?"

"Harlot. Harlot." the crowd murmured in a rhythmic cadence that softly underscored Father Caleb's raised voice.

"Think you that the Lord God Almighty was not repulsed by your unholy lust for that policeman?" His gravelly voice rose at the end as if in horror of such a deed.

Darcy almost expected him to spit on the ground at her feet. She wasn't sure if he were most offended that she'd slept with Hank when they weren't married, or that she would give herself to a policeman, an avowed enemy.

She tried to straighten her spine, but her knees were shaking.

The crowd continued their low, hypnotic, chant.

Two women joined the two men at her arms and began winding the lengths of yellowed, brown stained sheeting around her. In a moment of insanity, Darcy wondered if they reused the brown stained sheets repeatedly like a cheap motel. Only God knew how many people had been bound and stoned by these people.

Her shoulders and torso were now bound, and they were working their way down to her legs.

"Bind her legs firmly so that she may go to her God the way she should, humbly and submissive as befits a woman. Perhaps God will forgive her perversion once she has been punished," Father

Caleb instructed in a voice increasing in volume to override the chanting of his followers.

"Harlot! Harlot! Harlot! Harlot! Harlot!"

The chant was building, and Darcy knew it was only a matter of moments before they would finish the binding and work themselves into the zealous fury of a mob.

Her ears rang with their condemnation.

"What is God's punishment for a harlot?" Father Caleb bellowed.

"Stone her! Stone her! Stone her!" the crowd roared back.

Propping her up against the peeled bark of a tree that showed evidence of it being used for beatings as well as this fatal kind of punishment, The men tied a rope around her waist to keep her standing, then moved away.

Darcy concentrated on staying upright. She pulled her shoulders back and stared at Father Caleb and raised her chin defiantly. For some reason she couldn't fathom, retaining her dignity in front of these animals was imperative.

"One last time to repent before you meet your maker," Father Caleb said. He was so close to her she could smell the rotten, fetid odor of unwashed clothes and body. She almost gagged it was so repulsive. She turned her face away.

"So be it," Caleb stepped out of the way.

"Stone her! Stone her!"

The frenzy grew, yet when the first stone hit her forehead, she was shocked. Somewhere deep inside she hadn't believed they would kill her. The slim thread of hope that was holding her together snapped as stone after stone hurled against her body.

"What is the matter with you people?" she screamed. "What happened to 'Thou shalt not kill'?"

"Stone her! Stone her! Stone her!"

A large rock crashed into her kneecap, and she slid down but the rope held her partially suspended. Dignity forgotten, she tried to fold herself into a protective ball, but failed because of the bindings. The bruising continued.

She lost count of the different assaults, each sharp blow blending into another until her whole body throbbed. Even the chanting, which had grown hysterical, merged in her brain as a wave of indistinguishable sounds. Like swimming in the ocean, she ducked her head as she waited for more waves of pain and sound to crash over her.

Then the assault stopped, and though the chanting grew softer, it continued.

Darcy cautiously opened her eyes and saw the reason for the delay. They were out of stones. She saw a rush of children carrying plastic beach pails scamper around picking up used stones in a twisted parody of an Easter egg hunt.

Once the children returned to the line, the chanting grew louder, and the stones flew. In her delirium, Darcy thought she heard the squeal of sirens.

The stoning stopped abruptly as did the chanting. Screams, shouts, and sounds of stampeding feet filled the air. Darcy watched as Father Caleb attempted to escape in a rusty red pickup. He didn't slow down enough to let more than a handful of his followers jump in the open truck bed.

Many others ran for the safety of the van. Darcy watched as women and children tried to scramble in too, but the men callously pushed them out, shouting, "No women or children. Even heathens won't do much to women or children. We need the space for true disciples." Darcy watched as women and children plummeted to the hard ground. None of them whined or try to beg. Silent tears streaked through the dirt and dust on their faces producing small rivulets, more horrible because of the lack of sobs. They had obviously been trained to never to cry aloud. Darcy thought she had never seen such an absence of hope imprinted on all their faces. It reminded her of the pictures taken of holocaust victims she had seen—vacant eyes not seeing or understanding about what was going on all around them.

Escaping vehicles threw up gravel and dust in a filthy cloud that drifted in the air and slowly settled on the women and children huddled together, crying but immobile like robots whose batteries had died.

Darcy blinked hot tears and began to sob in uncontrolled gulps.

Her aching body heaved with the need to howl her terror and relief.

She wasn't even aware when Hank had come. After he cut her loose, he held her crying in his lap and rocked back and forth as if soothing a fretful baby.

"Get me the hell out of this shroud," she ground out through clenched teeth and kicked her legs in frustration.

Hank took out his knife again from its scabbard on his belt and made short work of slicing through the sheeting and the duct tape that still bound her arms. He threw the rags and used tape away from Darcy, then began the survey of her injuries. Red splotches blossomed profusely on her arms and across her upper chest.

He gently lifted her shirt to examine the damage.

"Stop it," Darcy shouted as she pulled her shirt down. "Please don't touch me."

"Okay," Hank replied sympathetically. He stood with her in his arms.

"Put me down. She kicked her legs but the contusions all over her body shrieked in protest.

"Nope." He carried her to his glossy black pickup and gently placed her in the seat and fastened her seat belt.

By the time he got in, she was sobbing again while curling her arms protectively around her middle.

"They killed Mac, Hank. Kicked him against the fence like so much garbage." She was unsure what hurt worse, the emotional pain or her aching ribs.

"They didn't kill him, Darcy."

"What?" Her tear-filled eyes widened and glinted with hope.

"I said, they didn't kill him. Oh, he's bruised up a bit, but Abby called to tell me he was doing fine."

Darcy cried even harder but with a smile on her face and tears glistening in her soft brown eyes. "Thank you, God. Thank you!"

"Not that I'm in the same category, but you might thank me too. If I hadn't given you that GPS medallion, we'd have never found you."

"It worked? I wasn't sure I pushed it hard enough."

"We got here, didn't we? It took a lot of time to organize a collaborative force of Cheyenne police, Albany County Sheriff's Department, and the Federal Forest Service just to ride to the rescue of some pushy reporter who got crosswise with a fundamentalist cult."

"Sorry. Sorry." She grabbed his right hand from the steering wheel and squeezed it. "Will you cut me a little slack if I tell you that several of those rocks hit my head?" She swiped at trickle of blood running down her cheek.

Darcy saw the muscle twitch in his jaw. "Yeah. You can have all the slack you need."

"Do you think they got them all?" she asked in a small voice.

"They damned well better have."

Wisely, Darcy didn't say much else on the drive back to town. When the truck pulled up at the emergency room entrance, she broke her silence.

"Oh no, Hank. Take me home. I want to see Mac and—"

She was alone in the cab.

Hank came around, gently lifted her her from the seat, and began carrying her in.

"Hank Nelson, put me down."

"Nope." he said, but he smiled and kissed her cheek gently.

It took the better part of two hours to check her over. The results were a smorgasbord of injuries ranging from contusions and lacerations on up to a bruised kidney and a broken rib. A black eye was already turning an alarming array of colors and was swollen shut. They wanted to keep her overnight for observation in case she had a concussion.

"Please, Hank. I'll be careful. Don't make me stay here."

"Okay, but you have to promise to do whatever Abby says. You got that?"

She nodded. "I will. I promise."

In the end, they gave her a prescription for pain, but told her she couldn't use it until tomorrow because it might mask symptoms of a concussion or other injuries.

She used the drive to her apartment to convince Hank she could walk and preferred to.

"What will the neighbors think if they see you carrying me up the stairs like I'm drunk or something?"

"Don't kid yourself. By now, they know almost everything that happened to you. That's quite an underground telegraph system going on in that building."

She smiled and let him help her down from the cab but insisted on walking slowly up the steps. She grimaced and sucked her breath in a couple of times, but she made it. She clung to Hank's steadying arm. By the time she reached the doors, she felt like she'd climbed the Alps.

Abby met them at the door holding Mac. Abby's eyes were reddened, and Mac had a large white bandage wrapped around his middle, but they looked wonderful to Darcy.

No one would let her hold Mac until she was ensconced on the settee with a couple of soft pillows at her back and a knit afghan across her legs.

When she finally got him in her arms the tears began again. "Mac, I'm so sorry. It was all my fault that you got hurt." She hugged him gently to her chest, and he licked her tears away. By the next morning, the adrenaline and shock had worn off and the real pain began. Abby wouldn't leave Darcy, so Hank ran the prescription by. Darcy practically snatched the pill bottle from his hands. "Tell me all the news. What happened after you left?" She washed the pills down with some now cold coffee left over from breakfast.

"Would you like some coffee, Hank?" Abby asked as she bustled around picking up dishes and scattered newspapers.

"No thanks, Abby. I have to get back." He turned back to Darcy. "Okay, the short version is that we caught all of them. Some will be accused of attempted murder and kidnapping while most will be evaluated for mental instability."

"Not Father Caleb, though." Darcy imbued his name with venom.

"No. Not Father Caleb. He'll stand trial and do time for what he did to you. We're also hopeful that a couple of his followers will will flip on him and we can put him away forever for Shawn Dobson's death and probably others."

Darcy hadn't been aware that she had been leaning forward

until she relaxed back into the arms of the settee. "Thank God," she whispered and closed her eyes. Her eyes popped open as another thought occurred to her. "What about the women and children left behind. You should have seen those savages throwing them out of the van like so much garbage. Will they ever be able to recover and have any life worth living?"

"I don't know, Darcy. They were probably pretty damaged when they joined the group. Most of the children had been born into the group though we did find a couple of boys who had been kidnapped. It is going to take a long time to evaluate the depth of the abuse these women and children suffered." Hank added, then stood as if embarrassed to be caught with his tender heart dangling from his chest. "Got to get back. Someone will be by today to get your statement and I'll see you later tonight. Okay?"

Darcy closed her eyes, the painkiller already working. "Uhm hmmm. Thanks, Hank."

Hank kissed her on the forehead, trying to avoid the large lump there and left.

Darcy spent the morning in a blur. Zach called and beyond assuring him that she was all right, she didn't remember much of the conversation.

Later, propped up with Mac lying by her side, she flipped on the television to watch the News at Noon show. The top story was her near death experience. To add more injury to more insult, Bryce Adkins was doing a stand up by the 'bones' house.

"—all we know right now is that over 30 people are being held at both the Cheyenne City jail and the Laramie County jail as law enforcement attempts to get statements from all of them. Department of Family Services has been notified and will be picking up the children as soon as possible. A reliable source in the Police Department told KCWY today they are hopeful that this will also lead to closing the case of the brutal murder of Shawn Dobson in the house behind me. We will keep you informed as the investigation progresses. And if Darcy Moreland is listening, we hope you get well soon. We miss you." Adkins flashed his signature capped-tooth smile into the camera.

"Horse puckey!" Darcy snapped off the TV. "I'm going to skin Zach Horton alive!"

Abby sitting across from her, doing a crossword puzzle looked up. "Now dear, I'm sure Zach—"

"Knows how much I hate that weasel. How dare he give him my story?"

"Be fair, Darcy. You're hardly in a position to do it yourself right now. Should I get you a mirror?"

She scratched Mac's ears. "You are evidently the only friend I have left in the world, boy." Mac rolled on his back, so she could scratch his belly. Darcy laughed and reopened her split lip and groaned. "Okay, I admit I can't do it," she dabbed at the blood on her lip, "but why Adkins? Couldn't he find anyone else?"

"I don't know, dear, but until you do, don't you think you should give Zach the benefit of the doubt?" Abby handed her another dose of her pain medication.

Darcy swallowed them gratefully but felt compelled to protest. "You can't keep me drugged forever, you know. "Abby bent down without comment to swing Darcy's legs back around and tuck the afghan around her legs.

Midafternoon, Darcy got a call from Netters.

"Hi, Darcy. Did I wake you up?"

"No. I'm between drug-induced stupors right now. What's up?"

"I knew you'd be pissed about Adkins taking your story."

"Way beyond pissed but go on."

"I talked to Zach and if you're willing, I could come over tomorrow and we could do a 'What did the truck that ran over you look like?' story. Or does vanity preclude?"

"You donkey's patute! Of course, I'll do it."

"Make some notes about what you want to say, and I'll be over about ten, so we can preempt another noon news broadcast from Adkins. Okay?"

"Okay. And Netters—"

"Yeah?"

"Thanks."

CHAPTER 21

When she wasn't groggy from the pain medicine, Darcy tried to sketch out some notes. What could you say in a minute or less about almost being stoned to death?

She slept fitfully, dreaming of small children with brightly colored beach pails and hollow-eyed women with shabby clothes and no hope.

In the morning, she convinced Abby that she was well enough to go up to her own apartment.

"I just need a bath and a nap in my own bed. I promise, if I have any problems, I'll call you."

Abby stood, arms akimbo, and looked down at her. "Fine, but don't think I won't check on you. I promised Hank."

"I'll be fine."

Darcy swung her legs off the settee and slowly heaved herself up. Abby reached to help her, but Darcy waved her off. "I have to do this myself. It's important."

Every movement hurt somewhere, but she was determined to avoid being an invalid. She refused to let them win. Climbing the stairs was tortuous but being in her own apartment with her things around her soothed her aching heart.

Mac sniffed around for a while then found his bed in the corner and sank into it. Darcy thought she heard him yawn.

"Good to be home isn't it, boy?"

She headed for her bedroom gingerly stripping clothes off as she went. Abby had brought her some clean clothes to change into, but at first, Darcy hadn't been strong enough to shower or bathe. More than rest, she needed to scrub herself all over.

She ran a tub and poured liberal amounts of apple blossom Epson bath salts into the water. In moments, the bathroom filled with the clean spicy scent and soothing steam.

Making sure she had a towel nearby, Darcy stepped carefully into the deep cast iron tub and sank into the silky lukewarm water. She wanted a hot bath but knew that wouldn't be good for her bruises. She leaned her head back and cried a little because it felt so good, and because she was alive.

Once the water cooled to uncomfortable, she pulled the plug and stood, closing the surrounding curtain, and started the shower, stepping to the back of the tub and pulled the shower curtain closed while the water warmed.

A bath to sooth and a shower to clean, she thought as she lathered her hair. Watching the suds run into the drain she thought, "So much for you Father Caleb."

Drying her hair and doing her make up felt therapeutic, like she was coming back to herself somehow. She slipped into a long-sleeved shirt to cover most of the bruises but had to settle for sweatpants because her knee was so swollen.

"Not half bad," she said to her mirror, though make-up could do little to disguise her puffy black, blue, and purple eye, still swollen shut and the size of a golf ball, her bruised and scratched cheek, nor her distended split lip.

She brewed herself some tea, mostly for the comfort of it, grabbed some frozen peas for her knee, and sat in the streaming sunlight from her bay window.

Her knee was so painful, she had almost left the door ajar, so she wouldn't have to let Netters in, but quickly reconsidered that piece of lunacy.

Even though she was prepared for it, the loud knock made her stomach clench and her heart beat faster. Struggling out of her wing-backed chair, she hobbled to the door and peered through the lens of the small glass spy hole. She accidentally bumped her bruised eye. "Shit."

"It's okay, Darcy. I can come back another time," Netters shouted through the door.

She swung the door open.

"Get in here." She cupped her hand around her throbbing eye.

She limped back to her chair, lifted the bag of peas off the table, and held it to her eye.

Netters winced. "'Shit' hardly covers it. You *do* look like a truck hit you. Do you want to do this another time?"

"And let Adkins steal my story? Are you insane? Can you shoot me here?"

"No problem." Netters set up his tripod and handed her the mic.

"I'm just going to tell a shortened version and I'll have to trust you to edit it for me. Okay?"

"Whenever you're ready."

"'Candy is dandy, but Liquor is quicker Dorothy Parker" she said to check her levels. She looked at Netters who nodded. Count it down for me." On the visual two, one signal, Darcy sat up tall and began.

"This is Darcy Moreland reporting for KCWY News. For the past few weeks, I have been covering a story about two skeletons found buried in an old house.

As information on the most recent set of bones became available, I reported that one of the bodies belonged to Shawn Dobson, an award-wining journalist.

His documentary film *Faith and Judgment* won acclaim at the Synergy Film Festival but it also, in my opinion, cost him his life. Dobson had been filming his documentary among a little-known religious fundamentalist cult led by a man called Father Caleb.

John Jacob Walker, the murdered neighbor, remembered seeing Dobson and Father Caleb together in the rented house across the street. It was my interview, in my opinion, that cost John Walker his life.

The alleged murderers, Father Caleb, and his cohorts, were captured yesterday in the Medicine Bow Forest through the joint efforts of the Cheyenne Police Department, Albany County Sheriff's Department, and the U.S. Forest Service. They were apprehended in the act of attempting to stone me to death.

I have every confidence that all the guilty parties responsible for the murders of Shawn Dobson and John Walker will be brought to justice.

As for me, I am grateful for the swift action of the combined force that saved my life yesterday. After that experience, I can honestly say I know how Shawn Dobson died both in theory and in fact.

This is Darcy Moreland, reporting for KCWY News."

Darcy signaled to cut. "Okay?"

"Sure fire. Zach's going to love this. And as a bonus, Adkins's head will probably explode." Netters began packing up his camera equipment.

He didn't look at her. "I'm glad you're okay. If I had known . . ."

"Don't be asinine. I'm fine."

Netters head jerked up, and he stared at her. His eyes narrowed at this obvious lie.

"I mean I'm getting better . . . and, hey! I'm still alive."

"Yeah. There is that." He swung the heavy duffle over his shoulder and walked to the door.

Darcy followed to lock it behind him.

"If you need anything . . . I mean . . ." Netters began.

"Thanks." She went on tiptoe and kissed his cheek. "I love you too."

Netters was blushing and speechless when she closed the door behind him.

Darcy spent the rest of the morning napping and reading from her stash of romance paperbacks. She forced herself to get up and move around every so often to keep from stiffening up even more.

Around noon, Abby appeared at her door with some homemade chicken soup and warm French bread.

"Hungry?" she asked as she bustled past and into the kitchen.

"Yeah. I guess I am." Darcy followed her and leaned against the door for support.

"I saw that nice Bill Netters come and go. Just visiting?" Abby passed Darcy and set the bowl and plate on the table.

Darcy sat, but couldn't stifle a laugh then gently press her swollen lips. "Give it up, Abby. Who do you think you're kidding with the soup and sympathy routine?"

Abby chuckled and set her own bowl down. "That's why you're such a good reporter. You see right through people." She and Darcy sat at the table and sipped a spoonful of soup each. "So?"

"So he came to do a short recap video. Bryce Adkins wanted to take over my story and Netters helped me take it back. That's all."

"So when is it going to be aired?"

"At noon, five, and ten would be my guess. Depends on Zach." She scooped up a spoonful of chunky chicken and celery. "Yum. This really hits the spot, Abby. Thanks."

Abby pulled the TV around and squinted at the remote buttons. "Don't know why they can't make these damn buttons a reasonable size."

"Gimme," Darcy held out her hand, turned the set on. She gave the control back to Abby. "Channel 23 I presume?"

"Very funny. I'm just trying to be supportive." She turned the volume up.

The anchor, Tom Lewis, was just introducing her clip. Darcy leaned back and munched on her bread.

The screen filled with Darcy's battered face. "Oh, Abby! Turn it off! Turn it off!"

"Shhhh. I'm listening."

Darcy hunched over her soup bowl and slurped her noodles loudly. She didn't look up until she heard the tag line at the end.

Abby clicked the TV off. "Sometimes, you are very rude. I wanted to listen to your report, and I could hardly hear it."

"Sorry. I wasn't prepared for how awful I looked. I mean I see my face in the bathroom mirror, but somehow with that mega closeup it was like starring in a horror movie."

"It was a nice report . . . well . . . except for when you talked about them almost stoning you. Now *that* was a little horrific."

Abby got up to take her bowl into the kitchen. "I'll leave the rest of this in your refrigerator for later."

Darcy could hear her rinsing off the dishes and loading Darcy's tiny dishwasher.

"Thank you so much. You're a real sweetheart," she shouted over her shoulder.

"Nothing of the sort," Abby kissed the top of Darcy's head. "Now, if you need anything, call. I'm going to the movies with Mrs. Daniels, but we won't be leaving for a while." She opened the door. "Try to get a nap. You've had a busy morning."

Darcy curled up with Mac on the big brown sofa. She turned the TV on an old movie channel but kept the volume low. The white noise soothed her to sleep.

When her phone began buzzing on her coffee table, Mac barked at it. Darcy struggled up to grab it. Wiping the sleep from her eyes, she said, "Hello?"

"Hi. It's Hank."

"Mmmm" she relaxed back onto the sofa.

"Darcy, wake up. I'm going to come get you in a few minutes so do your fluff and buff thing."

"Ahhh, Hank," she whined. "I don't want to go anywhere. I look awful and . . ."

"Yeah, I know. I saw the noon news."

"Well that was friendly." She sat up and Mac jumped to the floor.

"Gary Romero called."

"What?" She started to stand but pain in her knee made sit. "Why?"

"He saw the report too and wants to meet us at Marie's apartment. He was insistent that I bring you with me."

"What does it mean, Hank?"

"It means that the longer we talk, the longer it will be until we find out. Be there in five."

Darcy clicked her phone off. "I wish he wouldn't do that," she said as she passed Mac. "He could at least say goodbye before he hangs up on me."

She exchanged her long-sleeved blouse with a bright peach

t-shirt and a hoodie that matched her sweatpants. She'd only worn the blouse for the update, but it looked silly with her sweatpants and her knee was still huge.

She ran a brush through her hair just as Hank knocked on her door.

"I thought you said five minutes. Did you call me on the way?"

"Found a great parking space right in front. Got your keys?"

Darcy grabbed them from the table. "Be good, Mac. I'll be back soon."

Hank guided her out the door. "You do know, don't you, that all he hears is 'Blah, blah, Mac. Blah, blah.'"

"Shut up, you insufferable man."

He stopped her at the stairs. "I'm going to carry you down. I don't think you should go up or down stairs for a while."

"I went up them this morning okay." She squared her shoulders, looking for a fight.

"Yeah, well, I wasn't here this morning." Hank scooped her gently her into his arms, carried her down the stairs, down the front steps, and lifted her into his pickup.

"That was fun," Darcy said. "Planning on hauling me all over town?"

"Just might if you don't stop being sassy." He went around and got in his side. "I could introduce you as my slightly-crippled girlfriend with the smart-ass-mouth." He buckled her in and went around to his side. He put the truck in gear.

"Hilarious." She crossed her arms and refused to speak for the ten minutes it took to get to Sage Hill.

Hank jumped out. "Stay put," he ordered.

He returned with a wheelchair and lifted her into it.

"I can walk, Hank." She started to get up, but he pressed her back down.

"You shouldn't be on that knee any more than you can help. Just enjoy the ride." He pushed her into the lobby and maneuvered the chair into the elevator after a couple of attempts.

Darcy admitted to herself that this was better than trying to walk or stand.

"Here we are," Hank said as he knocked.

The door swung open almost immediately. Gary Romero nodded to Hank then his eyes dropped to Darcy. "My God! What did they do to you?"

"Tried to kill me, I think." She tried to smile but her split lip threatened to crack open again. She raised her hand to her lips tenderly.

"I saw you on the news, but it is a shock to see you up close. I am so sorry, Darcy." He glanced up at Hank. "Come in. My aunt is in the living room."

Hank pushed Darcy's chair next to Marie. She noticed the coffee table was littered with pictures and papers. Hank took a seat across from the women and Romero sat in a white wing-backed chair that mirrored Marie's flanking the fireplace. An anemic fire flickered on the grate.

"How are you, Marie?" Darcy reached out to squeeze her hand.

Marie smiled at her and nodded. "Better," she answered haltingly.

"Oh Marie. You can speak. That's wonderful."

Marie shook her head and Darcy saw her eyes were red-rimmed and swollen from crying.

Darcy looked at Romero.

"What my aunt means is she is getting better, but she can't speak very much yet. Even without speech, my aunt can be formidable. It was her idea to ask you to come." He patted Marie's hand that rested in her lap clutching a lace-trimmed handkerchief.

Marie smiled at him.

"We'd like to clear up the mystery of Thomas McCaulley's body."

"You discovered who was responsible?" Darcy asked Marie. Marie looked at Romero and then nodded.

Hank took out his small notebook.

Marie looked at the table in front of her and reached out with a tremulous hand and picked up a picture. She handed it to Darcy.

Darcy looked at a yellowed photograph of a slim young man wearing a light colored 1940's style suit and two-toned wing-tipped shoes. He leaned back against a convertible with rounded fenders.

She handed the picture to Hank, then turned to Marie. "Who is that?"

After a couple of tries, Marie said, "C.J."

Darcy looked at Romero.

"It is my Great-Uncle C.J. He's about 23 in that picture. It must have been taken just before he left for California." He pointed to the picture Hank still held. "That's the car he drove out there and wrecked."

"He died in that crash, didn't he?" Darcy asked.

"Yes. He was always a little out of control."

"What does he have to do with McCaulley?" Hank asked.

Romero looked bleak and ran a hand through his hair, but when he looked at his Aunt, she pursed her lips and nodded emphatically.

"Uncle C.J. evidently killed Thomas McCaulley."

Hank's face was impassive. "How?"

"It was an accident," Romero began, and then took a sip from his water glass. "McCaulley was in love with my aunt, and he'd come to talk to C.J. about his intentions. Technically, he should have talked to my grandfather, Robert, since he was the head of the Romero family at that time."

"What happened, Gary?" Darcy asked softly. She could see how difficult this was for him. Who wouldn't have trouble admitting someone in your family was a murderer? She took Marie's hand once more.

"Thomas came over to talk to C. J. but the story I heard was that C. J. was drunk and got in a shouting match with McCaulley."

"What about? Do you know?" Darcy asked, shifting seamlessly into reporter mode.

Marie dabbed at her moist eyes.

"The way I was told the story was that C.J. didn't think Thomas was good enough for Great Aunt Marie. My Great Uncle Robert said it was partially his fault. C.J. had been a screwup for most of his life, and Uncle Robert tried to encourage him to be more mature. He said Marie's safety was his responsibility and to take that charge seriously."

"I don't quite understand how that lead to the tragedy," Darcy said.

"According to family stories, C.J. could never do anything by halves, He wouldn't let Marie go out alone unless he accompanied her. As you might imagine, Aunt Marie hated that."

Darcy glanced at Marie's face. Her eyes were narrowed, and her lips squeezed into a slash that told volumes without sayin a word.

"Aunt Marie called my Uncle Robert and told him to get C.J. under control or she would lock him out of the house and the devil take the hindmost." Romero smiled at his Aunt. Darcy was quite sure he admired his Aunt's grit.

Hank kept writing notes and left the questioning to Darcy.

"So did your Uncle Robert rein him in?'

"He thought so. He explained that he didn't need to hover over her all the time. He said Marie had a right to have some freedom. She was a grown woman. C.J. argued that Robert needed to get to town more often. He said the whole city was awash with soldiers coming from God knows where for training and then leaving to go to the war. C.J. said the men often behaved badly because they didn't know if or when they'd come home. C.J. said it made them bold."

"What did Robert say to that?" Darcy prodded.

"He said to just do the best he could to keep Marie safe without ruining her social life. C.J. argued but finally agreed to back off a little."

"And did he?" Darcy looked from Romero to Marie, who nodded solemnly.

"The trouble was, C.J. was frustrated and felt like his brother didn't trust him to look out for their sister. The angrier he got, the more he drank. There were many nights he didn't come home at all." Gary was pacing back and forth now. This can't be easy for him, Darcy thought.

"John Walker said the same thing. He said he would often see C.J. obviously drunk, try to get into his house. Once John walked across the street to help him and C.J. took a swing at him," Darcy said.

Marie grimaced. She hated being reminded of how out of control C.J. was back then.

Anyway," Romero continued, "fists flew. As I understand

it, there was pushing and shoving on both sides, and Thomas McCaulley fell and hit his head on the andiron in the fireplace. C.J. tried to wake him but knew almost instantly he was dead. C.J. panicked and wrapped the body up in an old rug, stashed it in a dark corner in the crawl space, and drove out to the ranch to talk to my grandfather."

"And what did your grandfather tell him to do?" Hank asked.

It took a moment for Romero to clear his throat and take another sip of water. He looked at Hank with haunted eyes. "He said, 'Let the dead bury the dead.' He told C.J. to leave town, and he'd try to clean up the mess."

"So C.J. left for California, got in a fatal crash, and your grandfather decided it was in everyone's best interest to tell Marie that Thomas was killed in an Army training accident. Is that it, Gary?" Darcy asked.

By now, Romero was sitting, shoulders hunched in and holding his head in his hands. He didn't look up, just nodded.

"How long have you known this, Mr. Romero?"

Darcy's head whipped around to look at Hank's steely eyed gaze. Clearly, Hank was seeing Romero as a criminal, an accessory after the fact.

"Since my dad died last year. He told me I had to take the secret to my grave. It was family."

"How long has your aunt known?" Hank asked.

Romero looked at his watch. "About two hours. She made me tell her and then call you."

Hank snapped his notebook shut. "Thank you for the information. We'll be in touch." He stood and swung Darcy's chair toward the front door.

"Wait a damn minute, Hank. You may have turned into Robocop, but Marie is as much a victim in this as Thomas was." Darcy swiveled the chair toward Marie and gave her a soft hug. "I'm so sorry." Marie patted her back. "I'm sorry you had to find out this way."

Marie leaned forward and kissed Darcy on the cheek, then smiled. Tears crept into Darcy's eyes, but she blinked them away.

"I'll see you again soon, if it will be okay." She looked first at Romero slumped dejectedly in his chair and then back to Marie who was nodding and smiling.

CHAPTER 22

The District Attorney finally decided not to press any charges against Gary Romero. The official view was that since all the primary players were dead, Marie Romero would be the one to suffer most if they put her great-nephew on trial.

After about two weeks, Darcy's wounds had mostly healed, at least her physical ones. She could now open her eye and even though it was still colorful, the eye still worked. She was still incensed at what she saw as Hank's lack of humanity. They hadn't spoken since he took her home from Marie's apartment, ostensibly, because they were both busy, but, because they knew when they finally dealt with it, it would probably be ugly.

Darcy did a final stand-up in front of the 'bones' house

"Captain Thomas McCaulley died in a tragic accident here in this house almost 60 years ago. His remains have now been buried in his fiancé's family plot.

Shawn Dobson's remains were retrieved by his sister and interred his family's plot in Chicago.

As heartbreaking as their deaths were, it is satisfying to get justice of a sort for both men and to solve the mysteries of their passing.

It is also an intriguing reminder of the saying: "If walls could talk, what amazing stories they could tell.

This is Darcy Moreland reporting for KCWY News."

When Netters turned the camera off, she heaved a deep sigh of relief. She dabbed at the few tears in the corner of her eye, feeling like a huge weight had been taken off her shoulders.

Her eyes drifted beyond Netters packing up his camera and saw Hank leaning against his pickup. Darcy's heart did a flip. It had taken her time to reach the conclusion that Hank would always do the ethical thing and follow the law to the letter. It was a part of him, like the color of his eyes. She knew from experience, though, he had a good heart. Honor and compassion was a good combination. She walked slowly toward him, and he stood straighter.

"Good report," he said.

"Yes, it was," she reached up to twine her arms around his neck. "We must discuss the details sometime real soon."

Hank nodded. "But not tonight."

"No. Not tonight."

Hank followed Darcy home. He had some grocery bags in the bed of his truck that he grabbed out and followed Darcy who was still painfully walking up the front stairs.

It hurt Hank to see how broken she still was, but he kept his mouth shut, because he knew it bruised her pride.

"You coming?" Darcy asked as she braced herself to climb the rest of the way.

"Yup," Hank answered biting back an offer to carry her up. She would hate that.

When they got to the apartment, Hank unlocked the door, leaving Darcy free to pick Mac up as he raced around her feet.

"For heaven's sake, Mac. I wasn't gone that long." She scratched his ears and put him down still cautious of his rib injury.

Hank walked into the kitchen and began to unload the groceries. He put the yogurt and milk into the refrigerator. Then he filled a large bowl on the counter with fruit.

Darcy was sitting in the middle of her brown sofa and allowed Hank to help her like this. She got so tired these days. The smallest thing would wear her out. And she hated it.

"How about I make you a grilled cheese sandwich? My culinary skills are not as good as Abby's, but I do C&F pretty okay."

"C&F? What does that mean?"

"Cheap and Filling. I can make a great fried egg on toast if you'd rather."

By now Darcy had turned to look at him. A small grimace of pain crossed her face, but she beat it back. "I am not hungry, Hank. Could you just bring me some water and come sit down?"

"Sure. Okay," Hank said. He would give her her weight in gold if he could wipe out her pain. He poured water over some ice cubes and took it to her.

As soon as he sat down next to her. She slumped against him. He raised his arm and placed it on her shoulder, trying to avoid any still tender spots.

"I am not a China doll, Hank. You don't have to be so careful." She boosted herself up a little and kissed him with enthusiasm. She had needed to kiss him for a long time now, but her split lip wouldn't allow it. It was worth the wait. She could feel his soft breath on her face. She inhaled the spicy masculine musk that she always associated with him. Passion rose thrumming like a soft drum in the back of her head. She felt it rise like a tsunami. Before it could crash, she turned to sit astride him. She could feel him stiffen. And not in a good way.

She held his face between her hands. She kissed him again deeply then ran her tongue delicately over his top lip and slipped her tongue into his mouth. She felt him shiver a little and his hands on her waist slipped deliberately down to her butt. Her stomach did a flip-flop like a trout brought to shore.

She placed her hands on his shoulder and pushed away so she could see his face. His blue eyes turned almost silver as he stared back. "Hank, again I am fine. Yes, I have some places that are very tender yet, but I won't break. I need you now to help me wipe away the last bit of that horrifying terror I felt when I thought I'd never see the people I loved ever again." She pulled him close and kissed him again.

Hank slipped his arms under her and lifted her up. He had had a lot of practice with that move over the last few weeks. For once, she didn't protest. He moved to her bedroom and laid her down in the middle of her bed.

His hand dipped into the waist of her sweat pant and pulled them off, trying to avoid the still bruised and swollen right knee. Next, he lifted her sweatshirt and drew it off as well. Darcy watched his face grow rigid with suppressed rage as he surveyed the still livid bruises on her otherwise creamy white skin.

She saw him pull off his boots and jeans faster than she thought possible. Then, there he was lying beautifully naked alongside of her. She touched his lightly-furred chest and ran her hand enticingly lower.

"You have no idea how much I wanted this. This must have been the longest recuperation ever." Darcy whispered in Hank's ear.

"Sure feels like it. I am not altogether sure we should even be thinking about this until you are completely healed." His hand rose between them and cupped her breast. He was careful not to apply any pressure, but he bumped her sore rib on the way up.

"Ouch! Watch the ribs." She pulled back a little. Darcy started to laugh.

"What are you laughing about?" Hank said a little exasperated.

"I was just remembering a scene between Aubrey Hepburn and Albert Finney in a film called *Two For The Road.* They laid out on the beach so long that they got terribly sunburned but wanted to make love anyway. It was so funny."

"There is not a damned thing funny about you almost getting killed."

She tried to swallow her smile, but it just ended as a smirk. "Sorry. Sorry. Not funny." Darcy ran her fingers through his hair the base of his neck and pulled him to her. She kissed him deeply.

Hank rolled on his side and ran his hand slowly from her hip to under her breast once more. Darcy snuggled closer, then threw her right leg across his body. "Okay if I'm on top? I think I can minimize the pain if I am."

She reached across him and fished a small foil packet from her bedside drawer. "Here you do this thing. I can't balance that long."

Hank rolled away briefly, then without losing a beat he lifted her hips on top of his. Darcy rested on him. It only took a few seconds for the pain of her bruises to recede because Hank was using both hands to run up the back of her legs gently until he cupped her butt and continued the slow massage all the way up her back to concentrated on her shoulders. "You are still a little stiff across your shoulders here."

"I know. That's normal for me."

Hank began to kneed the taut muscles in her shoulders. Darcy melted.

"That's better." Hank use both hands to caress down the sides of her body. Darcy squirmed in appreciation of what felt like electric shocks coursing through her veins.

"Let me know if anything I do is uncomfortable or causes you pain."

Darcy mumbled against his neck. "Too slow," she said.

Hank pushed her up slightly so he could see her face. "You're in no condition for mad jungle sex right now. So just enjoy the softer rain forest." Darcy smiled down at him. She closed her eyes and spread her arms. She tried to remain limp and focus on the sensations, but Hank's warm, gentle hands were arousing.

Occasionally murmurs of pleasure escaped from deep in her throat, but generally and uncharacteristically she was losing her ability to speak.

Hank positioned his hands on her inner thighs and lifted her so he could find her wet center. She began to thrash, so he stopped. "Easy, love." "Take it easy."

Darcy raised herself up higher finally appreciating all of those plank exercises she did at the gym. "Now!" Darcy said fiercely through gritted teeth.

Hank obliged and positioned himself then let her take the lead as she slowly lowered herself down. She felt him slide inside her. She rested for a moment enjoying the exquisite fullness of him. It felt like an inside-out hug. She didn't even know how much she needed that. Tears blurred her vision for a moment.

"What's the matter?" Hank looked worried.

"Nothing. I just feel so safe, and I haven't felt that way for such a long time."

Now it was Hank's turn to squirm. His large hands cupped her butt and caressed it. He never tried to increase her pace, but she could tell he was practicing amazing restraint. With her hands resting on his chest, Darcy levered up a little again and began to pulse up and down the whole length of him. She contracted her muscles around him as she rose to his tip then slid back down again. She watched his face contort until finally his eyes opened and stared into hers. They looked like a clear, blue mountain lake. She smiled down at him and increased the pace moving back and forth and up and down taking charge of her own pleasure and making Hank quiver with need. Finally, mercifully, she brought them both to a mutual crescendo. She collapsed on top of him with just enough energy for a gentle kiss before she rested her head on his shoulder and softly nuzzled him.

"Mmm," Darcy hummed against his neck.

"That was a bravura performance," Hank said running his hand up her back again.

Darcy allowed herself a giggle. What would you know about a bravura performance?"

"I'm not a total barbarian. I watch movies."

"What kind of movies?"

Hank laughed. "Not the kind you're imagining in your salacious little mind."

"Oooh salacious. I like the sound of that."

"I just bet you do," Hank lifted her off him and headed for her bathroom.

Darcy enjoyed the view of his broad shoulders and narrow hips as he walked away from her. She laid there a while and listened to hm splash around in the shower. She decided to join him. Limping slightly she walked to the door, knocked, but didn't wait for an answer.

Hank peered around the shower curtain. "Hey, I'm showering here."

"So I see," Darcy said and came toward him. "I thought we could share, you know, as an ecological thing. Save the planet and all that." She put out her hand so he could help her step into the high sided tub.

Hank reached down and swung her into the shower without even a grunt. She appreciated his eagerness.

She stood under the large hand held shower head, one of her few luxury purchases when she moved in. She let the water splash all over them both.

Hank smiled. He held up a bar of soap he had been using. "Need this?"

"Thanks." Darcy worked up a thick lather and handed the bar back to him. She began rubbing the sweet-smelling bubbles on Hank, starting on the back of his neck and working her way down his torso. She looked down.

"Well he's awake," she said with a smile.

"My turn." Hank lathered up and began to caress her breasts and her belly. As he slipped lower, the shower steamed with more than hot water.

It took half an hour to run out of hot water. Hank lifted Darcy out and he followed. She handed him a towel and they both dried off.

Darcy left to put on a clean pair of sweats and put the tea pot on to boil.

"I only have instant coffee or tea," she said leaning out of her tiny kitchen in time to see Hank pull on his black t-shirt. He was already dressed in his black pants but was still barefoot.

"It just occurred to me that since you always wear the same black outfit, you never have to do the 'walk of shame' because no one can tell you've had a sleep over."

"Is that what this was?"

"Well we didn't braid each other's hair, but I think it qualifies." Darcy smiled.

"I love how you always make up your own rules."

"Rules? What rules?"

"Exactly," Hank laughed and pulled her into a heart melting kiss.

Ryan Erickson Elevate Photography

PAULLA HUNTER is the author of the Darcy Moreland Mystery series. She's a former teacher turned writer. She has a passion for history, reading, theater, travel, and of course, writing murder mysteries. She is a member of Rocky Mountain Fiction Writers, Sisters in Crime, and Wyoming Writers. Paulla and her husband live in a historic downtown area of Cheyenne, Wyoming.

CPSIA information can be obtained
at www.ICGtesting.com
Printed in the USA
JSHW031902250423
40801JS00005B/27

9 781684 920617